An
Amish Man
OF ICE MOUNTAIN

Center Point
Large Print

Also by Kelly Long and available from
Center Point Large Print:

The Amish Bride of Ice Mountain

**This Large Print Book carries the
Seal of Approval of N.A.V.H.**

An *Amish Man*
OF ICE MOUNTAIN

KELLY LONG

CENTER POINT LARGE PRINT
THORNDIKE, MAINE

The text of this Large Print edition is unabridged.
In other aspects, this book may vary
from the original edition.
Printed in the United States of America
on permanent paper.
Set in 16-point Times New Roman type.

ISBN: 978-1-68324-279-6

Library of Congress Cataloging-in-Publication Data

Names: Long, Kelly, author.
Title: An Amish man of Ice Mountain / Kelly Long.
Description: Center Point Large Print edition. | Thorndike, Maine :
Center Point Large Print, 2017.
Identifiers: LCCN 2016050026 | ISBN 9781683242796 (hardcover :
alk. paper)
Subjects: LCSH: Amish—Fiction. | Large type books. | GSAFD:
Christian fiction.
Classification: LCC PS3612.O497 A84 2017 | DDC 813/.6—dc23
LC record available at https://lccn.loc.gov/2016050026

For Young Woman's Creek
and Scott and for Hollie John

Prologue

Ice Mountain, Pa.
Seven years ago

She watched him move in the hot sun, her eyes narrowed like a hungry hawk's, but she was careful never to let him see what she truly wanted. Oh, he was so delightfully young. So incredibly perfect. She'd spent most of the summer grooming him to fit her needs; an initial light touch on his strong, tanned forearm, standing near enough so that she knew he caught her scent, and then persuading him to work without his shirt when his tall body was soaked with sweat. She would have had him by now if his almost puritanical Amish upbringing hadn't stood in her way. Yes, she would have had him . . . any way she desired. She continued to gaze at him, biting the inside of her cheek until she tasted blood and savored the sensation.

"Joseph?" She kept her voice as melodic and sweet as her hidden vice of chain-smoking and her age would allow.

He plunged a shovel into the garden's earth and looked up at her. She couldn't help but smile. His long, dark hair fell in damp, natural waves around his beautiful, naïve face. His deep-set, green-gold eyes were clear and always attentive to her call. Her gaze traveled to his bare chest glistening in the sunlight. She loved his innocence, his maleness in its strong beginnings. *Sixteen . . . today.* Desire snaked through her abdomen.

She snapped back to the moment as he approached on long, black-wool-clad legs, his suspenders hanging loose about his lean waist.

"Ma'am?" he asked in his husky voice.

"It's your birthday today, right?" She smiled at him and he returned the gesture, his perfect white teeth revealed for a moment.

"*Jah.*" He nodded. "My sister's going to make me a cake."

"Oh, how charming, but . . ."

He frowned in confusion. "Ma'am?"

She waved a hand. "It's nothing, really. I'd made one for you too . . ." She looked away but flashed her gaze at him to judge his expression. As she expected, he appeared surprised—and pleased.

"That's nice of you, ma'am."

She cast him a demure but calculated smile. "It's your special day. Maybe you could . . . have a bite?"

He laughed. "*Ach*, surely. *Danki.*"

She touched his bare arm, her fingers tingling against his warm, slick skin. "Good. I hope you like whipped cream."

"I love it."

"Then by all means," she purred. "Come in."

Chapter One

**Late Spring, Commodore Gas Drilling Rig,
the Marcellus Shale
West Virginia
Present Day**

He worked from dark to dark; four weeks on, two weeks off. The job was exhausting—mentally, physically, and spiritually—but twenty-three-year-old *Amisch* Joseph King was used to hard living. And he told himself that he was driven by the need to keep his younger *bruder*, Edward, safe from the world's influence. If that meant being a roughneck on a gas rig in the middle of nowhere, then so be it.

"I don't see that you clocked out yet, Aim-ish! You still belong to me for the next three minutes unless you'd like to go back to mucking manure!" The resonating scream of the shift's "push," Edmunds, the man who was paid to keep the fellas moving, startled Joseph even though he was inured to the continual yelling. He tried to catch himself on the icy support bar of the metal walkway in the unseasonable sleet. But he lost his footing and his big body went down hard, slamming his right cheekbone into the muddy slush at his superior's booted feet.

Edmunds and some of the crew nearby roared with echoing laughter as Joseph got up.

"You can add another minute onto my time, Mr. Edmunds," Joseph said evenly, wiping at his face with the long sleeve of his coveralls and pushing his dark hair back beneath his hard hat. He resisted the urge to glance in Edward's direction. His *bruder* would probably be looking as shamed as Joseph should feel, but he'd learned, since coming to the rigs, to let a lot roll off his back. *This time it happens to be sleet . . .* He edged past Edmunds and the few other men gathered and made his way down the catwalk, looking at gauges, until he reached his younger *bruder*, who was leaning near a steam heater with a dangerous look of apathy on his twenty-one-year-old face.

"What are you doing?" Joseph snapped. "Straighten up. You know how easy it is to get too comfortable around this equipment. Do you want to get burned?"

"At least I'm not falling on my face," Edward drawled, half joking, the overhead lights playing on his blue eyes and strands of fair hair. *We are complete opposites,* Joseph thought with sudden insight. Edward as fair as he was dark, and his brother's disposition one of carefree living while he . . .

The shift whistle blew, and Joseph frowned, staring out into the dark fields beyond the artificially lit rig. His brother's insolence didn't hurt half as much as the discord and loneliness he felt whenever their two weeks off came up. It was too long a drive to go home to Ice Mountain—not that he would ever drive, of course. But he also knew that getting a ride somehow would put him at odds with wanting to come back to the rigs. It was enough, he supposed, that Bishop Umble hadn't suggested they be shunned for doing such work—yet.

He sighed aloud and couldn't wait for the luxury of the hot bath and dry clothes that he knew he would get at the Bear Claw Inn, four miles from the work site. Joseph much preferred to spend his time off at the inn rather than the so-called "man camps" that were on the drilling site itself. Even though the man camps had catered food and a laundry, there was too much alcohol about for Joseph and his *Amisch* upbringing, though it didn't seem to bother Edward—which was exactly why it bothered Joseph. His younger *bruder* fell too easily into drinking and playing cards during off time.

Now, they climbed down from the rig and Joseph clambered wearily into the cab of the company truck, pushing aside beer cans and potato chip bags from beneath his feet to make room for Edward beside him. Big Moe, a Texan roughneck, was driving.

"Whoo-ee! You boys stink to high heaven—sweat and wet dog got nuthin' on you two."

"Thanks, Moe," Joseph muttered dryly. He was trying to control the shivering that was part and parcel of twelve hours of standing in the sleet.

"So, y'all been here for two months thereabouts—you ready to go home yet?"

Edward grunted. "I don't quit."

Joseph elbowed him, knowing Big Moe was trying to make conversation.

"Ahh, I used to feel like that myself some 'til my girls came along." Moe smiled. "Now I'd do anything to be home with my wife and daughters, but there don't seem a better way to make money. Those young'uns go through clothes faster than a weevil through wheat, and it's my job to take care of them."

" 'So Gott made a roughneck . . .' " Joseph murmured.

"What's that, Joe?" the Texan asked, pausing to let another company truck ease out in front of him.

"*Ach*, nothing. Well, something I read actually —about how God made a roughneck."

Edward sighed. "You read too much."

"How's it go?" Moe asked, interested.

"I can't remember the whole thing, but it was something like . . . 'God said, "I need somebody who understands work—work that isn't pleasant or easy, but is rewarding, who takes pride in what they do, for they know that the work they do will . . . help others"—so God made a roughneck.' "

The truck bumped along and Joseph listened to the sudden silence in the cab until Moe cleared his throat. "That's right pretty-like. Makes a man feel like he can hang on awhile if he knows God's behind him. Thanks, Joe."

Joseph nodded, glancing sideways at his *bruder*, who appeared to have fallen asleep. *Maybe I do read too much . . .* He sighed to himself and concentrated on the welcoming bright lights of the inn up ahead.

Mary "Mama" Malizza ran the Bear Claw Inn with a soft heart and an iron hand. She knew how to handle rough men and understood that most of the time, roughness was a necessary guard against homesickness, weariness, and loneliness.

But the beautiful red-haired slip of a girl who stood before her desk now proved as tenacious as the most moody of her male customers, and Mary was uncertain of exactly how to proceed.

"You say you're twenty-four," Mary asked again, buying time. *The kid looks about seventeen . . . maybe I'm getting old.*

"Yes." The girl's voice was melodic and soft, maybe too soft for her to be any kind of a waitress at the inn, but there was something about her blue eyes that made Mary think of a proud, starving cat. And besides, she liked gumption when she saw it.

"You got a man?"

There, that made Miss Redhead flinch . . .
But Mary had the distinctly uncomfortable feeling that she'd touched a painful nerve from the way the girl straightened her shoulders even more.

"No, no—man."

There was something wry about the way the girl said it that made Mary decide to leave the subject alone.

"Well, I run a clean place, as far as can be, and I won't harbor no runaways. I ran away when I was about your age and nearly killed my ma, and I won't—"

"My mother's already dead."

"Oh," Mary said, deflated. "Well . . . we'll give it a week's trial and no hard feelings if it don't work. You can start tonight because I'm short-handed. But those trays are heavy and the men are hungry, and some might be hungry for a pretty little thing like you. Most ain't seen so much as a hair of a woman for a long month's time."

"I understand," the girl said, visibly relieved now that the brief interview was over.

Mary thought of something as she looked down at the sketchily filled-out application in front of her. "Hey, you don't list an address. I don't have any rooms open for board."

The girl flushed a bit but lifted her chin. "I wasn't certain of the last digit of the zip code. I

14

have an apartment down the road, but I moved only this week. I'll get the information for you tomorrow. Do you mind if I run out to my car for a minute?"

"Sure, but I don't hold with smoking—from the workers or the men on premises. I got asthma."

The girl shook her head. "I'm sorry. I don't smoke."

Mary nodded, half-satisfied, then peered again at the application. "I can't make it out. How'd you spell your name? I need it for your waitress tag."

"Oh, it's Priscilla." The girl gave the appropriate spelling, then slipped out of the office.

Mary shook her head. *The kid won't last a week . . .*

Chapter Two

Priscilla Allen unlocked the door of the brown station wagon with shaking hands as she tried to hurry in the downpour of sleet.

She worked the finicky lock and gained the front seat, turning around anxiously to search the mounded blankets on the folded-down backseat.

A head popped up suddenly, followed by a gurgle of laughter; Priscilla couldn't help catching her breath.

"Mommy, did we get it? Did we?"

"Yes, you silly. You scared me half to death." Priscilla clambered over the seat to check that the blankets were still properly positioned over the back windows of the old car. Then she squirmed closer to the mound and caught her four-year-old daughter, Hollie, in a close hug.

"Are you warm enough?"

Hollie nodded. "Uh-huh. I've got three gloves on one hand and three other ones on the other and three pants and four shirts and two coats and two hats. I'm hot!"

"Well, you keep it all on. I've got this job and I have to start tonight. So, you settle down out of sight like usual. I'll be out to check on you as soon as I can."

"Can you bring me a hamburger? I smelled them and I'm awful hungry."

Priscilla wet her lips and swallowed. "Yes, I'll wake you up when it's ready. I'm so sorry you're hungry, Hollie."

The child snuggled closer. "I'm not that hungry, Mommy. Not like that time when we ate frozen peas all by themselves."

Priscilla tried to smile. "All right. Remember, only Mommy has the key and don't—"

"Unlock the door! I know," Hollie declared, the tassel on her topmost hat bouncing.

Priscilla clambered off the seat and carefully got out, looking around with sharp eyes before relocking the door and running back to the inn.

• • •

Joseph leaned his head back in the tub with a deep sigh of contentment. Then he frowned as his *bruder* barged into the bathroom and snatched the last dry towel from the rack.

"Gotta hurry, Joe. I'm going downstairs to play cards with some of the fellas." Edward splashed water on his face, then dried himself with the towel, tossing it onto the floor.

"Hey!" Joseph yelled as Edward made to head out the door.

"Whaaat?"

"You get paid and then you go and gamble it all away. How exactly are you saving money for you and Sarah?"

Edward flashed him a faintly wicked grin. "I win, Joe."

Joseph sighed and splashed the warm water against his chest. "*Jah*, well . . . bring me up some fresh towels. You know we don't use the phone."

"*Ach*, all right."

"And Edward?"

"What now?"

"Remember your intended." Joseph kept his voice level.

"Ice Mountain's a world away, Joe. A world away."

Joseph listened as the suite door closed with a slam, then started to wash his hair. His *bruder*'s words tore at his heart because he knew they held a ring of truth . . .

Priscilla hastily changed into the yellow dress Mary provided for her and decided that the garment was plain and suitable. She'd been a bit afraid that it might be something skimpy, but Mary must have meant it when she said that she ran a clean place. She looked in a mirror in the small staff bathroom and pinned on her name tag, then tried to ignore the grumbling of her stomach, which made her think with some weariness of Hollie's hunger.

A tall man, obviously staff in his yellow shirt and black pants, approached her when she entered the hall. He had an armload of white towels.

"I'm Dan. You the new girl?"

Priscilla nodded, nervous, but knew she had to speak. She needed this job so badly.

"Yes, I am."

"Look, run these towels up to room seven, will you? I'm supposed to be training you, but I can't start until I've worked out a mess in the kitchen— one of the cooks wants to try some sort of pastry flan for dessert. Flan! For roughnecks!"

Priscilla smiled in spite of herself and took the towels he thrust at her, then she hurried off in the direction he pointed, looking for room seven.

She found the room at the end of a clean, carpeted hallway. A decorative pair of antlers hung on the door beneath the room number. She gave a tentative knock, and was wondering how quickly she might get something from the kitchen to take to Hollie when the door was thrust wide open.

"Edward! Where *en der weldt* have you . . ."

The tall, dark-haired man stopped abruptly, licking surreptitiously at a drop of water that ran down his chiseled cheek and past his mouth.

Priscilla took in the fact that he was nearly naked, clutching only a hand towel below his lean waist. A snapshot mental image of him seemed to burn behind her eyes. Then he muttered something in a hoarse voice and took a step toward her, snatching the towels from her arm and slamming the door in her face. She stood, stunned, for what felt like a full minute before she came back to the moment and turned to hurry off down the hall.

Still, even as she gained the kitchen floor, she had to blink to get the overwhelming vision of his dripping body out of her mind. *Heath never looked like that* . . . She shuddered in spite of herself. *Like what?* the practical part of her snapped back. And some reserved, hidden piece of her that she'd thought long defeated relaxed into the remembrance of the man: his eyes hazel green and deep set, his shoulders broad and strong, his abdomen well-defined, while dark hair ran in an arrow to where he held the towel. She felt herself color hotly. *I have a job to do, a hungry child, and here I am—daydreaming.* She swallowed and squared her shoulders, banishing the image of the man from her mind as she entered the dining room and scrambled to make herself useful.

Joseph leaned hard against the cold door, pressing his bare back into the wood and clasping and unclasping the towels he'd taken from the woman. He couldn't stop the waves of shame that ran over him at the fact that he'd stood exposed. *No woman has seen me that way since Amanda . . .* The name filled his mind with a strange mixture of dread and excitement, and he let his head fall back against the wood, his throat working. *I'm still not over it—seven years. Ach, Gott, seven years, and still I'm haunted. Will it never stop? Can it?* He drew a deep breath and remembered the scripture promise that *"All things are possible with Derr Herr."* And then, for some reason, his breathing leveled off as he recalled the cool purity of the girl's blue eyes. He was able to relax his stance and move to the business of drying, his thoughts resonating with a strange peace.

"You hire a new waitress here, Dan?" Joseph asked his *Englisch* friend as his eyes searched the dining room. Joseph had decided that he owed the girl an apology for his abruptness, but he couldn't seem to locate her.

"Sure did, Joe. But she stepped out to take her break a few seconds ago."

"Great. Thanks." Joseph ignored Dan's quizzical look and made for a side door leading outside.

The sleet had slowed to a lazy, misting fog and Joseph had to search the parking lot carefully before he caught sight of her red hair as she moved through the packed cars under the arc lights.

"Miss?" he called.

She stopped so fast that he realized he'd scared her, which was the last thing he wanted to do.

"Miss, I'm sorry. I mean no harm. I wanted to apologize."

Was it his imagination or did she seem to nearly wilt with relief? She turned to face him as he came closer, one of her small hands on the hood of a blue Pontiac, the other clutching a small brown bag.

He caught up with her, the car between them. "Miss? I'm Joseph King. You—uh—brought me towels earlier." He felt his face color but he plunged on. "I wanted to apologize for being rude. I was expecting my *bruder* and then it was you and . . ." He trailed off when he sensed her anxiousness to be gone. *Maybe I should have let well enough alone . . .*

"It's all right." She spoke quickly, her voice high. "Please forget it."

"Right," he agreed. "Okay." He turned to go because it was so obviously what she wanted him to do. Waves of anger, distaste, or something, practically radiated from her small frame.

He felt a wash of shame again, then forgot it when he couldn't resist a glance over his shoulder and saw the red-haired girl scurrying to a brown station wagon parked toward the back of the full lot. There were blankets covering the back windows of the car, he noticed, and she seemed to look around before unlocking the door. He turned back toward the inn with a shrug when the unmistakable high-pitched shriek of a happy child echoed across the damp lot and left him thinking seriously about what the girl with the towels had to hide in her own life.

Priscilla's heart beat fast when she climbed into the relative safety of the car. She handed Hollie the bag with the hamburger and fries, thankful for the food, even while she couldn't get the big man's words out of her head.

He apologized even though it was my mistake. Heath never said sorry, not once, not for any-thing, but why should he? The world thinks he's perfect . . . She shuddered—if only everyone knew the truth. She pushed aside her train of thought and took a single fry from Hollie's mittened hand. It tasted so good, she knew the faintness of hunger before she rallied.

"I've got to go back now, love. Try and go to sleep."

Hollie chewed with visible contentment. "All right, Mommy, but who was that man you were talking to?"

Priscilla froze. "What man?"

"I peeked out the back window, over the top of the blanket. The big man with the funny black hat and coat."

"Nobody. And no more peeking."

"Nobody must be somebody," Hollie sing-songed matter-of-factly.

"Well, he's not. Now be good."

Priscilla got out of the car and made her way back to the inn, but first she stopped at the garbage cans outside and lifted one of the lids. She knew the bag she had carried out was still on top because she'd crimped the tie far to the left. Hurriedly, she opened the bag and caught up the piece of toast and scrap of bacon and ate as fast as she could, forcing herself past the nausea that always accompanied such maneuvers. But tomorrow would be better. *Three meals* . . . She forgot all about the man and went back to her shift.

Chapter Three

"You've got a fine black eye." Edward's voice sounded laconic from where he slouched in the bathroom doorway.

"*Danki*," Joseph answered, peering closer into the steamy mirror. He did have some *gut* bruising around his cheek and eye from his fall on the slippery catwalk the day before, but it was nothing to worry about. "Want to come fishing with me today?"

Edward snorted. "And sit still in this cold? *Nee, danki*. Me and some of the fellas are going to take the four-wheelers out for a ride up in the mountains."

Joseph caught his *bruder*'s eye in the mirror. "Don't drink and ride those things. And you shouldn't be riding them anyway."

"There's no bishop here."

"But Gott is here," Joseph retorted, feeling his temper rise.

"There's *nee* distinct mention of four-wheelers in the Bible, Joe. Get with it."

Joseph turned. "You know as well as I do why we keep to the Ordnung. Why it matters that we be *Amisch* even when there's no one to see. Too many of our people were persecuted—tortured, so that we could live."

Edward gave him a sour smile and adjusted the ball cap he'd taken to wearing. "And that's what I'm doing, *bruder*. Living."

"What about Sarah?" Joseph's voice was quiet and he knew he'd struck home when Edward flushed.

"Not fair, Joseph. She's not here. And besides, every day I work is to make money for her and me."

"Uh-huh."

"I'm leaving." Edward spun on his heel and Joseph sighed when the door of the suite slammed.

I'm tired of being the big bruder . . . *the rule-keeper . . . the guard. But that's why I'm here.* He viciously pushed away the truth that echoed inside—that there was more to his being away from the community and the mountain than he was willing to admit. He closed his eyes for a moment, then spoke aloud into the silence of the room. "I'm here for Edward and I'm not doing a very *gut* job of it—and that is why I'm going fishing."

"I don't like fishin'." Hollie's voice was plaintive.

Priscilla sighed and adjusted the lines. She'd noticed the big, relatively secluded pond near the inn when she'd driven past for the interview and was glad for it today. Mama Malizza had told her not to come in until three, and even with the

25

tips from the previous evening, she had nearly no money. The station wagon's tank had to be filled. Hollie needed vitamins and milk and so . . . out came the fishing poles. Thankfully, the day was clear and not too cold.

"I don't like it either," Priscilla admitted. "But we're good at it." She held up the line of six trout and Hollie rolled her eyes.

Priscilla stilled when she heard a rustling in the woods near the pond. She glanced at the station wagon and wondered how fast she could get Hollie there. She was about to abandon the fish and pick up her daughter when a big man broke out from the treeline. He carried a fishing pole and wore a black hat and black coat along with black wool pants. Priscilla released a quick breath. It was the *Amisch* man from the inn.

He stopped when he saw them, looking somehow awkward and surprised at the same time.

"Hiya," he said finally.

"Hello, we were getting ready to go. We won't disturb you." Priscilla started to drag in her line when she got a bite. She threw him an exasperated look and reeled in the big fish.

"Never leave when the fish are biting." He laughed suddenly as she added the fish to her catch. "And it looks like they're really biting."

"I saw you last night," Hollie announced.

The man had stepped closer and Priscilla resisted the urge to hush her child. She didn't want to raise any suspicion on this stranger's part.

"Did you now?" His voice was kind.

"Yep. From our car. Why do you dress funny?"

Priscilla suppressed a silent groan, but the man seemed to take no offense as he answered easily.

"I'm *Amisch*. I come from Pennsylvania."

"Oh," Hollie said. "What's Amish?"

The man eased himself onto a large rock nearby and opened a bait box. "*Ach, Amisch* is a way of believing, a way of living."

"Oh," Hollie repeated. "So Amish believe in dressing funny?"

"Hollie," Priscilla snapped, embarrassed by the sidelong smile the man threw their way. *He really is impossibly handsome . . . and here I go again . . .*

"She's all right," the man said, loading his hook.

"What's your name?" Hollie persisted despite Priscilla's glare.

"I'm sorry. I should have said." He removed his hat, revealing overly long, wavy dark hair, and nodded at them. "I'm Joseph King. Pleased to meet you."

"I'm Hollie and this is my mommy, Priscilla. Aren't they nice names?"

"Sure are." He clapped his hat back on and cast in his line.

"Why do you have a black eye?"

"Hmm? *Ach*, I fell on the rig in the ice."

Priscilla felt a sick premonition inside, almost

27

as if she could see where the conversation was headed. And sure enough, Hollie spoke up again.

"Mommy used to have black eyes too. She had to learn things from Daddy. So he gave her those eyes to remember. What do you remember from your fall?"

Priscilla swallowed a lump in her throat and stared down at the water. She was mortified, but she had not been able to come up with any way to wipe certain memories from Hollie's mind. She didn't want to look up and see the pity on the *Amisch* man's face. She'd seen it enough times in the eyes of certain friends . . . *But why do I care what he thinks anyway?* She lifted her chin and turned to face him directly, but to her great surprise, she was met with a look of respect.

He spoke slowly, his voice low, as his green-gold eyes seemed to gleam with an emotion she couldn't understand. "I learned, Hollie, that falling means getting up. Standing up again and again. Until the falling doesn't matter as much as the standing."

"That's smart," Hollie said, then went back to jostling her pole.

Priscilla's eyes welled against her will and she gave a brief nod to the *Amisch* man. He smiled in calm return.

Joseph had to look away from her finally. He knew about wife beating, had read about it and heard of its effects at rare times on the mountain.

But to beat a young girl . . . Dear Gott . . . How auld *could she be actually? And with a child?* He swallowed hard, determined not to let her see anything but the true respect he felt for her, bravely fishing—probably to feed her and the *kind. What had the little* maedel *said? "I saw you last night—from our car."* The realization hit him hard enough to make his heart slam in his chest . . . *They are living in the car . . . in the car!*

His eyes searched the water frantically, as if he'd find an answer there. He knew instinctively that asking the girl about her living situation would make her bolt like a hunted deer. *Nee.* He had to think. He cleared his throat and ran his line through his fingers, wanting something real to hold on to, because the living closeness of a woman struggling so badly, alone with a child, was a reality he did not fully understand. At home, on Ice Mountain, or in any *Amisch* community, a widowed woman was cared for, lifted up by the community. *A widowed woman . . . the child had said "her daddy." Perhaps Priscilla is still married—then who am I to interfere? But . . . still. She must be running from this man, who would teach her things through violence. Surely she deserves as much help as I'd give a kitten in the snow . . .*

"We should have a fish fry for lunch," he said suddenly, the words coming from nowhere into his head. He turned to look at her. "I get homesick on the days off, and my brother likes to run around. I'd truly enjoy the company."

Hollie began to bounce in response, but he almost held his breath as he waited for Priscilla's reply. *She's cautious and probably rightly so . . .*

But then she lifted those clear blue eyes to him and shrugged. "Where would we have it?"

"Well, here," he improvised quickly. He gestured with his chin toward an outside grill and picnic table. "If you two don't mind the chill in the air."

"Please, Mommy! Please. We were going to cook the fish here anyway."

She nodded slowly. "Well, all right. I—I could drive down the road and get some batter mix if you don't like them grilled."

He thought about her probable lack of money. "Sure. I can stay here and get the fire started." He reached into a pocket and grabbed a handful of money, then decided against it, not wanting to offend her, and offered two bills instead. "Maybe you can pick up some ice cream too—for Hollie."

"Yay!"

He watched Priscilla wet her lips, eyeing the bills. "I don't usually let her eat sweets."

"Only for today then." He smiled. "But it's up to you. I mean no disrespect."

"No—no, I know you don't." She set her pole on the bank and rose. Joseph couldn't help himself; he ran his eyes down her trim, jeans-clad figure, and thought her red hair looked like a

30

triumphant pennant, lifted by the breeze. *She's beautiful* . . . Another realization that made his heart pound.

She took the money from his hand; careful, he thought, not to let their fingers touch, though his palm seemed to tingle for want of the contact. *I'm losing my mind* . . . He caught a firm hold on his emotions; he knew what stupid thinking could bring and he wanted none of it ever again.

"I'll clean and fillet the fish," he muttered. He sensed that she seemed confused by his sudden withdrawal, but he'd go to hell and back before he let himself be caught by his waywardness with another woman. *I am so screwed up* . . .

"Thank you," she said softly.

He gave a stiff nod and waited, conscious of her loading Hollie in the car and then driving off before he got to his feet. *I'm having a fish fry with her, and that's all. This will be the end of it* . . . He tramped to the outside grill, telling himself that he was comforted by the thought.

His hair is more brown than black. I couldn't tell so much when it was wet . . . Priscilla blinked at herself in her rearview mirror in disgust while Hollie chattered happily about the picnic to come. *Maybe we should keep driving away from here; he's dangerous to my peace of mind. But I have his money* . . . She knew she was rationalizing over twenty dollars, but—

"Mommy!"

"What?" she exclaimed, startled out of her thoughts.

"I said for the fifteenth thousandth time—he's nice, isn't he?"

"I suppose. We don't really know him, Hollie. He's a stranger and we have to be careful."

"He's not a stranger and I'm tired of always being careful. His name's Joseph. That's a nice name. Why don't you like him?"

"I didn't say I didn't like him."

Hollie huffed. "You don't have to. I can tell."

"How?"

"Never mind. Can we get rainbow sherbet? Is sherbet ice cream?"

"Sort of . . ." Her mind drifted back to the fluted sorbet glasses Heath's relative had bought them for a wedding gift. How Aunt Miriam would have cringed to know that he'd used a shard of one of the elegant gifts to carefully make a slit in each of Priscilla's cuticles when she'd broken a glass by accident . . . only small cuts that would never show, never need bandaging. The black eyes had been harder to explain, but she had— both out of duty and necessity.

A car blared its horn and she hastily realigned the station wagon, then pulled into the small market, trying to focus on ice cream and fish batter.

Chapter Four

Joseph looked up from the copy of *The Budget* that his *fater* regularly mailed him, when Edward unlocked the door and walked into their room at the inn. His *bruder* was mud-stained and reeked of alcohol.

"Tell me you spent all afternoon waiting around here for me." Edward belched, then groaned.

"Actually, not."

"Well, why do you have that stupid, moon-eyed look on your face? Don't say you met a woman?"

Joseph resisted the urge to shift in his chair and kept his expression deliberately calm. "You're drunk."

"*Jah*, I am. And hungry too. Let's go get supper once I've had a bath." Edward walked into the closet, obviously aiming for the bathroom.

"If you can find the tub," Joseph said dryly. He went back to his paper while Edward muttered a curse and slammed the bathroom door. Then Joseph realized that he'd read the same line over five times. He lowered the paper and thought back to his spontaneous afternoon picnic.

He'd deboned and filleted the fish easily with the knife he carried when he wasn't working. Then he'd struck a match and got a wood fire going in the semi-rusted outdoor grill. He heated his knife and used it to scrape off the grill, enjoying the feel of doing something simple with his hands, and missing Ice Mountain.

Priscilla had returned with Hollie after twenty minutes or so; and against his will, and despite his earlier resolve, he'd felt his pulse pick up as he realized that he couldn't, in all decency, let them go on living in a car for much longer. But he had no idea how to solve the problem. *Spend time with them . . . Get to know them better.* The words had come from deep within his spirit and he knew they were from *Derr Herr.* So, he'd applied himself with vigor toward fixing the food and making simple conversation.

Priscilla had gotten a small plastic bag from the back of her car and he'd watched her deftly shake the batter onto the fish in the bag.

"Mmm." Hollie had sniffed the air when he'd started to fry the fish. "That smells good. I'm awful hungry."

Something had pulled hard inside of him, and he'd glanced at the child with deep sympathy. His own *dat* might not have done the best job raising him, but he'd never gone hungry.

"What's your favorite food?" he'd asked Hollie, then could have kicked himself when the little girl's blue eyes took on a wistful look.

"Ohhh, Mommy's meatloaf and mashed potatoes, but we haven't had it in a while, 'cause there's no oven in the car." She'd giggled then, though he saw Priscilla's discomfiture and did his best to change the subject.

"Me," he spoke up, "I like apples and onions, but I'd say fish and ice cream will do as well, though I find I'm not so hungry myself today. I think I'll only have a bit."

"Please, don't," Priscilla said low. He looked into her blue eyes and saw the pride there. "There's enough for all of us."

He'd nodded, realizing he'd put a foot wrong by wanting to give them his share. "All right," he'd answered, looking back down at the tender fillets. *My, but she is a proud little thing, and brave too . . .*

They'd eaten in quiet companionship, and afterwards he'd taught them both how to skip stones across the pond. He'd had to resist the urge to touch Priscilla when he'd wanted to show her the way to bend her arm, and decided that the girl awakened hazardous feelings in him he'd long suppressed . . .

"Joseph!"

"What?" He looked up at his *bruder*, startled out of his reverie.

"Are you coming down to dinner or what?"

Joseph gave him a wry smile. "Can you find the dining room now?"

"*Hou je bek*, will you?"

Joseph laughed. "All right. Let's go." *And I'll*

see Priscilla again . . . He didn't want the thought to matter, but somehow it did.

Priscilla knew she was a fast learner and, even though it was only her second day at the inn, she found herself catching on to the hectic rhythm of the place. For the most part, the roughnecks were respectful and cheerful, eager to talk about their wives and children but never crossing any lines. So it was a great surprise to Priscilla when a lean, wiry man she'd heard called Edmunds, muttered a ribald remark to her as she walked past. She felt herself color a bit but decided to ignore it and focused on serving steak to a table of four men from Texas.

She was aware when Joseph entered, wearing a light blue shirt and suspenders with his dark pants. By their similar build, she decided that the man with him must be his brother, though the brother was as fair as Joseph was dark. She pulled out her order pad and was easing through the crowd toward their table, her heart beating a bit faster as she recalled his kindness to Hollie at the pond that afternoon. Then someone brusquely reached a strong arm around her waist and she found herself flat in the lap of the mean-eyed man, Edmunds.

She struggled to rise, desperately wanting to handle the situation without causing much notice, but the man had a hand in her hair.

"Well now, what do we have here? As fine a filly

as I've seen in quite some time. I wonder which way she likes to be rode, boys. What do you say?"

Priscilla pushed against his chest and noticed that someone clapped a large hand on Edmunds's shoulder. She looked up in mute fury and saw Joseph towering over them. Edmunds turned his head slowly, without releasing her.

"Aww, it's the pretty Aim-ish boy come to the rescue. What you gonna do, Aim-ish? Fight me for the first ride?"

"Joseph, it's all right," she hissed.

Edmunds laughed. "Oh, it's Joseph, is it? So you two have met before? Tell me, Joseph, how was she?" He jostled Priscilla against his lap suggestively.

"I'd like to see you outside, Edmunds. Whether you let her go and come or not is up to you, but I promise you won't like the consequences either way." Joseph's tone was level, almost pleasant.

Priscilla found herself summarily dumped onto the floor as Edmunds rose. "Be right back, little filly."

She scrambled to her feet, noticing the sudden quiet of the place, as Joseph turned and started outside, with Edmunds hard on his heels. She longed to follow but decided it would only cause more fuss, so she swallowed hard and returned to where Joseph's brother sat.

"May I help you?" she asked clearly, and the place began to resume its hubbub of conversation.

Joseph's brother narrowed his blue eyes and half smiled. "*Nee*, I don't think you can. I say you won't be able to concentrate until my *bruder* walks back in that door. You know, the *Amisch* don't fight, as a rule, and Edmunds is a snake. But Joseph wouldn't take kindly to me interfering. I'm Edward, by the way."

"Priscilla," she whispered, gesturing to her name tag. "I'm sorry for this; I hope he's all right."

Edward nodded. "Don't apologize for Edmunds . . . and don't underestimate old Joe."

Priscilla nodded, but she wasn't fully convinced . . . she knew the brutality of men like Edmunds firsthand.

Joseph turned in the shadows to lean casually against the back wall of the inn as Edmunds gave a low growl and lunged at him. Joseph stepped aside and put a restraining hand on the wiry man's shoulder, holding him easily at bay.

"You know, Edmunds, we Aim-ish are a strange lot. We've got certain customs that they won't tell you about in books."

Edmunds gave an ineffective swing and grunted. "Shut up and fight!"

"*Nee*, not until I tell you what you're up against." Joseph smiled.

"I've laid low bigger men than you, Aim-ish."

"That may be"—Joseph pulled Edmunds close, holding the other man's arms to his sides—"but I want to tell you that you can't stay awake all the time . . . not for long anyway. And when you sleep, I'll be there, with a knife, and a neat *Amisch* trick that'll make sure you don't . . . *bother* another woman ever again."

Edmunds froze. "What are you sayin'?"

"I think you understand."

"I'll have you fired," Edmunds blustered.

"I'll still be there—sometime—when you sleep."

Edmunds struggled to step back and Joseph let him go easily.

"You're sick, you Aim-ish freak."

Joseph almost laughed at the gullible man but managed to keep his expression serious as Edmunds staggered off to his truck.

"I'm going back to the man camps, and I'm going to sleep," Edmunds roared out the window as he drove by.

Joseph lifted a hand and hollered back, "Pleasant dreams."

Then he did laugh and made his way back inside.

Priscilla turned in amazement as Joseph walked calmly back in. He appeared completely unruffled, and none of the men bothered with him much except one of the big Texans, who called out, "Hey, Joe, should we be lookin' to scrape that cowpoke up outta the mud out there? He is the boss, after all."

Joseph merely smiled and took his seat, glancing up at Priscilla. "Are you all right?"

"Yes, but what did he mean, 'the boss'? I didn't cause you to beat up the boss, did I?"

"Nope." He raised both his hands. "See, no blood. No nothing. Edmunds simply chose to go back to the man camps for tonight. And I think you'll find in the future that he won't be a problem here."

"He better not be," Mama Malizza boomed, making Priscilla jump. "You all right, honey? I warned you some of these men could get feisty, but that wiry fella rubs me the wrong way. You're lucky you had Joseph here to watch over you."

"Yes, I know," Priscilla said, wetting her lips, grateful there was to be no repercussion from her own boss; the older woman might be loud, but she was kind.

"Well, if you're up to it, let's get back to work. These *Amisch* boys are partial to our T-bones, I think."

Priscilla watched Joseph give Mama Malizza a quick smile, then he turned his gaze back to the menu. "I'm also partial to trout, fried over an open fire," he said, apropos of nothing.

But Priscilla couldn't contain the flush of happiness she felt for a second and ignored the considering look Edward gave her. Instead, she took their orders and went on with her work, the unfamiliar feeling of contentment in her heart.

"Well, what did you do to him, for heaven's sake?" Edward hissed when Priscilla was out of earshot.

Joseph looked at him and shrugged.

Edward flopped back in his chair in disgust. "The only time the perfect *Amisch* man does something not *Amisch*, and you won't share the details? *Kumme* on. And since when is it your style to rescue a beautiful girl?"

"She doesn't need rescuing. And you think I pretend to be the perfect *Amisch* man? Maybe you don't even know me, little *bruder*."

"*Ach*, I know you, and you are as near to perfect an *Amischer* as I've ever met. You think it's been easy growing up in your shadow?"

Joseph shook his head with a faint smile. "Remind me to enlighten you sometime, but right now, I want to eat."

Chapter Five

"I wish we could see the stars," Hollie whispered sleepily.

Priscilla stared up at the underside of the roof of the car as she and Hollie cuddled for the night. It wasn't much of a view, but it was a small sacrifice to make while she tried to save and gain stability and safety for them somewhere.

"I could tell you a story about the stars," she suggested, recalling a college astronomy class she had taken what seemed like light-years ago. She'd done dual enrollment her senior year, doubling up her last year in high school and her freshman year of university. *I thought I knew so much . . . then I met Heath.*

"No story," Hollie slurred, drifting off. "I like the real stars better."

Priscilla frowned in the darkness. In some ways, her daughter had more sense than she did herself. She'd always loved stories, especially the romantic ones. But now, she wished every glass slipper might be smashed before another girl fell prey to the illusion of a prince on a white horse. Against her will, she thought of Joseph and that slimy man, Edmunds. Given another two minutes, she probably would have clawed the boss's eyes out, but as it was, Joseph had stepped in.

She wondered what Joseph had done or said in such a short period of time to change Edmunds's attitude, but she also told herself that it didn't matter. She didn't need a hero. She didn't need anyone—except Hollie. *And what about God?* Her conscience got the question in before she'd even had a chance to thrust it aside, and she thumped her pillow, feeling the car shake. *I don't need Him most of all . . .* And thankfully, she was too tired to refute those words as she drifted off into a fitful sleep.

• • •

Joseph closed his Bible and placed it on the bedside table. Then he switched off the electric lamp, wishing he had a candle to douse instead, and settled down beneath the crisp sheets. It was hard to relax in the comfortable bed when he knew that Priscilla and Hollie were outside in an uncomfortable, unheated car. He'd wanted to tell Edward about the situation but had gotten sick of being plagued all evening with questions from his *bruder* about Priscilla as a person . . . *nee*, as a woman. If he revealed what he knew about Hollie and their homelessness, Edward would have him married off mentally before the conversation was over. And marriage was not something he wanted to consider . . . ever.

He sighed and sat back up and switched on the light. He opened the bedside table drawer and withdrew a flyer he'd taken down from a telephone pole. The mini poster advertised a local farm that boasted a petting zoo. *I'll still be off for a while . . . I bet Hollie would love it— I bet Priscilla wouldn't. Still, to give the little girl a chance at some fun, it might be okay to ask. After all, it wouldn't be like a date; it would be for Hollie.*

Satisfied, he put the paper back in the drawer and lay back down to sleep, reaching for the light once more. A few hours later, he was awakened to the angry slash of lightning illuminating his room and he sat up to listen to the booming thunder and the pounding of rain against the window.

Immediately, he thought of the station wagon outside. He dressed haphazardly in the dark as fast as he could and grabbed his coat and hat. Then he quietly left the room, not wanting to rouse Edward in the other bedroom of the suite, and made his way downstairs. He slipped out into the terrible din in time to feel small pebbles of hail begin to fall as he made his way through the parking lot until he'd located the station wagon.

Louder than the din of the storm were Hollie's screams of terror coming from within the vehicle. He approached the driver's door, knowing he'd probably frighten Priscilla but unable to see any help for it, and started to bang on the glass window. After a few soaking moments, the window was rolled down halfway and Priscilla's pale face appeared in stark relief against a flash of lightning.

"What do you want?" she demanded in shrill tones as Hollie's cries magnified in intensity.

"Give me the child," he said as levelly as he could without yelling above the noise.

"Are you crazy?" Priscilla cried. "She's terrified!"

Joseph didn't feel like arguing as hail pelted his neck, but he kept his calm. "I know that. Let me take her inside where it's quiet until this passes. You come too."

"I can't! Someone will see."

"Not in my room. *Kumme* on."

He waited precious moments while he watched her struggle to decide; then she rolled the window back up. The rear door opened and he moved to quickly grasp the blanket-wrapped, screaming child in his arms. He watched Priscilla struggle out, then turned to run back across the parking lot.

Once under the awning of the inn, he gently rocked Hollie against him. "Shh, shh, *boppli*. I want to take you inside, but you must be still. Nothing will harm you."

Priscilla had joined him, and he took in her shivering form and her red hair clinging to the perfect oval of her face. *Still beautiful; maybe more so . . .* He bounced Hollie against his hip and was amazed when the child began to giggle. His ears rang with the abrupt change in decibels and he had to smile. "All right, there's a *gut* girl. Now, we must be very quiet because my *bruder*, Edward, is sleeping and we don't want to wake him."

He paused when Priscilla grabbed his coat sleeve, and he looked down at her.

"We'll be all right," she said. "We can go back to the car."

He raised an eyebrow when Hollie's mouth began to pucker. "Really? I think not." And then he shouldered through the wooden door of the lobby. He sensed Priscilla's presence behind him, but he still turned so that Hollie could see her mother.

"There," he whispered. "Now remember, *kind*, very quiet. My *bruder* turns into an ogre if he's wakened." He took the stairs to the next floor two at a time, feeling Hollie's soft hair brush his cheek, and he caught the sweet, baby scent of her. Ach*, Gott, but life was fragile. What kind of* fater *would leave a child and mother such as these to . . .* He swallowed and managed the card key to his room with one hand, then switched on the small bedside lamp.

Thankfully, Edward's door was closed, and Joseph moved to lay Hollie in her bundle of blankets on his bed. But, like an errant puppy, the child rolled out of the covers and sat up, fully alert. Joseph drew off his coat and hat, tossing them over a chair, and went to the bathroom to fetch dry towels. He handed one to Priscilla, who was standing stiffly, the closed bedroom door behind her. Then he gave the other towel to Hollie, who giggled.

He quickly put his finger to his lips and Hollie did the same, quieting immediately. He turned to smile at Priscilla, who was assiduously applying herself to drying her hair, so he went to the closet and found another towel for himself.

He watched between swipes at his hair as Priscilla finished and went to his bed to begin to unbundle Hollie from her outdoor clothes in the warmth of the room.

"That's quite a storm," Joseph whispered as the lightning continued to illuminate the room.

Priscilla nodded, clearly not wanting to speak for fear of being overheard. Then she turned from Hollie and stopped still, gazing at Joseph with some emotion he couldn't fathom . . . *Was it anger? Confusion?*

He looked down at his person to find his shirt all askew and mostly undone. Dismay filled him. *What must she think?* He hastily worked the pins in the dim light. "I'm sorry," he said softly. "I was in a hurry—well, to check on you both—and I threw my clothes on."

Again, Priscilla gave a stiff nod, and he wanted to groan aloud. *Twice now, this woman has seen me in a state of undress. And why? Because of my carelessness.*

Then he noticed that Priscilla was shivering in her soaked clothes. He turned to the tall closet and pulled out the long nightshirt he'd packed but had never worn since he'd first come to the rigs.

"Here." He crossed the room and handed it to Priscilla, then backed away.

She peered down at the bundle with a look of suspicion.

"You're freezing in those wet things," he said. "Put that on."

She thrust it back at him and he shook his head

in exasperation. "I don't want—I mean . . . please don't stay cold on my account. That flannel is warm and you can—uh—change in the bathroom or I could go in the bathroom while you . . ." He drifted off when she set her chin and pulled the nightshirt back to her chest.

"All right," she whispered. "Hollie, I'll be right back."

Joseph sighed. *She probably thinks I'm* narrisch, *but at least they're out of the rain . . .*

He stood awkwardly in the middle of the room while Hollie started to bounce on the big bed. Soon, Priscilla was out of the bathroom, swathed from neck to heel and then some.

"Mommy, come lie down with me like you do in the car."

Joseph watched Priscilla shake her head. "No, Hollie. Be still. The storm will soon pass."

"But, Mama!"

Joseph couldn't help glancing in the direction of Edward's door and knew Priscilla must have seen him, because she marched with reluctance back to his bedside. "I'm sorry," she whispered, but barely glanced at him.

"*Nee, nee,* please. I will sit in the chair here." He pivoted to sit with haste, unsure of what to do with his hands, so he simply shoved them deep into his pockets and leaned his head far back against the chair. But he could hear Priscilla move and he gritted his teeth against the intimate sounds that followed—the sheets rustling, the gentle creak of the comfortable bed, the light being turned out, and finally, a small feminine sigh of contentment. He closed his eyes in the flashing dark and tried to pray, but he found himself slipping into sleep before he could get very far and finally gave in to the pull of slumber.

Priscilla tried to relax in his bed. *His bed . . . the* Amisch *man's bed . . . How in the world did I end up here?* Hollie turned on her side to spoon against her and Priscilla couldn't help nestling against her daughter, but the motion brought her in closer contact with his pillow, his sheets. She couldn't help but catch the manly scent of him; something like pine and nature and sunshine all rolled into one. Heath had smelled like strong soap—always. He'd believed in being overtly clean and she couldn't have picked out his natural scent in a million years, but this *Amisch* man—she would probably never forget . . . or cease to remember his willingness to share his bed with two near strangers.

She listened and the storm raged on, convincing her that she might as well try to sleep as the man opposite her seemed to be doing. His head was tilted back, his chest now fully covered, and his long legs were stretched out in front of him. She felt bad for staring at the breadth of his bare chest earlier . . . *but I hadn't expected it, that's all.* She snuggled closer to Hollie, pushing aside the memory of the other time she'd seen him, and near naked at that. She sighed to herself and drifted off, reluctantly allowing herself to enjoy the comfort of a real bed.

Chapter Six

He knew he was dreaming, but he was caught in that nether world between sleep and wakefulness and couldn't seem to escape . . .

She came toward him while he sat in the chair, and he reached out to feel for the hem of the brief shift she wore, pulling it up, urging her to him. He was hot and frantic, desperate in the desire of his flesh. "Please," he rasped, knowing she liked to hear him beg. But she teased him, holding back, until he caught a handful of her bleached blond hair and pulled hard . . .

He gasped and awoke with a jerk, his gaze searching the room in the early morning light. *Dear Gott . . . Amanda. I dreamed of Amanda. Why?* Then his darting eyes took in the two figures curled up on his bed in obvious slumber. He saw the red hair against his pillow and sat back, working for breath. Then he understood. His dreaming mind had gone where his body would not. It was safe to think of Amanda when he truly had desire for the woman who slept so peacefully with her child before him. The realization was devastating, and he was trying to deny his feelings when Edward's bedroom door suddenly opened.

Joseph stood up and crossed the room in long strides. He saw Edward's sleepy gaze sweep the bed.

"What the—?"

Joseph caught his *bruder* and unceremoniously dragged him back into his own room, closing the door behind them with a quiet click.

"I can explain," Joseph whispered.

Edward grinned at him. "Did I see the redheaded waitress in your bed?"

"*Nee . . . Jah.*" Joseph sighed in exasperation. "Did you also happen to notice her child?"

Edward rumpled his blond hair. "No, but Joe, what—?"

"Listen, Edward, they're homeless—Priscilla and her little girl. They live in a car out in the parking lot. It was raining last night and I worried for them, so I snuck them in. Now you can help me get them out."

Edward's blue eyes looked suddenly sober, and Joseph breathed a sigh of relief. No *Amisch* man from Ice Mountain would think of allowing such a circumstance for a woman and child, and he was glad he had Edward's attention.

"All right, big *bruder*. What do we do?"

Joseph looked at the clock on Edward's bedside table. Nearly five thirty a.m.

"We'll have to hurry," he said, trying to think. "Get dressed and let me go and wake them. I don't want her to be frightened."

Joseph started to open the door when Edward caught his shirt sleeve.

"What?"

Edward smiled. "It's nice to see you care, Joe."

He shook off his *bruder*'s hand and rolled his eyes as he quietly entered his bedroom. *But I don't want to care . . . I don't deserve to care . . . not ever.*

Priscilla turned her cheek into the subtle warmth of the touch on her face; then she bolted wide awake with a gasp.

Her eyes frantically searched the half-lit room, looking for Heath.

She gazed up at the tall *Amisch* man in confusion for a moment, then remembered where she was.

"You touched me," she accused in a hoarse whisper.

"I'm sorry. I had to wake you. You were sleeping so heavily." Joseph's deep voice registered true apology in her mind and she nodded, sinking next to Hollie to catch her breath. Then she rolled back and stared up at Joseph.

"Don't ever touch me again."

"I won't. I understand." He took a step away from the bed and she fought back the tears that came to her eyes.

He understands . . . but how can he? How can he know that every touch from Heath was merely a prelude to shocking violence, that our marriage bed was a place of scorn and brutality and . . .

"We have to hurry if you would like to be outside before others see you. The rain's stopped."

Priscilla felt her anxiety pulse upwards again at his words and frantically pushed away the covers. "I'll change fast." She rose and scurried to the bathroom, nearly tripping on the long nightshirt. She stripped off the flannel and grabbed her still damp clothes, careful not to look in the mirror as usual when she was naked. She dressed, then opened the door, only to stop dead still at the sight of Joseph's brother sitting on the bed, smiling at Hollie.

"What's going on?" She hated that her voice came out as a mere squeak. Joseph walked toward her as Hollie giggled out loud.

"Don't be afraid. I told Edward about your—situation. He's a *gut* man . . ."

"Thanks, Joe," Edward called from the bed with a wry look. "Priscilla, you have a beautiful daughter here. Why is she living in a car?"

Priscilla saw Joseph startle at his brother's words, and she almost reached out to touch his

53

arm. But she dropped her hand and lifted her chin instead, speaking with determination.

"Because it's home for now. It doesn't matter where you live—it matters who you live with," she quipped, then crawled onto the bed to start pulling on Hollie's outdoor things.

"Fair enough." Edward smiled.

"This is Joseph's brother, Mommy," Hollie announced proudly.

"I know, but we have to hurry. Now be still." Priscilla hated Hollie's sigh of discontent, but it was imperative that no one see them.

"What time are you on today?" Joseph asked quietly.

"Three to eleven." She gathered Hollie in her arms and scooted off the bed. "Can we go now?"

She watched as Joseph seemed to hesitate.

"I hate to think of you both in that cramped car. Would you—be willing to go out, maybe to a local farm where Hollie could pet the animals?"

"Are you asking her on a date, Joe?" Edward drawled, stretching his lean length back against the pillows.

Priscilla saw Joseph's handsome face flush and her heart beat faster.

"*Nee*, I—uh—wanted—"

"That would be nice," Priscilla interjected, telling herself that she didn't like Edward's mockery, and that was why she'd agreed.

Hollie wriggled in her arms. "Yay! A real farm. Can I ride a pony?"

"Maybe, little one. We'll see."

Priscilla liked the way his green-gold eyes softened when he looked at Hollie. Then he held out his arms. "May I carry her? She must be heavy for you."

Priscilla didn't have much choice as Hollie practically leaped from her into Joseph's grasp. *This is getting out of hand. Hollie cannot get too attached to this man . . . and neither can I.* She frowned at the sibilant whisper of her consciousness.

"Don't worry so much," Joseph whispered, almost as if he could read her thoughts, and Priscilla did not respond. Instead, she marched ahead of him to the door, nodded to Edward, and stepped into the hallway.

Joseph breathed a sigh of relief when he deposited Hollie into the back of the station wagon. Mercifully, no one had been about.

"I need to change out of these damp clothes," Priscilla said pointedly, and he took the broad hint in good form, though images of her bare arms and legs raked through his mind. *It must be hard to change in a car . . .*

"Surely," he said, snapping back to the moment at hand. "I'll—uh—go get us some breakfast to go."

He shut the car door and walked back to the inn, entering the dining room. A few roughnecks were gathered at the tables, and Edward beckoned him over.

Joseph took a seat next to his *bruder* with a faint sigh.

"Don't do it, Joe."

"Don't do what?"

Edward played with the rim of his ball cap for a second. "Fall for an *Englisch* girl and one with a *kind* at that."

"I thought you said it was nice to see me care," Joseph pointed out with a sour smile.

Edward leaned forward, his elbows on the table. "I was—wrong when I said that. And don't get all mad because I'm trying to be serious for once. You need a *gut Amisch* girl, who'll put up with your moods and cook and—"

"I am not moody," Joseph snapped.

Edward half smiled. "*Jah* . . . right."

Joseph drew a deep breath. "Look, I'm helping her out—that's all. I don't want anything else."

Edward picked up the menu and leaned back. "All right, Joe. Have it your way, but don't say I didn't warn you."

"I'll never give you the satisfaction."

Edward raised a sardonic brow. "And I'll dance at your wedding, big *bruder*. But tell me, will it be *Englisch* or *Amisch*?"

"Shut up."

"Don't mind if I do."

Joseph wanted to throttle Edward for stirring up such a churning caldron within him . . . After all, Priscilla had given him warning, and he had no doubt she meant it. *"Don't touch me ever again."* He swallowed hard, staring at his menu but not seeing the words as his mind scrabbled over the past. *"Don't touch me . . ."*

Chapter Seven

Priscilla tried to be casual about the excitement Hollie expressed over the amount of breakfast food that Joseph had provided.

"I wasn't sure what-all you both like, so I got a little of everything," he explained matter-of-factly as she let him climb into the car behind a towering stack of plastic takeout containers.

"Yay!" Hollie cried. "Are there pancakes?"

"Yep. Blueberry."

Priscilla watched Joseph out of the corner of her eye without intending to, noting that he'd removed his hat and accommodated his tall frame with relative ease in the cramped confines of the front passenger seat. He handed out containers with easy grace, his lean fingers adept at satisfying Hollie's request to cut up her pancakes. *He probably does many things well with his hands* . . . She shivered and pushed the thought

57

away, concentrating on biting a perfectly done strip of bacon.

When they'd finished, Joseph put the few remainders of food in a single container and Priscilla observed him settle more comfortably in the passenger seat. "All right, ma'am . . . How about that farm?"

She put the key in the ignition. "I don't know where to go. Do you want to drive?"

Joseph laughed. "I don't know how."

"Why can't you drive? Daddy could drive," Hollie announced.

Priscilla saw Joseph shrug good-naturedly. "I could probably figure it out in a pinch, but the *Amisch* where I come from don't drive and don't own cars."

"I should have remembered," Priscilla murmured, feeling the weight of Joseph's questioning gaze. "My mother was raised *Amisch*, but she gave it up to marry my father."

"She must love him a great deal then."

"She's dead," Priscilla said flatly, then added, "He's not."

Joseph's beautiful eyes met hers and the question hung eerily in the balance between them: *Do you wish he was?* Priscilla wet her lips and turned her head to put the car into drive. *Well, do I? Lord knows it would make my life easier, given the way dear old Daddy urges Heath to . . .* She drew a deep breath, reminding herself that she had determined to try not to be poisoned by the past.

"I'm sorry," she said briskly, glancing at Joseph.

He smiled a bit. "Families are complicated."

"Is yours?" she asked, then could have bitten her tongue at expressing an interest in his personal life.

"Well—" He rubbed his strong chin in thought. "This past summer, my sister married an *Englischer*, but then he became part of our community. My *daed* wasn't too thrilled with the wedding at first—neither was I, come to think of it. But my new *bruder*-in-law is a good man. His name's Jude and my sister is Mary. I miss them . . ."

"But you're here."

"*Jah* . . . and so is Edward. That's why I came—to look out for him."

Priscilla caught the introspective look on his face and couldn't resist asking him another question. "Is that the only reason you're here?"

She glanced at him, surprised by the intensity of his gaze, but then she shrugged. "You don't have to answer that. I've grown rather adept, out of necessity, at reading people, and the way you responded—I don't know—made me think there's more."

He cleared his throat and looked sober. "There is . . . I guess."

But Priscilla understood that the ensuing silence meant he had no desire to talk and concentrated instead on his quiet directions to the farm.

Joseph watched her small, competent hands on the wheel and wondered at her ability to read him so well when he barely understood himself at times. Certainly, he'd never tell anyone about his wayward nature and unholy desires—even the thoughts he'd already had about Priscilla would be enough to scare her. *And Gott knows she needs no more fear in her life . . .*

He assumed a jolly expression for Hollie's sake as they pulled up beside a large, bright red barn. It was still early in the morning, but he knew farmers were up for long hours before others. They got out of the station wagon and he was surprised and touched when Hollie slipped her small hand into his palm and swung his arm back and forth.

"This is gonna be fun, right, Mommy?"

Joseph glanced at Priscilla and saw her reserve. *Probably she doesn't want Hollie to get too close to any man after what happened with the father . . .*

An elderly man in a straw hat and overalls came out of the barn and smiled widely at them, displaying a large gap between his front teeth. "Hi, y'all. Come for the petting zoo, have you? I'm Mr. Green. Ben Green." He extended a hand over the fence and Joseph liked his firm grip.

"*Amisch*, are ya, sir? Not many around these parts."

"I'm from Pennsylvania," Joseph explained. "I work on the rigs."

"So ya got some time off for the missus and young'un? Well, step right this way. The petting zoo's been a success so far, but it was really my wife's idea. She passed from the cancer almost six months ago now, but I keep it going in her memory, like."

"I'm sorry for your loss," Priscilla said before Joseph could get the words out, and he noticed Priscilla didn't correct the man's assumption that they were a family.

Ben Green waved a gnarled hand and pulled on the barn door. "Not a loss, surely. For I'll go to her one day. So I pass the time with hope, and it makes things a mite easier."

"Do you have a pony?" Hollie piped up.

"Three of 'em, honey. You can take yer pick at the end here on which to ride."

"Yay!" She tugged on Joseph and he squeezed her hand gently in response.

They went through the barn happily, petting goats and sheep, looking with pleasure on a new lamb and its mother, and watching a variety of feathered-legged roosters parade past. Soon, Hollie broke away to walk with Mr. Green, and Joseph found himself near enough to Priscilla to catch her scent—something refreshing and delicate that sent his pulse racing and made him think of summer and sunshine and home . . . *You smell so good. I want to bury my face in your neck and touch your red hair and the creamy white skin of your throat and . . . Gott help me— I've never felt like this since—*

"Joseph?"

He nearly jumped, confused and caught in the pleasure of the fantasy. He felt his face flush and was glad for the dim interior of the barn as he turned toward Priscilla's voice.

"Did you farm in Pennsylvania? I always wanted to live on a farm." She was leaning on a support fence, gazing at some nursing piglets, and he had to take a moment to regain his equilibrium.

"I—we, my *daed* and I, did a bit of everything . . . farming, maple syrup making . . . I especially like woodworking, but that all seems a long way off."

She sighed aloud. "At least you had some freedom to choose. My father was—very controlling."

"Did he expect you to be perfect?"

"You got it, and I was far from that. In fact, I—" She broke off when there was a sharp, piercing cry from the other end of the barn. "Hollie!"

Joseph reached the stall first, taking the situation in at a glance. A horse's slashing hooves battered the barn wall and Hollie cried out again from inside the stall. Mr. Green was desperately trying to extract Hollie from the confined space and was doing so at his own peril. Joseph grabbed a bridle hanging nearby and got it around the horse's neck and began to speak low to the animal. At the same time, he bent and stretched into the stall to catch hold of Hollie's jacket. He pulled and the little girl ran out. At the same time, one last glancing kick by the horse caught him in the rib cage and he couldn't help the groan that escaped his lips. But then he got the horse settled and closed the stall door, turning to lean on it and breathing heavily.

"Lord have mercy," Mr. Green panted. "Is the young'un all right? She got away from me and was into that stall in a flash. I should have known better. I'm sorry."

Joseph felt his side dizzily and watched as Priscilla ran shaking hands over her daughter.

"I'm okay, Mommy. I'm sorry. I wanted to pet the horsie." Hollie began to sob in the aftermath.

"It's all right," Priscilla soothed. "Joseph, are you okay?"

"Right as rain," he managed, not wanting to make a big deal out of the pain that was making him blink.

"You don't look it, young man," Mr. Green said. He caught hold of Joseph's arm and gave it a brisk tug. The move made Joseph's world swim and he grasped the ridge of the stall door.

"Joseph," Priscilla said in a sharp voice.

"I'm fine." He straightened with a faint smile.

"Everything's fine." He took a step forward and promptly collapsed to his knees.

Mr. Green caught his shoulder and Priscilla rushed to his side. "We are going to a hospital!" she cried.

"Sounds *gut*," he gasped, then watched in fascination as the straw-strewn floor rose up to swallow him whole into blissful darkness.

"Shouldn't we get him a balloon, Mommy?" Hollie whispered the question from where she perched on Priscilla's lap. They were within the confines of a white, curtained emergency room unit, and Joseph lay asleep on a portable bed.

"No, honey, he has to rest."

Priscilla drew a deep breath as she watched the even rise and fall of his bandaged ribs. *He risked his life to save my little girl . . .*

The curtain was briskly drawn aside and a comfortable-looking nurse entered. She cast an eye over Joseph, then patted Priscilla's shoulder.

"You can take him home, honey, as soon as he comes around. The doc gave him something for the pain when he set his ribs, and that's making him sleepy. He's lucky he didn't puncture a lung. If you'll sign these papers for him, I'll find a Popsicle for this little one, and you can help him get his shirt on."

Priscilla opened her mouth to protest, but the nurse had already left the papers on a nearby tray and whisked Hollie outside the curtain. Priscilla rose, biting her lip, and approached the makeshift bed. His body was so big, so . . . male, and she felt guilty at the sensation of pleasure that skimmed the back of her brain as she ran her fingers gently along his bare forearm. He stirred, the heavy fall of his dark lashes lifting a bit at her touch.

She was surprised when she touched his shoulder that he murmured and seemed to want to get closer to her hand, arching his neck and half sighing. She glanced at the curtain, then allowed herself to brush the backs of her fingertips over the brown male nipple nearest her and caught her breath at his reaction. Seemingly unhindered by his injuries, he lifted his arm and slipped it behind her, pulling her inexorably, intimately close, so that her mouth hovered a bare inch from his. She wanted to struggle but wouldn't risk hurting his ribs further, so she waited a moment, her heartbeat thrumming in her ears. She stared down at him and thought about how kind he'd been to her and Hollie. *He's so good and innocent . . . how could he ever understand?*

"You're so beautiful," he breathed, his eyes still closed. "But I can't—not if you knew."

"Knew what?" she whispered, amazed at how her toes tingled at the intermingling of their breath.

"Everything," he slurred.

"I think I know enough," she was amazed to

hear herself say, then dipped her head so that her mouth touched his.

He made a strangled sound in his throat; half protest, half want, and then she lost track of who was kissing whom as he lifted his head and she tangled her hands in his dark hair.

Chapter Eight

The last vestiges of the pain medicine cleared the edge of his consciousness and he came fully awake to the odd sensation that there was something important he should remember. But Priscilla was urging him into his light blue shirt, and his side ached something awful. He remembered the old farmer helping her get him into the station wagon and then the brutal drive to the hospital. He even remembered the brusque doctor sticking a needle in his arm and starting on his bandaging before the full effect of the drug kicked in. But something else niggled at his mind, then drifted away.

He stood up from the bed with some encouragement from the motherly nurse and winced when Priscilla offered him his right suspender.

"I'll only use the one. *Danki.*"

She nodded, ducking her head, and he barely got a glimpse of her face, but something about her posture made him sense that she was nervous.

"Is everything all right, Priscilla?" he asked quietly when she handed him his coat.

She looked up at him, her beautiful blue eyes luminous, her pupils dilated. He shook his head. *I could get lost in those eyes . . . like swimming in warm twin pools that envelop and slicken and speak of wet mysteries and secret places. I am losing my mind . . . maybe it's the drug. I hope it's the drug . . .*

"Let's worry about you, all right?" she asked, and he nodded dutifully, feeling foolish for his thoughts.

"Thank you for saving me, Joseph," Hollie chirped between loud sucks on a purple Popsicle. She sat on a nearby chair, her thin legs swinging, and he had to smile.

"You're welcome, little one."

The nurse bustled over to Priscilla. "Here's a prescription for pain medicine, if he needs it. Now, y'all take care." A buzzer sounded from down the hall and she hurried out.

Priscilla gave him his hat and he tried to lift his arm to put it on, but she took it back at his obvious grimace and stretched to place it on his head.

"*Danki*," he said, noting that she quickly took a step away from him.

"*Gaern gscheh*," she muttered.

He smiled in surprise and she shrugged. "I still remember a little Penn Dutch from my mother."

"You sound like Joseph, Mommy . . . How come?" Hollie asked.

"It's only a few words, Hollie, in another type of language. Now finish up. We've got to get back to the inn. Mommy's got to go to work."

Joseph glanced at the clock on the wall, surprised to see it was after noon.

"Well, let's stop somewhere and get you something to eat before your shift," he suggested. "I know I'm starving."

"Me too. Mommy, please?"

Priscilla sighed aloud. "All right. I think the hospital has a cafeteria."

Joseph found that walking was not exactly comfortable, but he followed gladly in Priscilla's wake with Hollie clinging to his left hand.

They entered the small but bright cafeteria as sunlight poured in from large windows, high-lighting Priscilla's bright head. *Her hair looks so soft . . .* Joseph mused. Then remembrance slammed into him and he knew instinctively that he'd touched her hair, stroked her throat, kissed her mouth . . . He stopped dead still.

"Joseph, what's wrong?" Hollie tugged on his arm, then let go.

Priscilla turned around and searched his face and their eyes locked. He saw the tumult of emotions in the blue depths and knew his thoughts were true.

"Dear Gott—I . . ." He choked out the words,

watching her face flame in acknowledgment, and was vaguely aware that Hollie had darted off in the direction of the food. "Priscilla, I'm so sorry . . . I didn't mean . . ." *Monster! I'm an unholy monster—she's been through heaven knows what, and there I was touching . . .*

She stepped near him and shook her head. "Of course you didn't mean anything. You were—drugged and I, well, I . . ."

"Mommy!" Hollie cried loudly, breaking the moment. Joseph looked where the little girl pointed to a bulletin board on the cafeteria wall. "Mommy, look! It's your picture."

Joseph saw Priscilla's face drain of all color and for a scary moment, he thought she might faint.

"Oh God," she whispered, and started to walk toward Hollie.

Joseph followed slowly, watching the tension in every line of her slight frame. He'd tracked wounded animals on the mountain and had the eerie feeling now that he was following a trail of misery that could end in nothing good.

Priscilla caught her daughter's pointing hand and pulled her close. Then she went to the bulletin board and ripped the homemade flyer with her picture from the corkboard. She crumpled the paper in her free, damp hand and yanked Hollie in the direction of the nearest exit.

"Mommy, wait! I'm hungry!"

"Hush, Hollie. We have to go."

"Where are you going?"

Priscilla stopped as Joseph's voice broke into her panicked thoughts. She stared up at him, his worried visage seeming to fade in and out before her eyes.

"Priscilla?"

She whirled and focused on the way they'd come in, ignoring Hollie's increasing wails.

"Priscilla, wait." Joseph got in front of her and she stubbornly moved to go around him, but he was equally fast. "*Sei se gut* . . . let me help you."

She shook her head mutely, trying to ignore his palpable concern and watched him pull some dollar bills from his pocket. "Hollie," he said low, breaking into the child's sobs. He crouched down in front of her daughter, despite his injured ribs. "Be a big girl and go and get what you want to eat. I need to talk to your *mamm* for a minute, all right?"

"Yay!" Hollie ran off and Priscilla blindly scrambled into a plastic chair, aware that he sank into a seat beside her.

"You don't understand," she muttered, gripping the edge of the table with her free hand.

"I want to." He reached for her hand beneath the table and gently pulled the crumpled paper from her fingertips. She let him, too tired to care for a moment. *All of my plans, again . . . gone. Why?*

She watched Joseph spread open the paper, smoothing it against the artificial grain of the table. He read for a brief moment, then looked at her squarely, his handsome face taut and white, but somehow reassuring at the same time.

"How long have you been running?" he asked.

She covered her face with her hands, then dropped them again, shrugging. "Nearly eight months. This time—I thought maybe . . ."

She watched him stare down at the words; then he looked at her again, his unusual eyes more green than gold now. "I have to know, Priscilla . . . are you still married?"

She would have laughed if she were not so near tears. *Of course you want to know that, because you're Amisch and you're innocent while I'm—*

"Priscilla?"

She shook her head. "No, Joseph. We were divorced almost two years ago, but Heath has never—he's never been able to accept it, or the fact that I received full custody of Hollie—as you can see." She eyed the flyer bitterly from an upside-down angle—it always said the same thing . . .

HELP ME FIND MY BELOVED WIFE. MISSING WITH YOUNG CHILD. LARGE REWARD.

CALL HEATH ST. CLAIR AT . . .

"Has he ever found you?"

Priscilla dropped her gaze. *Ah, this man and his dark hair and beautiful mouth and probing mind . . .* "Once. He kept me locked in a room for four days without food, kept Hollie from me.

71

I got away—found Hollie. We've been running ever since . . ."

Joseph drew a deep breath, then laid his hands flat on the table, as if in decision. "Look, do you want to be free of all of this running and hiding?"

"Of course," she said wearily.

He folded the flyer and put it in his pants pocket. "All right. Then come with me. I know a place . . . a world away . . . and he'll never find you or Hollie there, ever."

Priscilla knew it was more than a gamble, but she also understood the clear truth in Joseph's eyes. Something old and good resonated in her soul and the words were on her lips before she knew what she'd said.

"I'll go."

Chapter Nine

"Dang it all, honey. If I'd known you were homeless with a little girl, I would've given you my own bed to sleep in." Mary Malizza stood gaping at the little waitress she'd hired, after listening to her explain why she was leaving.

The pretty little thing sure didn't need to run off with another fella, though Mary knew that the *Amisch* brothers held a moral code that many of her patrons did not. Still . . .

"He's not forcing you in any way, is he?"

"Who? Joseph?" Priscilla shook her head vehemently. "Not at all. I'm tired of running, to tell the truth, and my mama was *Amisch*. He's just giving me a chance . . ."

"A chance at what? Don't you wanna know what his intentions are?"

She watched the girl's thin shoulders shake with a mirthless laugh. "I trust him. He doesn't have any intentions, and I don't want any, really."

Mary paced the confines of her office and could tell that the kid was itching to be gone. "Hey, I'm gonna give you some cash. You keep it for an emergency and you can consider it a loan, because I know you're gonna be all huffy about it."

"I really don't need—"

"Hush!" Mary snapped, pulling on her big glasses and rooting in the desk drawer. "I keep a little petty cash around. Now, here's an envelope. It's five hundred dollars."

Priscilla stared at her, clearly speechless.

"If you woulda told me the truth, I could have done more for you sooner. Remember that when you go. Tell the truth. Not all folks are as wacky as that ex-husband of yours."

The girl nodded and Mary sniffed and rose to come around the desk. She enfolded Priscilla's small frame against her robust bosom and squeezed long and hard. *Poor kid . . . probably hasn't had a hug in years.*

After the embrace, she gave Priscilla's shoulder a firm shake. "Now you take care, you hear? And take care of that young'un."

Priscilla nodded and left, and Mary stared at her office ceiling while she counted to ten, determined not to cry.

"Are you out of your mind?" Edward demanded.

Joseph concentrated on folding a shirt and put it in his satchel, despite the resulting ache in his side. "I'll only be gone long enough to ask Bishop Umble to give Priscilla and Hollie safety—sanctuary—for a time."

"*Jah*, right . . . and then you're going to worry about her, and then you're not going to be able to leave her, and then you'll obsess over her, because you have chosen to fall in love with her—a runaway woman who probably wouldn't know the truth from a—"

His *bruder*'s words penetrated, and Joseph spun, grasping Edward by his shirt front.

"Shut up." He punctuated the words with hard shakes, ignoring the pain in his ribs.

Edward rolled his eyes. "What are you gonna do, Joseph, Mr. Perfect *Amischer*? Beat me up for telling the truth?"

Joseph realized that he'd laid hands on his *bruder*, laid hands on another in anger for the first time in his life, and his arms went slack in an instant. He dropped his hands and sank down onto the bed. "Edward . . . I'm sorry. Forgive me. I don't know why I . . ."

"Forget it and listen to me."

Joseph lifted his eyes as Edward tugged down his shirt. "Look, Joe, it's only that I don't want to see you get hurt. And I'm the one who owes you an apology. I don't know Priscilla or what she's been through, but my point is that you don't know either. And I'm running out of time here to convince you before I go."

Joseph studied Edward's serious expression with a frown. "What did you say? Go? Where?"

Edward sat down beside him on the edge of the bed. "Joseph, I've been offered a better job with the rigs and I'm going to take it. But it's in Texas."

"What? How am I supposed to . . ." Joseph felt the weight of his *bruder*'s strong arm across his shoulders for an instant.

"You—are not supposed to do anything but go home. I don't need you to watch over me, and whether you want to admit it or not, you've gotten yourself tangled with a woman."

Joseph straightened his shoulders. "I am not tangled."

"Worse than a trout with one of Daed's blue slicker flies, Joe."

Joseph felt a faint smile come to his lips at Edward's analogy. "At least not that bad."

"Worse." Edward laughed.

Joseph nodded slowly. "What about Sarah?"

"I've written to her already. She knows I'm planning on going, and I can make twice the money in half the time. Don't worry. I'll not abandon the woman I courted with intent to marry."

Joseph felt his world whirl at his *bruder*'s seemingly calm and mature words. *Maybe Edward is grown up and I'm the one who's really got things to figure out.*

A tentative knock sounded on the door and Joseph rose to answer it, expecting Priscilla.

"I'll get it, Joe. Finish packing."

Joseph glanced briefly into his brother's eyes. "Hey . . . I'll miss you."

Edward ducked his head, then smiled. "I think you'll find you're too busy to do much of that . . ." He flung open the door with a flourish. Joseph stared at Priscilla's beautiful, pale face as she held Hollie, and he knew his little *bruder* was probably more than right.

"Are we going on another adventure, Mommy?" Hollie's voice was plaintive on the night air coming in through the open windows of the station wagon.

Priscilla tightened her grip on the wheel and resisted the urge to glance sideways at Joseph. She'd stopped at a small pharmacy about an hour from the rigs and had gotten his pain medicine prescription filled. Now he appeared to be drowsing in the passenger seat, but she had the strange feeling that he was listening to every word.

"We're going to some place special with Joseph."

"Where?" Hollie demanded, clearly needing some sleep.

"I don't know." *I don't know and I'm trusting this man with my life, my child, my future . . .*

"But where?" Hollie whined.

Priscilla sighed aloud in exasperation.

Joseph sat up a bit straighter in his seat and opened his eyes. "We're going to the place where I grew up—it's a mountain. Ice Mountain is its name. It's peaceful—real pretty."

"Will we have to stay in the car?"

Priscilla caught the smile that lifted the side of his handsome mouth. "*Nee,* in fact, there's no road to the top of the mountain. We'll have to leave the car at the bottom with an *Englisch* friend of mine."

"Oh." Hollie yawned. "What's *Eng—lisch?*"

"*Ach,* well, like you and your *mamm*—someone who's not *Amisch.*"

"Okay."

Priscilla glanced in the rearview mirror and saw her daughter's head slowly nod to one side against the door.

"Whew, she's asleep at last, I think," Priscilla whispered after a moment. "Sometimes I get tired . . ." She stopped. *Am I going to admit to this man how tired I actually do feel at times?* She felt tears prick the backs of her eyelids and hastily swiped a hand across her face, telling herself she didn't want anything to affect her driving.

"Hey." The rich timbre of his husky voice soothed her. "Are you all right? I wish I could offer to drive . . . or we could stop at a hotel soon."

She shook her head. "I'm fine, thanks. So, do we really have to hike to your community?"

He relaxed back in the seat. "Yep, and Mr. Ellis will take good care of the car, I'm sure."

"How can you be sure? He doesn't even know we're coming." She couldn't keep the faint note of anxiety out of her voice.

"Don't worry," he soothed.

Don't worry . . . She wondered what he'd do if she gave in to the sudden hysterical laughter that bubbled behind her tight lips.

"What will your bishop say? How do you know anyone will accept us and what if—"

"Priscilla, all will be well. Derr Herr goes before us."

It was easy for him to speak of God with such confidence, she thought ruefully. *He probably hasn't ever been hurt badly.* But she was able to lay aside her fears for the moment despite her lingering doubts, and concentrated on the dark stretch of road in front of them.

Joseph stared out the window at the dark trees passing in a blur. He'd had to speak with confidence to Priscilla; there was nothing else to do. If his sister hadn't managed to get an *Englischer* into the community, he'd have no true point of reference as to whether or not Bishop Umble would allow a divorced woman and her child such access. But he decided he'd figure something else out if this didn't work. *What had Edward said? Tangled . . .*

"So, your—uh—Heath—was . . ."

"Is," she corrected succinctly.

"*Ach.*"

"I know it's most likely hard for you to imagine, but sometimes people who seem like they are doing one thing with their lives—maybe a kind thing—are really up to something else."

The thought of Amanda drifted across his mind. *I was seemingly kind, wanting to help, and then I . . .*

"You have that look on your face," Priscilla interjected. "I can tell, even in the dark."

"What look?"

"Like you're someplace faraway—maybe a complicated place."

"*Jah.*" He sighed and then was silent.

After a moment, he saw her shrug. "You don't owe me anything, Joseph. Even this—mountain you're taking us to. You can back out. I could take you somewhere nearby and you could—"

"Priscilla, *sei se gut.* I've told you, all will be well."

She nodded and he felt like the scum on a pond when he suddenly recalled kissing her in the hospital. Somehow, all of those pulse-pounding moments had been lost in the tumult since Hollie had seen the bulletin board. He swallowed hard now and gazed at her pale profile in the shifting shadows.

"Priscilla?"

"Hmm?"

"Back at the hospital, when I was drugged— I touched you. I broke my word not to touch you." He turned away toward the passenger window, then closed his eyes tight. "Don't worry. It won't ever happen again."

Chapter Ten

Priscilla gazed with deep appreciation on the rolling mountains of Northern Pennsylvania, full of the myriad greens of late spring.

"Not much further now," Joseph said encouragingly.

She could tell there was a tense excitement about his big body. *He must have missed home a great deal.* And then a pressing thought came to her with insidious power. *Perhaps he's missing his betrothed or even his wife. But he kissed me. Yet he didn't know what he was doing.* She forced her tired mind to focus on the mountainous road and resolved not to become any more emotionally involved with the handsome *Amischer.*

Hollie chattered happy questions from the backseat, which Joseph seemed to answer with seemingly endless patience.

"What's wrong? Do you need to stop and stretch your legs?" Joseph asked, leaning over a bit in the seat, so that she caught his scent.

"Nooo . . . I'll be glad to get there. I guess I was wondering—what your girlfriend or wife might think about us arriving together." Priscilla felt her face flame even as she spoke the unbidden words and was surprised when Joseph's face took on an ashen hue.

"I'm not married. I don't have a betrothed. That's not—it's not the life for me."

"Oh." Priscilla felt worse for some strange reason. There was something about the way he spoke that seemed mournful. *Maybe he lost a girl to sickness . . .*

"So, you don't have a wife, Joseph?" Hollie asked, breaking the moment.

"Nope, little one."

"That's good," she gurgled. "Then you can marry me when I grow up."

Joseph laughed, and Priscilla was relieved to see his good humor restored. "Now that will be a blessed man who marries you, *kind* . . . Turn off to the left up here."

Priscilla did as he directed and found her heart

beginning to pound hard in her chest, though there was nothing alarming about the neat white house bordered by spreading myrtle with purple flowers, which climbed the outside wall of the large adjacent garage.

"Mr. Ellis lives here," Joseph confirmed, opening the door and getting out.

Priscilla sat still behind the wheel, uncertain what to do. She caught Hollie's hand in a gentle grip when the child would have followed Joseph.

"No, honey. Wait."

"Aww, but Mommy!"

"Wait," she said again firmly.

She watched a pleasant-looking, middle-aged *Englisch* man with a mustache come out onto the porch and saw Joseph speaking and gesturing back to the car. Mr. Ellis appeared to take the situation in stride as he made his way down the front steps and Joseph hurried over to the driver's door to open it.

"*Kumme*," he said gently. "It's all right."

"Yay!" Hollie tore out of the car and Priscilla suppressed a mental groan.

But Mr. Ellis proved equal to the child, who was jumping about him like a rambunctious puppy, and the older man gave a hearty laugh as he shook Priscilla's hand.

"Quite a handful you've got here, ma'am."

"Yes, at times."

"Well, good times I'm sure. Joseph here

explained that you need your car kept for a bit. I'll put it in the garage." He glanced at Joseph. "It wasn't too long ago that I was housing an Expedition in there for your brother-in-law."

Priscilla saw Joseph's grin as he spoke. "A more humble vehicle here, Mr. Ellis."

"Yep. Well, if you'll give me the keys, I'll drive her in."

Priscilla paused before handing over the key-chain with its brass diver's helmet on it—a token of a long-ago vacation to the sea. She colored, then lifted her chin. "I'm afraid I've very little money to give you, Mr. Ellis. How much do you need for keeping the car?"

Mr. Ellis looked to Joseph, then shook his head with a kind smile. "It's all taken care of, young lady. No worries."

Priscilla turned to Joseph. "I can't let you . . ." she began, then stopped at his reassuring smile. "Oh, all right. But it's a loan." She gave Mr. Ellis the keys.

"Deal," Joseph said.

She watched the two men shake hands; then Joseph gestured over to where the road curved into a shadowed hollow. She watched him take Hollie's hand with a casual ease that seemed to calm her daughter. Then he gestured with his strong chin. "This way, ladies."

Priscilla nodded to Mr. Ellis and followed Joseph and Hollie into the greenery, discovering an earthen path, and feeling that her life was about to change forever.

Joseph pushed through the overhang of leafy branches and stopped still as he felt the familiar cool rush of a secret breeze soothe his heart and mind.

"Joseph," Hollie whispered beside him. "It's cold here all of a sudden. How come?"

He smiled down at the child. "It's a mystery, *kind*. Would you like to see more?" He glanced over his shoulder at Priscilla and thought how right her bright hair and pale skin looked among the chill green. *She's like some exotic wild flower touched by the sun . . .*

He turned back, catching hold of his thoughts, then led them to the place a few feet away where the unusual, bright green ferns grew at the base of an outcropping of rock.

He let Hollie tiptoe near the jutting rock and heard her small exclamation of surprise and awe. "Joseph, there's a door here. Where does it go to? Is it a fairy house? Mommy doesn't believe in fairy tales, but I think that they might be true. Can we go in? Can we?"

"Wait, little one. Let's show your *mamm*." He stepped aside for Priscilla to peer into the alcove of the stacked rock.

"It is a door," she said in disbelief.

Joseph reached into a high crevice and found the

hammer he knew was hidden there. "Well, a boarded-up sort of door. I can open it, if you'd both like?"

"Please, Mommy?" Hollie begged.

"What is this place?" Priscilla asked, and Joseph was pleased to see the mystified look on her delicate features.

This place . . . was something he understood with clarity even when the rest of his life was a jumble of confusion. He knew true pleasure in removing the planks of gray wood from the entrance, almost as if he was revealing a part of himself that he believed worthwhile.

"It's a natural ice mine," he said as he pulled the last board, heedless of the ache in his ribs, and laid it aside. He caught Hollie's hand before she could plunge into the black opening revealed by the wood. "Whoa! Let me get the light."

"There's a light?" Priscilla asked, doubt evident in her voice.

"Yep. Hold the little one's hand. It'll only take me a second and . . ." He reached inside the looming blackness and felt for the kerosene lantern and matches. He fumbled with the lantern for a moment; then the flame burned bright and he swung it into the darkness.

"Mommy! Look—it's all sparkly. It is a fairy house, made of ice!"

Joseph watched Priscilla, wanting her to feel his joy in the place, but instead he saw her cross her arms protectively and shiver visibly in the blast of cold air from the mine. He turned back to the entrance and shrugged to himself. *Well, it's not like I believe in fairy tales either . . .*

Chapter Eleven

Priscilla stepped cautiously onto the ice mine's dirt floor, skirting the large, deep hole near the center of the cave. She allowed her gaze to follow where the play of the lantern light caught on the giant icicles that formed the walls of the mine.

"I don't understand," she said, her voice seeming to echo in the chilly dampness. "It's spring. This all should be melting, right?" She glanced over to see Joseph wearing a bright smile that took her breath away almost as much as the cold did.

"You would think that, but actually, the ice is at its fullest in high summer, and this place is bone dry in winter. Scientists have actually come and tried to explain why it happens, but I guess I look at it as an example of Gott's providing when it's needed most."

She didn't answer, not wanting to offend him with her doubts about God's presence here. *After all, if He never took care of me, why would He care about a cave filled with ice, no matter how pretty it is?*

"What's the big hole in the floor, Joseph?" Hollie asked, and Priscilla could tell that her daughter was in awe of the place.

"Different people have tried to dig over time, down into the ground. They looked for silver, but all they ever found were some old bones and plants frozen in ice."

"I want to dig . . . Can we dig, Joseph?" Hollie jumped and Priscilla caught her close, away from the edge.

"*Nee*, little one. The mine is not my people's. It belongs to someone who lives far away, so we *Amisch* sort of watch over it. I don't think digging would be the right thing to do. But now, up on the mountain, you can dig as much as you want. Maybe your *mamm* will want to start a garden."

Priscilla shook her head. She had no idea how long they'd even be staying, yet here he was, speaking so casually about something as lasting as a garden. She opened her mouth to protest, not wanting Hollie to get her hopes up, but Joseph held up a large hand in the play of lantern light.

"Priscilla, I'm sorry. I shouldn't have spoken about a garden. I was thinking and . . . well, I apologize."

"Thank you," she murmured, ignoring Hollie's groan and focusing once more on how quickly |and easily he sought to make things right by admitting when he was wrong. It was a trait in a man that she'd never seen in everyday life.

"Well, we'd best head up the mountain. If you'll both step outside, I'll put the boards back up."

She watched him hold the lantern up with his left hand and she hurried Hollie out, blinking in the bright light of day. Joseph was quick with the wood, despite his injury, and Priscilla struggled to think of something to say, but she didn't want to plague him with questions.

Soon they were climbing the earthen track and Priscilla watched as mountain laurel gave way to bright shrubbery, then blueberry bushes, and finally a stand of tall pines. They stepped into a large meadow and she caught her breath, feeling winded not only from the climb but also struggling with a sudden bout of anxiety. The wide spread of grass and wildflowers seemed to question her very presence, as if each blade whispered to a leaf, wondering who she was, and she could not help but think that the *Amisch* themselves would probably do the very same thing.

"Who is she again?" Bishop Umble asked between large bites of thick oatmeal.

Joseph sighed and glanced through the kitchen window out onto the porch where Frau Umble was serving cookies and lemonade to Priscilla and Hollie.

Joseph turned back to the *auld* man who'd been the bishop on Ice Mountain since before Joseph was born. *Maybe he's getting hard of hearing . . .*

"Have you read 'Rime of the Ancient Mariner,' Joseph?"

And losing his train of thought as well as the hearing . . . "*Jah* . . . the sailor tells his tale over and over and the bird and—"

Bishop Umble stopped him with a raised, gnarled hand. "Right. Right. But my point is that sometimes a person needs to tell his story more than once to find what he's looking for in it. So tell me again, who she is . . . and what is it that you look for, young man?"

Joseph's head throbbed faintly and his ribs hurt. He wished he'd had the foresight to take one of his pain pills before this meeting with the bishop; the man wanted him to think, and he would rather have been sleeping at the moment. But he hung on to the thread of meaning and tried again.

"I'm not looking for a wife." The words were out of his mouth before he could stop, and he wondered if the pain was making him strange.

"Hmm. I asked what you looked for, *buwe*, not the opposite. Though sometimes it's easier to start in the other direction."

Joseph leaned his head in his hand for a moment. An image came to him and he lifted his head to look into the wise blue eyes opposite him. "Once, when I was about five, I was outside alone in the dead of winter. I put out my tongue to touch the metal runner of my little sled and I was caught, mercilessly. I, by my own doing, had to rip my mouth away in order to free myself. I went in the *haus* bleeding all over . . ." *Now why* en der weldt *did I think of that?*

"And?" the bishop prompted quietly.

"And . . . it hurt. I think—I think that's what Priscilla's had to do in her own life—rip herself away from everything familiar because she had no choice; she had to free herself—was forced into it even. I'm looking for sanctuary for her, sir. A place to bleed and heal . . . and for the child too."

"Then it will be Derr Herr who brings her that healing. Not you, Joseph King."

"I know that."

The bishop scraped his oatmeal bowl while Joseph held his breath.

"Well," the older man said finally, "I must speak to the elders of course, but as for me . . . I give my permission for Priscilla and Hollie Allen to stay. At your sister's *haus*. If she will have them . . . if her husband will have them."

"*Danki*, sir." Joseph felt a surge of relief, though he was disconcerted at the idea of Priscilla being so close, if Mary would have her. He'd thought maybe one of the widows would . . .

"Joseph?"

"*Jah*, sir?"

"Pray for Priscilla as she discovers her healing. But I'd like you to keep your intentions in regard to her holy. Remember, a prayer partner. But who knows, Derr Herr might find her a fine *Amisch* suitor as well in the process. Now, let's go and talk with her."

"*Jah* . . ." Joseph muttered, suddenly terrified at the idea of being a prayer partner in Priscilla's life. *A prayer partner—a man with a woman? What is wrong with the bishop's head? And where did the idea of a suitor* kumme *from?* But he had no time to consider further as Bishop Umble opened the front door and the sun caught the bright fall of Priscilla's hair, making him forget all else.

Priscilla gazed with pleasure around the simple living area with its pale blue paint and odd but beautiful drawing of a mermaid on the wall. Her hostess, Joseph's younger sister, Mary Lyons, stepped lightly into the room despite the rounded curve of her abdomen. The girl was truly beautiful and Priscilla wondered idly if all of Joseph's family were so gifted with good looks.

"There," Mary said, moving to press against Joseph's side once more. She clearly loved and had missed her brother, and Joseph returned the affection openly. "Your daughter's playing with little apple-pie pans and some leftover dough at the kitchen table. Jude should be home any minute. He's the local school teacher. *Ach*, please sit down."

Mary gestured to the comfortable-looking

couch, then took a place near Priscilla while Joseph eased into a rocking chair beside the open fireplace.

"When are you due?" Priscilla asked softly, casting about for something to say in the sudden quiet of the room.

Mary smiled brightly. "About another two months. Then Joseph here will be *Oom* Joseph. I only wish Edward might *kumme* home soon too." Priscilla watched the siblings exchange glances and wondered what it must be like to have grown up with brothers or a sister. *It might have made a difference in my life, yet Hollie will be an only child too, and . . .*

She looked up to find Joseph's beautiful eyes looking over at her, and she flushed at her thoughts. *The way I was kissing him in the ER, he probably thinks I'm looking for another man. Not that Heath was ever a true man, not one of honor or decency or hope.*

Mary laid a cool hand over the fingers Priscilla clenched tightly together in her lap.

"Priscilla, don't be anxious. I know Jude will agree with the bishop. We will be so glad to welcome you into our home, both you and Hollie."

Priscilla swallowed and wet her lips. "*Danki*, but you all will want to be alone soon with the baby and I don't even know how long we'll stay and—"

"And," Joseph rumbled gently, "stop worrying. You'll stay here if Jude agrees, which I think he will do too. Let tomorrow's worries take care of themselves."

The front door eased open as Joseph finished speaking and Priscilla looked up with some anxiety at the tall, broad-shouldered man who entered. But she realized she needn't have worried when Mary ran to meet him and he caught her close, then moved to pull Joseph into a back-slapping hug.

"You must be Priscilla." He turned to her and held out an easy hand.

She shook hands, noticing he spoke with a different accent from his wife and brother-in-law. He must have read her thoughts because he grinned.

"I'm from Atlanta originally. These *Amisch* were *gut* enough to have mercy on me and take me in."

"Like me?" Priscilla bit her lip, regretting her quick words. But Jude shrugged with good humor.

"If you'll have us all, yes," Jude said.

Priscilla's eyes filled with tears. "Oh, I'm sorry. Of course, I'll have you. Thank you so much."

Joseph cleared his throat. "Where's Bear, by the way?"

"You have a bear?" Priscilla asked in surprise and not a little dismay.

Jude laughed. "Something like that. He's at your

dat's. Abner's been a bit lonesome, it seems. It's *gut* you're back, Joe."

Priscilla saw the concern in Joseph's face.

"I'd better go see him then." He glanced at Priscilla. "Tell Hollie I said good-bye."

"Oh—are you—I mean. Will I see you soon?" She didn't want to admit it, but she felt as if her lifeline was about to leave.

Joseph paused for a moment, his hand on the door latch. "*Jah*, soon. I forgot to tell you, the bishop made me your prayer partner."

Something tight and harsh seemed to mask his face and she stared at him in consternation. *Maybe he wants to have nothing to do with me now that he feels he's done his duty or something . . .* "Oh, okay."

He nodded and slipped out of the door, leaving Priscilla to lay her worries aside and be warmly welcomed into her new home.

Chapter Twelve

Joseph trod the mountain path with familiar confidence, letting his fingertips trail over the odd bush or tree branch with the feeling of greeting *auld* friends. He found himself hurrying though as he approached his old home, not able to get Jude's brief words about his *fater* out of his mind.

He came upon the clearing and stopped still for a moment, drinking in the sight of the ramshackle, humble cabin with its trail of rose vines—a long-ago testament to his *dat*'s love for Joseph's deceased *mamm*. Then he realized that the roof needed some new shingles shaved and that the kitchen garden seemed thin. *Maybe Daed's worse off than Jude could say . . .*

He hurried down the grass hill and the cabin door opened as a large, tumultuous pile of dark fur and loping legs hurled itself at him.

Joseph laughingly greeted the wolf dog. "Bear! Old fellow . . . been up to hunting anything bigger than you lately?" Joseph was slobbered on for his trouble and he smiled into the single eye of the dog, the other having been lost in a battle with a real bear. "All right . . . down, *buwe*!"

Joseph straightened and blinked as his *dat* came out onto the porch of the cabin. His *fater* seemed to have aged ten years over the past months and Joseph was alarmed at his thinness and the pronounced gray in his dark hair and beard.

"Daed?" Joseph mounted the steps and paused, then caught the older man in a quick embrace. He pulled away, amazed to see his normally taciturn father's eyes well with tears.

"I'm glad you're home, *sohn*."

"I'm happy to be here—I've missed you and Bear and—everybody."

"Will you be staying on a bit? The bishop came by and said you brought a woman and child with you—*Englischers*."

Joseph felt his side begin to throb and he shifted his weight on the uneven boards of the porch. "*Jah*, Daed. Can we go inside, and then I'll tell you about it."

"*Kumme* in, *sohn*. It'll always be your home here, no matter what."

And no matter who I bring home? I have to wonder . . .

But his negativity melted when he entered the *auld* home. He breathed in the familiar smells of wood smoke and lemon polish and was glad to see the place was clean.

"Mary—she *kummes* over often, though I tell her not to bother with the babe on the way."

"She's probably glad to help, Dat." He patted Bear absently and took a seat at the small kitchen table while his father poured two mugs of coffee.

"You hurt your side somehow, *sohn*?"

"It's nothing."

His *fater* arched a shaggy brow and Joseph shrugged. "I broke a few ribs getting in the way of an angry stallion. Priscilla's little girl, Hollie, was playing around and—"

"Priscilla." His *dat* said the very *Englisch* name as if he tasted a drop of mustard.

Joseph suppressed a sigh. "What did Bishop Umble tell you?"

"Enough to know the woman's had a hard lot and with a *kind* . . . Somehow, I guess I thought that you'd be marrying one of our girls from the mountain though."

"I'm not marrying anyone."

His *fater* gave a gruff laugh. "You hold on to that thought, *sohn*. Maybe it'll save you some heartache."

Joseph smiled sadly. *If only he knew what I've done* . . . "Well, Dat, it seems Derr Herr doses out heartache to everyone now and then, and there's no sense trying to avoid it." He took a long pull of his coffee, then got to his feet. "I'm going out to the shed to shave a few shingles for the roof."

His *fater* snorted familiarly. "Well, you won't be laying them, *buwe*, not with your ribs. Jude can do that."

Joseph felt on more even ground at his *daed*'s brusqueness and grinned. "We'll see, Dat. We'll see."

Priscilla settled tentatively on the edge of the comfortable bed. The Lyons' guestroom was painted a pale yellow cream and she felt strangely comforted by the gentle swishing of Mary's skirt as she moved to smooth the quilt atop the carved hope chest at the foot of the bed.

"I hope you'll be happy here." The *Amisch* girl's voice was gentle and Priscilla struggled with sudden tears, not liking her vulnerability but willing to accept it for the moment.

"I can't—I can't thank you enough, really."

"And Joseph too?" Mary's question was even more gentle, not prying or grating, yet Priscilla could not control the flush she felt warm her cheeks.

"Yes . . . him especially."

Mary sat down in a ladder-back rocking chair with a smile. "My *bruder*'s not easy to know. I bet he didn't tell you how *gut* he is at figuring things and building. He was the master builder for this *haus*."

Priscilla shook her head and gazed around with new appreciation at the stained wood of the window casements and the gentle slope of the roof. "No . . . he didn't say. He did a wonderful job. Your *haus* is beautiful."

"You speak Penn Dutch?"

"I—my mother was *Amisch* but she left to marry my father. She—when I was little—would speak Penn Dutch to me when we were alone. I guess I feel close to her memory here with you." Priscilla fidgeted a bit with the handle of a bag she'd carried up the mountain.

"My *mamm* is passed from this world as well. I never knew her." Mary rocked in easy time to her solemn words and Priscilla felt the normal guard she held on her past slip a bit.

"My mother died of a heart attack when I was

fifteen. She and my father had been fighting. He left the house and she—well, she had the attack and died in my arms."

"*Ach*, what pain you have carried . . . I am sorry."

And that was all the other woman offered, except to sit quietly with Priscilla for a few peaceful moments. The lack of talk or trying to fix the situation was the *Amisch* way, Priscilla knew, and the quiet was somehow a balm to a sliver of her hidden heart.

Then she gazed into the bag beside her in consternation. "Oh no . . ."

"What's wrong?" Mary stopped rocking.

"Joseph's medicine and his clean bandages—for his ribs. He broke them, saving Hollie . . . I forgot to tell you. He needs these things."

"*Ach*." Mary rose in apparent relief. "That's all? *Kumme* . . . I'll take you to him. Jude is reading to Hollie. He loves the *kinner*, you know."

Priscilla nodded but felt a bit uncertain. Joseph's mention of being a prayer partner clearly bothered him. *And it doesn't sit well with me either.*

But she knew she owed him a great deal for saving Hollie, so she followed Mary out of the cabin, clutching the bag to her chest, and tried to concentrate on the beauty of the late afternoon mountain sunshine that surrounded her.

Joseph fingered the smooth edge of the wooden shingle with satisfaction as he held it up to the light spilling in through the shed window. Tiny dust motes played in the bright beam and he thought how much more comfortable he was around wood than he'd been on the harsh metal of the rig. He reached to rub absently at his side, aware that the warmth of the small work space was irritating his bandages. He looked up in surprise from where he sat behind the lathe when a tentative knock sounded on the door.

"*Kumme* in," he called.

He blinked in the fall of light, then rose to his feet as he recognized the bright red hair.

"Priscilla . . ."

She shut the door behind her and held out a bag. "I—uh—your sister brought me here and showed me the shed. I don't mean to bother you, but I have the supplies for your ribs. Are you—in pain?"

Yes, pain . . . because the sight of you makes me narrisch *and I can't move forward and I can't go back . . .*

"Only a little. I'm fine."

"The doctor said you—um—we could change the bandages, and I have your pain meds."

He stared at her in fascination. *Does she want to help me? Touch me?* He almost smiled at the thought of what his *fater* would say if he escorted Priscilla into the *haus* and proceeded to have her strip his shirt off. He shivered a bit despite the heat and carefully put the shingle down on a nearby workbench.

"Well, I . . ."

"Is there somewhere less dusty that we could go—to do the bandages, I mean?" He watched her lift her chin. "Will your dad mind?"

"Probably," he admitted with a rueful grin that quickly faded. *And you'd mind too if you knew who . . . what . . . you were touching. Don't you remember the way I kissed you in the emergency room?*

"Then we'll do it here," she said briskly, setting the bag on the workbench and sliding around some tools to come close enough for him to smell her hair; like lavender and mint and something even more delicate and heady.

"Uh . . . here?"

"Unless you'd rather not. I mean—when you left Mary's, you looked kind of upset." She lifted her small hands to the collar of his shirt, then slid her fingers down his shoulders and beneath his suspender straps. "Were you? I know I'm not all that happy about being assigned a prayer partner either, but it seems a small thing in exchange for the bishop letting us stay." She slid a pin from its place in the fabric near his throat. "But maybe it means much more trouble for you?"

He stared down into her questioning eyes, trying to find the thread of the conversation and failing utterly with her hands on him. "Trouble? Uh . . . trouble. *Nee.*"

"Joseph? Do you even know what I'm talking

about? You seem confused." Her fingers pulled a second pin and she laid it on the workbench, then reached up to place a firm hand beneath the hair on his forehead, obviously checking for fever. She dropped her hand after a few moments and frowned. "So you are upset?"

She'd gone back to his shirt, spreading the blue fabric and exposing the bandages around his ribs.

The breath caught in his throat; his body remembered what his mind held tight rein upon. It would be so easy to reach down and touch her, but he'd promised never to do that again. Yet he knew how . . . that much he realized. He took a step back and knocked his hip into a sawhorse.

"Joseph." She sounded as exasperated as she did with Hollie sometimes, and he had to smile. Then she pressed against his rib cage, and he gasped.

"I'm sorry," she murmured, clearly intent only on his bandages while his own mind switched hazardously between the present and his shameful past.

"The base dressing is to stay on until you can get to a doctor to remove it, but these outer bandages are damp. You shouldn't be working or sweating. You need to take some pain medicine and lie down."

Again she mothered him, and he watched while she put a delicate fingertip to her pink lips in apparent thought.

I want to do that . . . touch your mouth again. It

would be better than any drug and twice as potent.

"You are going to be able to see a doctor somewhere here, right?" she asked.

"*Jah.*" He pulled his shirt from her hands in a sudden decision. The Bible instructed a man to "flee from sin," and if he didn't get away from her hands, he had no idea what he'd do. And he'd only recently been instructed to keep his behavior "holy" with this woman. Jah, *right.* "Look, Priscilla, *danki*, but—I'll get Jude to fix the bandages. He's a professor and—"

"A professor of medicine?" She tapped a small foot, stirring up more dust motes.

"He's *schmart* enough." Joseph scooped up the pins off the workbench and hastily set about readjusting his shirt. He grabbed the bag of supplies and started to move past her. Then he stopped; he remembered his *fater*. "Uh . . . if you'd like to *kumme* into the *haus*, I'll introduce you to my *daed*." *Which ought to go right as rain . . .*

Her ivory face was stony and he felt a pang of remorse for being so abrupt. He moved to touch her arm, then dropped his hand before he made contact. "Priscilla, please, *kumme* meet my *fater*. I'd be honored."

She gave a small nod and he exhaled with relief, moving to put a hand on the door latch. The door gave way under his hand though and opened inward. Mary nearly fell into his arms from the outside. He caught her arm, then looked up to find his sister, her husband, his father, and Hollie all clustered with interest about the door with faces that held looks of distinct interest.

Joseph stared at them all, feeling Priscilla directly behind his back. "Are you spying on us?" he asked in disbelief.

"Yes!" Hollie squealed, breaking the silence, and everyone laughed. Joseph turned back to Priscilla, wondering what she'd think of his *narrisch Amisch* family. But she was smiling, a gentle smile that softened her lips and made him want to make her happy for as long as he was able. He set his jaw, but the thought lingered like the mountain mist, tantalizing and mysterious. *Happy for always*.

Chapter Thirteen

The following day Priscilla realized that she was finding her feet amongst the warm *Amischers* and felt brave enough to take the path that Mary said led to the makeshift post office at the Kauffmans' store—the only store on the mountain, set roughly in the middle of the sprawl of cabin homes. She brushed a bit nervously at her pink button-down shirt before she mounted the steps of the building, already seeing the curious eyes staring from the large storefront windows. *I wonder if I should ask Mary about wearing Amisch dress . . . maybe I'd be less conspicuous.* But it was too late now and she entered the store, catching the pleasant smells of spices, fresh-cut wood, and leather all mingled together in a comforting blend. The scents allowed her to focus on her steps through the small groups of women and men; some who smiled with open good will. Priscilla eyed the dry goods and fabrics with a longing eye—she loved to sew.

"Can I help you, ma'am?" A large, jolly-looking *Amisch* man in a yellow shirt and dark pants spoke to her from behind one of the wooden counters. "I'm Ben Kauffman. I run the place."

Priscilla smiled. "I need stamps, please."

"Surely," Ben boomed out. "A book of them?"

"Yes, please."

She'd completed the transaction with faint relief, feeling as if she'd passed a test of some kind, when Ben called to her as she turned to go.

"Uh, ma'am?"

She turned back. "Priscilla, please."

Ben nodded. "*Jah*, Priscilla. I know you're going to the Lyons' and past Joseph's *haus*. I've got a package for him that's been sitting awhile. Will you take it?"

"Of course." She accepted the rather bulky manila envelope with another smile and escaped the store to the relative comfort of the forest path outside.

She glanced down at the package wryly as she walked. It gave her a reason to see Joseph, but she doubted he'd appreciate it, not after the way he'd wanted to get away from her in the shed. *He probably thinks I'm a fast woman . . . unclean . . . while he's been so good and kind and pure.* She missed noticing the tree root in front of her completely and fell flat on the ground, the package slipping from her hands. She lifted her head, struggling to breathe for a moment, as a beam of sunlight shot through the trees and illuminated the photos that had spilled from the ruptured envelope onto a background of green moss. Priscilla blinked, wondering if she'd hit her head, as she stared at the mass of images splayed before her in stark relief. She lifted the edge of a single photo and drew it nearer. She caught her breath—it was Joseph, looking younger and brooding, and completely naked as he lay among the tangled sheets and quilts of a large bed . . .

"Where's Priscilla?" Joseph kept his voice casual as he spoke to his sister. He'd worked it out during a relatively sleepless night that he would obey Bishop Umble's suggestion and begin to meet with Priscilla to pray with her. *No matter what else I may feel . . .*

"She offered to go to the post office at Kauffman's for me," Mary said with a smile as she put down the heavy clothes iron and wiped her brow with her apron.

"Let me iron," Joseph said roughly. "You should be sitting."

She laughed. "For the next two months? Not much would get done around here. Don't worry so much, Joseph. I'm fine and your niece or nephew is too."

He grunted and turned to catch Hollie as she ran and flung herself at him. The little girl was clad in an *Amisch* dress of butter yellow and had her golden hair braided in a thick knot at the back of her small head.

"Joseph! Look . . . Miss Mary gave me an *Amisch* dress. Don't I look pretty?"

He smiled. "*Jah*, you're a beauty for sure. Has your *mamm* seen?" He set the little girl down on the floor and met Mary's gaze. "Did you do her hair too?"

"*Jah* . . . I think Priscilla will like it. She told me her *mamm* was *Amisch* once and—" She broke off as the front door quietly opened.

Priscilla entered, looking flushed and out of sorts. She ducked her head when Joseph moved to greet her and quickly crossed the room to hand Mary the stamps.

"What's wrong?" Joseph asked.

She turned in his direction but still did not lift her head, letting the heavy fall of her hair hide her face from him.

"Mommy! Look at my dress!"

Joseph watched her absently pat Hollie's head, and then she mumbled an excuse and made for the spare bedroom. The door closed quietly behind her.

Joseph looked at his sister, who shrugged with concern. "Should I talk to her, Joseph?"

"What's wrong with Mommy?" Hollie asked plaintively.

"I'll talk with her," Joseph said. *Now is as* gut *a time as any to become that prayer partner, even if she's probably mad enough to spit about something . . .*

Priscilla sat down in the rocking chair of the guest room and began to move in quick motion. She'd gathered up the photos as hastily as she could, but stuffing them back in the ripped envelope had been a problem and she'd ended up hiding them in one of the Lyons' sheds in an old toolbox.

She closed her eyes, then blinked them open again; she'd seen more of the flagrant images than she'd ever be able to forget. *He'd looked so casual, so carefree . . . and so very, very far from innocent.* She slapped her hands on the wide arms of the rocking chair and shook her head. "Fool," she whispered aloud. *I've been such a fool about him, thinking he is so perfect and innocent, and all the while . . .* She gritted her teeth. *This goes to show that I have absolutely no judgment where men are concerned, least of all this* Amisch *man who brought us here and who really—*

She snapped her head up when a firm knock sounded on the door. "Priscilla, may I *kumme* in?"

She dropped her head in her hands, suppressing a groan, while the images from the photos danced wickedly in her mind. "No," she said.

The door opened a bit. She'd forgotten that the *Amisch* had no locks on their doors, and she looked up to see Joseph's concerned face.

He slipped into the room and closed the door behind him. "Are you upset? Did someone say something to you at the store?"

She glared at him, feeling her face flood with color against her will. "No."

"Then what is it? Did Mary—"

"Everything is fine, Joseph King. Everything." *And we are so off this mountain as soon as I can manage it today.*

He gave her one of his oh-so handsome, perfect smiles. "Did I do something then?"

Oh, I bet you did. "No."

She realized that he wasn't going to go away without some explanation for her odd behavior, and she didn't want to attract suspicion before she took Hollie and found the path down the mountain.

"Priscilla?"

"Hmm? Oh . . . it's—well, it's a feminine thing, Joseph."

"*Ach* . . ." He backed into the door, clearly embarrassed. "I'll send Mary in then."

"No, thank you. I'll be fine if you give me a few minutes. I'll be right out."

"Okay . . . right. I—uh—had *kumme* over to see if you would have us pray together, but if . . ." He drifted off and exited the room as though he was being pursued by a pack of hounds.

She would have laughed if she didn't feel so miserable inside. The less cowardly thing to do would be to give him the envelope before she left and explain about her fall, but she wasn't feeling particularly heroic at the moment. And she knew she wouldn't feel it later, running away. But what other choice did she have?

"Is Mommy okay?" Hollie asked when he came back into the kitchen.

He smiled at the child and avoided his sister's eyes. "Of course, *kind*, now why not go out and pet the goat. He likes to eat clover."

"All right." Hollie skipped in barefoot excitement out the front door.

Mary pulled a batch of fresh chocolate chip cookies from the cooling rack and offered him the tray. He scooped up three cookies with an absent hand.

"Is everything really all right, Joseph?"

He remembered Priscilla's explanation and ducked his head. "*Jah* . . . I've got to get going, but I need my old toolbox. I left it over here when I was helping build this place. Daed needs a bit of work done at home."

"It's in the toolshed."

He snagged another cookie and bent to kiss his sister's cheek. "*Danki.*"

Chapter Fourteen

Priscilla felt faintly guilty at urging Mary to go into the master bedroom and have an afternoon nap, but she knew she needed to get down the mountain before nightfall. When she was sure enough minutes had passed, she slipped the satchel she'd brought with them from beneath her bed and went outside to find Hollie playing near the goat's pen.

"Hollie," she whispered. "Let's go for a walk."

"Okay. Where to?"

"I thought we'd look for blueberries." *It was probably too early but they were going to need something to eat later.*

They were mercifully out of earshot of the Lyons' cabin when Hollie noticed Priscilla's satchel. "Mommy, you're not going to make us leave again, are you? I like it here and I like my pretty *Amisch* dress."

Priscilla swallowed and spoke carefully. "I like your dress too."

"Then we're not leaving? Why do you have your bag?"

"I—um . . ." She tried never to lie to her daughter, but she could imagine the fuss Hollie would make if she told her the truth. Yet she was so tired of all of the sneaking and hiding. "I—yes, Hollie. We have to leave. I don't think it's the best place for us and—"

"No!" Hollie stamped a bare foot. "No, Mommy. I'm tired of moving and living in a car. I want to stay here with Joseph and Mary and Jude and the goat. I'm not going!" Hollie's words ended in a screaming pitch and she darted away, far ahead up the path.

Priscilla gave chase until she had a stitch in her side. Then she saw the Kauffmans' store as she rounded a bend and tried to slow her steps and appear casual to any potential onlookers. But as soon as she passed the large white building, she broke into a run again. She caught sight of the yellow dress in the far distance and tried calling. She saw Hollie pause and turn, then move toward the dense underbrush of the forest.

"Hollie!" Priscilla cried, trying to catch up, but her attempt was futile and she found herself plunging among shadowy trees, far from the direction of the path.

Joseph whistled to himself as he set his toolbox down on the workbench and eyed the shelves above, looking for his favorite hammer. He pulled the tool from behind a box of nails and tested its weight in his hand, enjoying the feel. He flipped open the metal hinges on the toolbox and lifted the lid, then stopped dead still, the hammer still poised above the box. He put the tool down and slid a photograph from the torn manila envelope, feeling his heart start to gallop with sickening intensity.

"Dear Gott . . ." he whispered.

He looked at the lurid image, remembering against his will. Amanda had wanted to photograph him, and he'd agreed, despite his people's belief that a photo was a graven image. *But I didn't care . . .*

He sank to his knees, cradling the toolbox, and pulled out another handful of pictures. *How* en der weldt *had they gotten here?* He drew a hoarse, half sob of a breath, then grabbed the manila envelope and turned it over, expecting to see a return address, but there was nothing. Then he heard the faint jingle of a chain and dumped the remaining photos into the box, peering into the envelope. He reached two fingers inside and shakily withdrew the familiar gold chain and bear claw necklace. He laced the chain through his fingers and closed his hand on the metal, squeezing hard enough to draw blood to the surface of his palm, as he remembered what he'd promised . . .

"Joseph?"

Mary's voice penetrated the thin shed door and he slammed the box shut, scrambling to his feet and kicking it beneath the bench, as his sister opened the door.

"What is it?" he asked hoarsely.

"It's Priscilla and Hollie. I lay down for a nap —and well, they're gone. Priscilla's things are missing also. I feel like maybe you should look."

He pushed off the workbench, stuffing the necklace in his pants pocket. "They probably went for a walk. Don't fret, Mary. I'll find them."

He walked with Mary from the shed into their *daed*'s house, then took off at a jog toward Ben Kauffman's despite the resulting pain in his ribs. If anyone had seen Priscilla and Hollie, it would have been at the store, he told himself. All of the major paths in the area sort of intersected at Ben's store, and Priscilla's unbound red hair was sure to catch every eye.

He took the front stairs two at a time and wended his way through greetings from neighbors as he tried to get to Ben without being too obtrusive. But Agnes Smucker, a benign older woman with a toothless grin, caught his arm as he passed.

"Joseph King, I saw that pretty *Englisch* girl pass by here not more than ten minutes ago. It looked like she was in a hurry." There was a question in the woman's tone, but Joseph merely shrugged.

"Out for a brisk walk, no doubt, Frau Smucker."

The woman nodded and Joseph was trying to extract himself from the store when Ben's big voice rang out over the heads of the customers.

"*Ach*, Joseph. I met Priscilla. Did she give you that package—the big manila envelope? It was lying around the post for a while since you've been gone."

Joseph froze and for a surreal moment, he remembered falling into an icy creek when he was ten and catching pneumonia. He felt the bone-wrenching cold and, for a moment, he wondered wildly if he'd be able to breathe, to speak. *Dear Gott, help me.* And then his world tilted and he found his voice, hearing himself in a distant echo. "*Jah. Danki*, Ben. I've got to get going." He somehow managed a polite nod at Frau Smucker and left the store to stand shivering on the porch for a few seconds in the bright sunshine. *She saw . . . Gott help him, she saw. No wonder she left.*

The realization hit him with brutal force and he set off at a dead run for the path that led down the mountain.

Priscilla groaned as she pushed through a tangle of mountain laurel and jaggers that caught at her shirt and jeans.

"Hollie!" Her voice echoed eerily in the confines of the woods and she realized with a sinking sensation in her chest that she'd completely lost all sense of direction. Even worse, she could no longer see or hear her daughter.

She stumbled on, snatches of prayers coming to her lips, then heard a loud shriek beyond a stand of pine trees directly in front of her.

"Hollie?" Priscilla ran into a clearing of pine-needle-laden forest floor and saw Hollie jumping up and down in obvious excitement. "Mommy, look, it's a bear cub! Can I pet it? Can I?"

Priscilla walked slowly toward her daughter and put a hand on her small shoulder. "Hollie," she whispered with a dry throat. "That's not only a cub . . ."

"What?"

"Shhh . . ." Priscilla tried to still the rampant beating of her heart as a mother black bear rose up on its hind legs from behind some bushes and stared intently at them with dark, menacing eyes . . .

Joseph took in the situation before him at a glance and very slowly reached down to lift a tree branch from the ground.

"Don't move," he cautioned gently. "Don't make a sound."

He struck the nearest tree with the branch, making as loud a noise as he could. Then he did it again, adding a savage cry from the back of his throat. The mother bear sniffed the air and turned her attention to Joseph, still on her hind legs.

"Now, when I tell you—begin to back away slowly . . . very slowly."

"But, Joseph—" Priscilla whispered.

"Hush," he ordered. "Do as I say if you value your life, Priscilla. Do as I say." He struck the tree again and motioned with a nod. "Now."

He continued to strike the tree as he watched from narrowed eyes as Priscilla led Hollie backwards away from the cub. The mother bear still would not take her eyes off Joseph and he was infinitely grateful for the fact. He struck the tree again and the cub bawled a bit, then turned its furry rump and headed back toward its mother. The big bear dropped to all fours and Joseph held his breath. Finally, the animal gave a deep grunt and turned with her cub, ambling off to the other side of the clearing. Joseph put the branch down carefully and realized that his hands were shaking. He slowly traced Priscilla's steps into the woods and found her and Hollie in the shadow of an old pine. They were clinging to each other, shaking with silent sobs. Wordlessly, he wrapped his arms around them and held them close, careless for the moment about his promise not to touch.

"Thank you," Priscilla whispered after a moment, lifting tear-filled blue eyes to meet his gaze.

He set his jaw and dropped his arms. "Don't thank me. Thank Gott. Your childish running away almost cost you your daughter's life."

Chapter Fifteen

Priscilla wanted to scream so badly, she thought her blood pressure would spike through the roof. But instead she followed, outwardly calm, in Joseph's wake as he carried Hollie and led them back to Mary's house.

Once there, he deposited a willing Hollie into Mary's care and stared down at Priscilla. "I'd like to talk to you—outside."

Priscilla saw Mary look at her and Joseph with a worried expression. "Surely Priscilla can wash up first, Joseph?"

"*Nee*, she can't."

"Are you going to hurt my mommy?" Hollie asked solemnly, and Priscilla was glad to see the appalled look sweep his face as he gazed at the child.

He sank down on his haunches and took Hollie's shoulders between his hands with visible gentleness. "I would never hurt your mommy, *kind*. I only want to talk."

"Okay." Hollie yawned and brushed at her dirty skirt. "I'm sorry about my dress, Miss Mary."

Mary smiled. "It's fine, Hollie. *Kumme*, we'll see if we can wash it while your *mamm* talks with Joseph."

Priscilla noticed that he waited until his sister

had left the room before he turned and opened the front door. "Outside, Priscilla. *Sei se gut.*"

She squared her shoulders, vaguely aware that if it had been Heath, she would have been scared to death, but with Joseph, she felt only raw anger. She flounced off the porch, following him until he'd led them a good distance from the house.

"What do you want?" she finally snapped at his broad back. He stopped and turned and she stood her ground, lifting her chin, though his unusual eyes seemed to burn like golden green flames through her thin shirt.

"I want to tell you that I once thought you brave, and maybe you are on some level. But mostly, you're only a scared little girl who would rather run than discover the truth."

Priscilla bristled at his calm words. "The truth? You think I'm the one with truth issues here? I have trusted you, told you things I've never told anyone, followed you across two states, and you—you've been playing me all along, haven't you, you perfectly innocent *Amisch* man?"

He tilted his head. "Innocent? Is that what you thought? Perfect? Like Edward believes? *Nee*, Priscilla. I'm far from it."

"Well, I know that now," she spat, unable to keep the rush of images from her mind.

He smiled grimly, as if he could read her thoughts. "So you opened my mail and you saw those pictures. No good comes to those who look for trouble."

She took an infuriated step closer to him. "Listen, I didn't open your mail. I was trying to bring it to you and I tripped and fell. The envelope ripped and there you were—all over the ground. I couldn't help but see . . ." She grimaced and felt her cheeks flush at the same time.

"So what do you want to know?" he asked.

"What?"

"You must be curious."

"I don't want to know anything about your private life. It's none of my business what you do in your free time and I—"

She broke off into a squeak when he closed the distance between them and bent down very close to her mouth. "Listen, you spitfire, I was sixteen years old in those pictures. Sixteen." He drew a harsh breath and he swallowed hard. "An *Englisch* woman rented the cabin on the other side of the mountain for the summer. She was older . . . maybe in her late twenties. I don't know—but what I did to her, I did many, many times." He punctuated the statement by gritting his white teeth and Priscilla could feel the heat of his breath on her lips. "It was my doing, my fault . . . every caress, every kiss, every photo." His voice had lowered and Priscilla felt her anger melt away into a simmering burn of sensation deep within her belly. She swayed nearer him, half closing her eyes, when she felt her chin caught in a firm grasp. Her eyes flew open in time to see his mocking smile. "So, remember, little spitfire—the truth burns, and I know its scars well. But the question is, Priscilla, do you?"

He released her chin and turned, stalking off through the trees, while she clutched her abdomen in mute confusion and frustration.

"Too tight?" Jude asked in what Joseph considered to be his "professor" voice. His *bruder*-in-law had been an intense student of *Amisch* studies when he came to Ice Mountain. *And that's what got him into trouble with Mary . . . Women,* he thought, knowing he was being unfair, but not in the mood to think about what he felt about Priscilla, especially not when he still carried the bear claw necklace.

Jude wrapped another layer of bandages around Joseph's ribs and pulled. For a moment Joseph saw stars, then swallowed hard, gripping the high dresser in his old bedroom with white-tipped fingers.

"Hollie told me about the bear and the cub," Jude said from behind him.

"*Jah,*" he managed.

"She also told me that her mother was ready to leave this afternoon."

"She was, I guess. It was only—a misunderstanding." When Jude finished, he drew as much of a breath of relief as he could with the tight bandage.

"You know, Mary and I had several big misunderstandings when we were starting out and—"

"Starting out?" Joseph lifted his pale blue shirt and shrugged it on with a grimace of pain. "I'm not starting out with Priscilla, Jude."

"Uh-huh." Jude was folding away supplies and Joseph snapped his suspenders into place in a frustrated motion.

"What do you mean, uh-huh?"

Jude looked up and peered at him over the top of his spectacles as if he was an object of study. Joseph could imagine his internal thoughts: *"Subject is in complete denial of any attraction."*

"Well, you brought her here."

"To protect her."

Jude shrugged. "That's as good a reason as any. Didn't you tell me once that there were no girls on the mountain you found attractive? If you'll excuse my bluntness and not tell your sister, from an objective viewpoint, Priscilla is attractive."

Joseph frowned. "I'm not denying that."

"Okay, then." Jude slapped him on the shoulder lightly and put his hand on the door latch. "Attraction is a *gut* place to start too, Joseph."

"I don't want to start anything." He felt his temper rise and Jude laughed.

"Then you'd better learn, my friend, that Gott

has a way of changing what we want into what He wants. I happen to know firsthand. Have a good night!"

Joseph rubbed his side wearily and sank down onto the old double bed he used to share with Edward. He gazed around the shadowed room, the light from the kerosene lamp on the bedside table illuminating the shelves of books and the odd wood carving that had been so much a part of his growing up. Then he reached in his pants pocket and pulled out the bear claw necklace. He thought tiredly about Jude's words and wondered if it had been Gott's will to send Amanda Stearn into his life. He rubbed a hand over his eyes, then stared at the beamed ceiling. *But surely I chose that sin, when I might have walked away at any time, leaving her in peace . . .* He swallowed hard as he blindly fingered the curve of the bear claw and knew that he could at least do one thing right at the moment. *I won't sin against Priscilla. I will keep my attentions holy and pray with her until she leaves and . . .* Something deep inside hurt hard at the thought of her leaving, and he rolled on his side in misery, but admitted to himself that she belonged to a world away from Ice Mountain and him . . .

Priscilla stroked Hollie's hair absently as they lay in the big bed they shared, taking in a deep breath of the flowered mountain night air that stole in through the screened window. She wanted to sleep, but she couldn't get Joseph's words out of her head—*"My doing . . . my fault."* He'd been sexually abused and he blamed himself completely, but of course, he'd probably never talked to anyone about it—maybe only Priscilla herself. And she'd . . . She swallowed hard. She'd been too caught up in the moment to even stop and tell him that he was wrong. She thought of his broken ribs and the stallion and then the bear— twice he'd saved Hollie's life. She owed him the chance to get free of his past and resolved to talk to him the next day, no matter how upset he might become.

Chapter Sixteen

Joseph leaned the ladder against the cabin roof and hoisted the bundle of shingles he'd shaved onto his shoulder. He ignored the warning pull in his side and climbed the ladder, glad that his *daed* had gone to the store so he couldn't nag about the work Joseph knew he was perfectly capable of doing. He'd reached the top rung and slung the shingles over onto the roof when a feminine voice rang out in anger.

"Joseph King, what are you doing?"

He bent his head with a sigh, then turned to look down on Priscilla's bright, unbound hair. She was wearing a white dress and her legs showed long and firm. He caught a tight hold on the ladder and forced himself to climb back down, dreading the temptation she represented.

"What are you doing here? Where's Hollie?"

"Jude suggested taking her to school with him—I thought it was a good idea."

Joseph nodded. "*Jah*, she's a bright little thing; she'll do well." Then he arched an eyebrow, clearly wanting his other question answered.

"Um, look, Joseph—I need to talk to you about what you told me yesterday."

He watched her toy nervously with her white belt and tried not to look at her legs. "What is there to talk about?"

"A lot," she burst out. "A lot—especially about that—that—woman who, well, who sexually abused you when you were underage."

He was glad the ladder was there to steady him as her words struck like a blow. *What the devil is she talking about?* His face must have registered his confusion, because she stepped forward and touched him earnestly on his bare forearm where his sleeve was rolled up.

"Joseph, I know I'm probably not handling this right, but I feel like I need to tell you—what that woman did to you was wrong. It was a crime."

He shook off her hand, feeling trapped suddenly. "Listen, Priscilla . . . I don't know what you mean or why I even told you, but if there is a criminal in all that happened—it's me."

"No, it's not!"

He caught her arm without thinking and pulled her into the empty cabin, not wanting any stray passerby to hear their talk. "*Jah*, it is," he insisted, releasing her arm.

"All right. Tell me how it started. The first time. The first day." She crossed her arms and he shook his head.

"What woman wants to hear tales of this?" he asked, embarrassed.

"This one does."

He turned his back on her for a moment as memories flooded unbidden into his consciousness. *The first time . . . the first time . . .* He stared out the cabin window at the beauty of the late spring day and remembered against his will. But his pride would not let him speak. He drew a deep, steadying breath, then faced her.

"I don't want to talk about this," he said slowly.

"It would be good for you."

He smiled at her. "What would be *gut* for me would be to have less of the spitfire and more of the prayer partner. *Kumme*, let's sit down and have some lemonade and talk about how we can pray together."

He saw the reluctance on her face, but she finally sat down in one of the carved kitchen chairs and glared at him. He half laughed and pulled two glasses down from the open shelf, then poured lemonade from the ice box. He gave her a glass and sat opposite her at the table.

He watched her drink, her ivory throat working, then looked away.

"This tastes like Mary's lemonade."

"It is," he told her. "My sister insists on hauling it over for Daed and me, though I tell her we're perfectly fine."

"She loves you very much."

"*Jah*. I am blessed with that." He took a long pull of his drink then put it down, folding his hands together. "So, how can I pray for you, Priscilla Allen?"

He noticed the look of discomfort that crossed her face. "You can't."

"And why is that?"

She shrugged. "My father was abusive, my husband was abusive." She gave a bitter laugh, which sounded more like a sob. "It was my father who actually urged Heath to 'control his wife' in the proper manner."

Joseph stared at her. "You mean your father knew that—that your husband was beating you?" He felt rage unfurl inside him at the absurdity of the situation and reached out without thinking to touch her hand.

"My father encouraged Heath, even after the divorce and custody hearings. I—think he's sick, as sick as Heath in some ways."

Joseph thumbed his way across her fingers, wondering what he could say to her unimaginable revelation. *Please, Derr Herr, help me.* "You came here today seeking to help me, but I know it's you who needs the lo—" He paused to correct himself, startled at his train of thought. "The support."

She curled her fingers slightly into his, and his breath caught. *She just told you that her father was a monster, you idiot. Settle down.*

"I'm used to doing without support," she admitted, lifting her gaze to his.

"I know that, but here you don't have to . . ."

She smiled sadly. "Maybe. But I can't stay here forever, Joseph."

"I know that." *But I don't know it, and I want you to stay—to stay and stay and stay . . .*

Priscilla couldn't help but notice his green-gold eyes darken in intensity. He looked as though he was struggling with something deep inside and she felt guilty for sharing her own problems when it was he that she had wanted to help. She drew a deep breath and clung a bit tighter to his hand.

"Joseph, do you think it was my fault that Heath hit me, that my father knew and even— even encouraged it?"

"What? *Nee,* Priscilla, you must not believe such a thing." His big body tensed, his eyes registering shock.

"Then why do you believe that what happened to you was your fault?"

He dropped his gaze, his thick dark lashes

fanning against his high cheekbones as he shifted in his chair.

"It's not the same."

She gently rubbed the calluses on his large palm. "How can I pray for you, Joseph King?"

She watched him carefully, instinctively understanding that he'd encased his true self in a barrier of ice for years. *But ice could melt with enough warmth* . . . She remembered kissing him in the ER and how good it felt, but now she understood why he had blamed himself and not her for that torrid meeting of mouths and hands . . .

"I—I worry for my *fater*'s health," he said finally.

She nodded. "I will pray for him."

"*Danki.*"

She sensed his restlessness and knew that the quiet moment between them would soon pass if she didn't do something to lengthen it.

"I haven't thanked you properly, Joseph, for saving Hollie and me yesterday." She lifted his hand and brought it close to her mouth. She heard his breath catch. "And what you said— about me always running . . ." She leaned forward a bit more and let the long strands of her hair brush his hand. "I think you might be right, Joseph." Then she brushed her lips across his knuckles, moving back and forth until her teeth grazed his tanned skin and she heard him gasp.

"Priscilla . . ."

His tone held warning and desire, and she pulled away only a bit to quickly begin speaking. "Dear God, please bless Joseph's *daed*. Bless him and bring to light anything that might be wrong with his health. Give Joseph time and peace with his *fater*. Amen." She slowly eased his hand down to rest against the table, sliding her own hands away with reluctance. Then she peered up at him, awaiting his reaction.

He was breathing deeply, as if he'd run long and hard through a sodden field. He brought his hand to his mouth as if trying to recreate the sensation of her touching him. She felt her heart begin to thump wildly in her chest in response and had to resist the urge to squirm in her chair.

"Priscilla . . ." he murmured against his own skin and she felt as if he was touching her, heating her, so that she shivered in delight, struggling to focus. "Priscilla . . . mmm . . . what you can do to me, reduce me to . . . I don't . . . I can't . . ."

The moment was shattered by the banging of the front door. Abner came in carrying a heavy bag, breathing hard. Joseph rose immediately to take the parcel from his father and steered him toward a kitchen chair.

"Sit down, Daed. Are you all right?"

Priscilla was alarmed by the grayish hue of the older man's skin and looked quickly to Joseph. "I think we should take him to a hospital."

"I'm fine," Abner huffed.

Priscilla watched Joseph consider her words then put the bag down with a decisive thump as his father labored to breathe. "Daed, Priscilla's right. We're going to Coudersport to see Doctor McCully. We'll get you down the mountain to Mr. Ellis's home and call an ambulance from there."

"Take me to Grossmudder May—she'll know what to do." Abner gasped the name of the community's healer, whom Mary had told Priscilla about in passing.

"*Nee.*" Joseph spoke with calm authority though Priscilla could see his pulse beat in his neck. "Jude says you've seen her thrice. I will not lose you, Daed. I've only now *kumme* home."

Priscilla sensed the desperation of the situation and remembered her mother's unexpected passing. "I think we should hurry," she said low to Joseph, and he nodded in quick, sober agreement.

Chapter Seventeen

Joseph longed for the chance to sit alone . . . *or even to be alone with Priscilla.* But the small waiting room of the Coudersport hospital was packed with Jude, Mr. Ellis, the bishop, and kindly Deacon Keim and his wife—all waiting as the hours ticked by. Mary had been feeling tired and Jude had insisted she stay on the mountain, and his sister had reluctantly agreed. Bishop Umble's wife was watching Hollie, and again Joseph silently thanked Gott for Priscilla's calm presence.

She was the only one who murmured occasional words of comfort, while everyone else, even Jude and Mr. Ellis, sat still and stoic in the oddly colored plastic chairs. Joseph understood that it was the *Amisch* way to wait and see what Gott's will would be, but their quiet made him restless and irritable for some reason.

He was about to fetch a drink from the pop machine when Dr. Luke McCully came striding into the room. Luke was a friend to the *Amisch* community and was helping to oversee Mary's pregnancy. Joseph trusted him completely.

"All right, we've run some scans and done some blood work," the doctor began. "I've called in an oncologist friend of mine—a cancer doctor—to consult. It looks like Abner's got lung cancer—stage four. But . . ."

He held up a hand to the listeners and Joseph felt himself clinging to the single word . . . *But*.

"But it's only one nodule in the right lung. It doesn't appear to have spread anywhere else. We can treat this."

Joseph cleared his throat. "How?"

The doctor shot him a direct look. "Radiation. Then chemotherapy. It'll mean coming here every day or possibly staying nearby for about six weeks initially."

"My *dat* will never do it. He's as stubborn as

an ox." Joseph spoke absently while words rang with aimless pain through his mind. *Cancer. Chemotherapy.* He looked at Priscilla, who met his gaze squarely.

"It's the getting up that matters," she said softly, reminding him of his words to her at the pond when they'd fished together.

He nodded. *She's right . . . I can't go into this from a beaten perspective. I'll talk to Dat, convince him. We'll work it out.* "Thank you, Doctor. Can we see him?"

"Sure." Dr. McCully nodded. "He's free to go home tomorrow actually. I've started him on some medicine that'll help his breathing."

"If he uses it," Jude muttered, and Joseph looked at his *bruder*-in-law.

"I'll see that he does," Joseph replied. *Which ought to be as easy as wrangling a timber rattler . . .*

"Good." Dr. McCully smiled briefly, then peered at Joseph. "I hear your ribs could probably use a once-over as long as you're here."

Joseph threw a sour look at Jude, who shrugged innocently, then glanced back at the doctor. "*Jah,* I suppose so."

"All right, I'll tend to you in a bit. *Gut nacht,* everyone. I'll be seeing quite a lot of you, I expect." Joseph watched the other man skim his eyes over those assembled, pausing momentarily on Priscilla, but he asked no questions—for which Joseph was grateful.

•••

Priscilla passed the heavy brown door in the hospital labeled "Chapel." She would have kept going, but she noticed that a bright light shone from beneath the door despite the relative lateness of the hour, and something drew her inexorably to put her hand on the metal knob. She heard the low rumble of a man's voice inside and almost drew away, not wanting to disturb the person, but there was some-thing familiar about the cadence of the tone. She gently opened the door and peered inside to find Joseph on his knees in the small, intimate room. She drew back and would have closed the door, leaving him to pray, but his voice stopped her.

"Priscilla—*kumme* in, *sei se gut.*"

She entered in surprise. "You didn't turn," she whispered. "How did you know it was me?"

He moved his broad shoulders, his back still to her. "I suppose I'll always know."

She had to be content with his strange words and moved to sit on the edge of one of the padded chairs. Joseph rose and came back to take a seat next to her, his hat in his hands.

"I have to thank you," he said after a moment. "Your prayers that whatever ailed Daed would be brought to light were answered."

She bowed her head. "I didn't want them answered like this."

"We rarely want what Gott chooses to give us, but that is part of being in relationship with Him.

We take the gifts wrapped in bright paper and the ones in oil cloth all the same."

"Being in—relationship with Him?" she asked curiously, not having heard things explained in quite this way before.

She felt the weight of Joseph's gaze as he explained. "I suppose you could call *Amisch* living, an organized religion, with all of its rules, but I learned from Bishop Umble young that religion doesn't matter much—it's the kind of relationship you have with Derr Herr that means the most. So . . . I try to know Him, in the trees, the ice, in those I love . . ." His voice trailed off and she sat in the silence for a long minute, thinking of Heath and her father and the way they used fear to preach. But how Joseph spoke was a balm to some wound in her soul and she felt her eyes well with tears.

"Do you cry because you don't have that feeling about Gott, Priscilla, or because you do? I cannot help but remember that you told me earlier I couldn't pray for you."

She drew a shaky breath. "I—I'm so angry with God, I guess."

She felt him turn toward her, and his fingers carefully stroked her hair back from her face in exquisite tenderness. "Angry because you saw Him modeled by an earthly father who only hurt you, a husband who abused you? But I promise, He is much, much more."

"Maybe," she admitted on a sob, feeling that ice was melting in her veins, her heart.

He pulled her close to rest her head on his shoulder and she allowed herself to be truly still for the first time in forever.

"Thank you, Joseph," she whispered. "I will keep praying for your *daed*."

"*Jah*," he said on a deep sigh. "We must pray. I talked to him and he refuses treatment. He says he will go back to Ice Mountain to die in peace, and I cannot sway him."

She lifted her head and saw his look of acceptance.

"But there must be some way to change his mind . . . to convince him . . ."

He smiled sadly. "Gifts in oil cloth, remember?"

And she leaned forward to let her tears fall on his dark coat.

Joseph stroked Bear's thick fur as the dog attempted to huddle on the couch beside him. He'd finished a letter to Edward about Daed and now the cabin seemed strange and empty without his *fater*'s presence. Joseph wondered for the fourth time whether he should have stayed at the hospital overnight. But Mr. Ellis had promised to run Joseph back the next morning to pick up his *daed*, and Priscilla had needed to come back to the mountain for Hollie.

He thought about the time with her in the

chapel, her genuine tears for his *fater*, for her own brokenness. It took strength to admit all that she had, and he knew that he admired her on a level unmatched by any woman. He shifted restlessly on the couch, exhausted but almost too tired to sleep. A warning growl from Bear made him look up, and soon a brisk knock sounded on the cabin door.

Joseph got up to answer the knock, wondering fleetingly if it might be Priscilla. But when he opened the door, holding Bear back with one leg, he discovered John Beider, an older neighbor and friend. John held a lantern high and spoke to Bear, and the dog soon wriggled in greeting.

"Joseph, Derr Herr convinced me, though the hour be late, to pay you a visit. I thought you might be having trouble sleeping and I'd spin you a yarn or two to help you drift off."

Joseph smiled. John Beider's talent in life was that he could literally talk a man to sleep with his stories, and Joseph welcomed him heartily.

"*Kumme* in, John. Should I make some tea?"

"*Nee, sohn*, just take a seat there on the couch."

Joseph did as he was told and Bear soon resumed his position next to him. John sat with his back to the fireplace, setting his lantern on the floor.

The older man rubbed his hands together, as if conjuring the story he would tell, but first he dropped his gaze for a brief moment. " 'Tis fair sorry I am about your *dat*, Joseph. The bishop passed our way and let us know."

Joseph swallowed and nodded. "As Derr Herr wills."

"*Jah*," John said dryly. "Easy to say—not as easy to accept . . . But I *kumme* here to tell you a tale. So, settle back and relax . . ."

John's face took on a meditative glow as he began his story. "Now, a *gut*, unmarried *Amisch* woman went for a holiday to the seashore. She settled her bare toes deep in the wet sand, lifted her skirts, and walked along the beach. But soon she stepped on something hard and bent down to pick the thing up, thinking it might be a shell. Instead, she found an *Englischer*'s class ring— what they wear when they graduate high school. She read the name inscribed on the golden ring. It said Louis Clark—Remember Me."

Joseph settled deeper in the couch, feeling lulled by the idea of the sea and its waves. John went on, his voice seeming to waver in time to the flicker of flame in his lantern.

"The *Amisch* woman put the ring in the pocket of her apron, hiding it away, for you know that we have no jewelry. And she returned to her home down Lancaster way, putting the ring far from sight in the back of an *auld* cupboard. Years passed, but the single *Amisch* woman could never find a man to suit her and when her *grossmudder* started to ail, the woman packed up *haus* and prepared to go and take care of the older woman.

"But when she moved the old cupboard, the ring fell to the floor and she picked it up, reading the man's name and his decree to be remembered. She grew frustrated with the keeping of a childish secret like the ring and threw it in the compost pile before she left the *haus*. The next spring, a neighbor boy brought fertilizer to the *grossmudder*'s *haus*, and when the *Amisch* woman spread it around her kitchen garden plants, lo and behold, her fingers closed on the ring, hidden in the rich earth. She cleaned it with her apron and wondered why *en der weldt* she could not seem to be rid of the ring. She rose, deciding to take the ring to the creek and throw it in, and she went to the front yard. But suddenly, overhead, she heard a man's voice and looked up to see a large orange hang glider, struggling to make a safe landing. She ran to help the man when he was on the ground, ignoring the way he studied her aged but still beautiful face. And, as she bent over him, the ring fell from her hand onto his chest. He lifted it in wonder, gazing at the inscription, then looked to her—and she knew.

" 'Louis Clark?' she asked with a breathless sigh.

" 'Yes,' he said with a smile.

" 'I-I haven't tried to remember you, but your ring wouldn't let me go.'

" 'I lost it long ago, as a marine at sea. But now . . . will you marry me?'

" 'But I'm *Amisch*,' she gasped.

" 'Then I will become *Amisch* too. I have found you at last and I'll never let you go.'

"He slipped the ring on her slender finger, a promise of a love that would endure for many years to come."

Joseph breathed deeply, completely relaxed. He smiled at John. "*Danki*," he said.

"*Jah*." John laughed. "But let me tell you the moral of the story . . . Sometimes things will pursue you, both *gut* and bad. But Derr Herr can turn them for good, for His glory. Be it a ring, a woman, or even a disease . . . He can turn them for good."

Joseph nodded and adjusted the cushion under his arm, preparing to rise. John waved him back, picked up the lantern, and quietly left. Joseph sat in the dark, in the flickering light of the low fire, and reached into his pants pocket. He pulled out the bear claw necklace. *Sometimes things pursue you* . . . He stuffed the necklace away, pulled the afghan from the back of the couch, and drifted slowly off to sleep, knowing now what he had to do.

Chapter Eighteen

"Mary," Priscilla whispered softly, patting the other woman's back in the bright morning sunlight of a new day. "Please don't cry so much. This stress can't be good for your baby."

Mary lifted her beautiful but tear-stained face to Priscilla and rubbed at her eyes with the backs of her hands. "*Jah*, you are right. And I promised Jude, if he went to teach, I wouldn't cry."

"And your *daed* wouldn't want you to be crying either, I bet."

"*Nee* . . . And I appreciate your caring. I'm due to go visit Grossmudder May today to see how the pregnancy is going. Would you like to *kumme* with me later?"

Priscilla smiled. "I'd love to. I've yet to meet this wonderful woman who is the healer of your community."

"*Gut* . . . I've got another dress that I hemmed for Hollie when she wakes. It's purple."

"Thank you." Priscilla bit her lip for a moment, thinking hard of how else she might distract her beautiful hostess from her worries over her father —then an idea came to her. *It's a risk, but for Joseph's sister, it's worth it.* "Mary, I've been wondering what you would think about me starting to—well, starting to dress *Amisch*?" She went on hastily. "I mean it with the fullest respect and honor and thought maybe if you had an old dress, we could make it over or something." She plucked at the leg of her worn jeans. "I don't feel right in these somehow."

Mary smiled in delight. "I have many things, thanks to my loving husband. And I think it's a *wunderbaar* idea, Priscilla. *Kumme*, let's go look in the cedar chests."

An hour later, Priscilla found herself standing on a sewing stool while Mary sat comfortably on some cushions on the floor, letting out the hem of a burgundy dress. Hollie was practicing tiny stitches on a pretty piece of cloth that Mary had given her and laughed out loud each time the needle missed her small fingers.

Priscilla smiled in remembrance. "My mother taught me to sew from the time I was Hollie's age. I grew so proud of all of the pin pricks on my fingers."

Mary smiled up at her. "You sound like an *Amisch maedel* . . . Can you quilt?"

"I suppose—though I doubt my stitches would match those of the women around here."

"It doesn't matter. You must *kumme* to my baby quilting. It's supposed to be a surprise, but Jude cannot keep a secret from me for long."

"I'd love to come," Priscilla agreed. Then she wondered what it must be like to have a husband who told you everything, loved you enough that no secret could stand between you. *Certainly Heath didn't reveal his true self until after we married, and Joseph, well . . .* She felt her face flush at the thought of linking Joseph with marriage. Hadn't his whole attitude been one of standing apart since she'd known him? *Except for his kisses in the ER,* her mind whispered.

"You must be hot standing up there," Mary said. "Your face is red."

And Priscilla felt herself flush even deeper. "I'm all right."

"*Nee* . . . jump down and help pull me up. I've finished with the hemline. Let's add the apron and *kapp* and see how you look."

Priscilla agreed, gently helping Mary up, then pausing to lift her skirts for a moment to scratch at her bare leg.

"Perhaps you shouldn't go barefoot," Mary said thoughtfully. "Your feet will get sore."

But Priscilla shook her head. "It's freeing. I'd like to try."

"Yay, Mommy!" Hollie clapped, wiggling her own tiny bare toes.

Mary laughed and led Priscilla to the main bedroom, where she helped pin up her masses of red hair into an intricate and beautiful bun.

"Such hair," Mary exclaimed in a complimentary tone. "It's like all the colors of the sun."

"Mary, aren't you to guard against vanity as an *Amisch* woman?" Priscilla teased.

"We are friends," Mary said simply.

Priscilla smiled as the words drifted into her heart . . . *I'm becoming bound here, to this place, these people, by cords of tenderness* . . .

Mary pinned a prayer *kapp* into place to cover her handiwork on Priscilla's hair, then held out a small mirror. Priscilla took it, staring at her image for long moments, seeing herself transformed, clothed with a dignity that she knew would please her mother, and she couldn't resist giving Mary a huge hug.

"*Danki,*" Priscilla whispered, then wondered with excitement what Joseph might think.

Joseph settled his *fater* into a comfortable chair, grateful that many of his *daed*'s *gut* friends had gathered to greet him upon his return from the hospital. In truth, his father was looking better than he had in days, his breathing eased by the numerous medicines that were lined up as foreign objects on the kitchen counter.

Joseph drew near when his *daed* called him close.

"*Jah*, Dat?"

"You're anxious, *sohn*. I can tell. Itching to be about some errand or another."

Joseph opened his mouth to protest and his *daed* held up a hand. "Go on with you, *buwe*. I've plenty of company here and I'm not dead yet. Besides, that big black gelding of yours has been eating his head off for want of exercise. Ben Kauffman's *sohn* can barely keep him in rein when the lad comes over to run the beast."

"All right, Daed." Joseph pressed the old man's shoulder with affection and made room for jolly Deacon Keim to have a spot as he took his leave. *Besides, riding Ned will make what I must do all the faster.*

Soon, Joseph was astride the big black horse, putting fair distance between himself and his community, as he passed the graveyard and started to canter to the other side of the mountain, where the *Englisch* took cottages for rent . . .

"Are you sure you'd like to walk?" Priscilla asked Mary anxiously. "Isn't it a bit far to Grossmudder May's?"

"I walk every time. It's *gut* for me and the *boppli*." She rubbed her growing abdomen and gave Priscilla a pretty smile.

"What's a *grossmudder*?" Hollie piped up as she filled her dress pockets with pebbles.

Mary laughed. "A grandmother, *kind*. But we call Grossmudder May 'grandmother' because she cares for all of us here on the mountain."

"Will she be my grandma too?"

Priscilla felt the weight of Mary's gaze and nodded faintly.

Mary smiled at Hollie. "Most surely."

"Great!" Hollie danced ahead on the path.

"She is such a happy child," Mary praised.

"I don't know sometimes. She—well, she saw a lot of things that I couldn't keep from her, even when she was much younger. My husband—he was a brutal man."

Mary slipped her hand into Priscilla's. "But you have Hollie."

Priscilla couldn't subdue the shudder that passed through her body when she thought of the night Hollie was conceived. It had been a nightmare that she tried not to relive, but it flooded back now and she swallowed hard.

"*Jah*, I have Hollie." Her voice quavered.

Mary sighed. "Priscilla, sometimes it's the bitterest water that gives life to the sweetest fruit. And surely, Hollie is such a blessing."

Priscilla had to smile, though her eyes were damp with tears. "You're right, Mary, and you *Amisch* seem to have a *gut* saying for every situation."

Mary gave a delicate shrug. "I think we try to speak the truth."

"And that, my friend, is exactly what I need. Sometimes, when you've lived with someone who hurts you, you start to believe that you're not worth much, but here—I feel—I feel alive to possibility."

"And with Joseph too?" Mary asked gently.

"Yes," Priscilla admitted in soft tones. "With Joseph too."

• • •

Joseph drew rein at the edge of the small cabin's property. From where he sat on Ned, he could easily survey the eerily familiar garden, the front yard, and the porch with matching buckets of bright flowers. *Maybe I have the wrong place— the garden looks freshly worked. But I'd know the way here if I walked it blindfolded . . .*

He slid down and tethered the horse to a large tree limb, then began to move toward the cabin. With each step, he felt his heart rate increase and his palms begin to sweat. Memories swept through his mind like the onslaught of flood water: dark, murky, and treacherous. Somehow, the words Priscilla had spoken to him about what had happened here seemed all the more striking in proximity. *Abuser . . . criminal . . . Who was really who?*

He swallowed hard and put his booted foot on the bottom step. The cabin door creaked open and Amanda Stearn stepped out onto the porch. Joseph steeled himself to meet her eyes and then felt his mouth tighten with tension when she smiled.

"Joseph, you came."

He reached in his pocket and produced the bear claw necklace, handing it out to her. He tried to ignore the blatant brush of her fingertips against his hand, wanting to jerk away. Suddenly, he felt a new clarity about the situation and wondered if she'd tricked him into coming to the cabin by using the necklace and the promise he'd made to be there if she ever sent it to him. *But what do I owe her . . . What can I gain from her? Forgiveness? Absolution? But only Derr Herr can truly give those . . .*

"I came because you sent me a token of an old promise—one made by an ignorant *buwe*, Amanda."

He watched her eyes narrow and realized how much older she seemed, older and almost malevolent. *How different from Priscilla . . .*

"I can assure you that you were far from ignorant, Joseph."

He shook his head at her insinuating tone. "I have the pictures . . . you have the necklace. Now tell me why you sent for me." *And tell me why I was foolish enough to come . . .*

Priscilla thought that Grossmudder May's cabin looked rather like a gnome cottage, perched on the edge of a thickly planted hill. Even Hollie appeared entranced by the mingled smells of fruit blossoms and herbs that filled the air and intrigued the senses.

"Oh, Mommy, it's like the ice mine that Joseph showed us. I think the fairies live here too."

Priscilla smiled as Hollie bent to attempt to tease a bright yellow butterfly from an apple blossom. The insect fluttered away and Hollie laughed, trying to jump after it.

"*Ach*, there's nothing more blessed than a child's laughter at my door."

Priscilla looked up to see an aged *Amisch* woman standing on the cabin's porch, a grin of wrinkles and dimples upon her old, intelligent face.

"Grossmudder May," Mary said, slightly out of breath. "*Sei se gut*, meet Priscilla Allen and her daughter, Hollie."

Priscilla almost wanted to look away from the keen eyes of the elder. She felt for some reason that her very soul was laid bare under the compelling gaze, and she wasn't sure she liked the feeling.

Grossmudder May smiled. "Don't fret, miss. I see only what Derr Herr gives me, and it looks as though you have some spirit and fight within you. 'Tis a *gut* thing, I'm thinking."

Priscilla dipped her head in polite acknowledgment, very conscious of her *Amisch* dress, not wanting to be an affront to the healer. But before she could speak, Hollie bounced up the stairs.

"Hello. Are you the fairy queen?"

"Hollie," Priscilla shushed in embarrassment.

But Grossmudder May waved a wrinkled hand, dismissing Priscilla's concern. "Allow the *kind* a bit of fancy, for it fades soon enough in this world. *Nee*, child, I am no fairy queen but a daughter of a King just the same."

Hollie frowned a bit in thought. "You mean God, don't you?"

"*Jah*, I do. 'Tis bright you are."

"My mommy's mad at God."

"*Ach* . . . well, we'll have to see about that. *Kumme* . . . *kumme* inside, Mary Lyons and Priscilla Allen. The child can play in the back garden."

Hollie let out a whoop of pleasure and darted behind the cabin while Priscilla followed Mary and the old woman inside, feeling a curious sense of expectancy.

"I find that I am short on money," Amanda said stiffly. "I married since the time we were—together, but my husband died recently and I was left with very little."

Joseph shrugged as casually as he could, though his throat hurt and he felt again a wave of uncertainty. Then he remembered Priscilla's endless resourcefulness, and fishing with Hollie. He squared his shoulders. "Yet you rented this cabin, Amanda, and are still young enough to work."

Her mouth dipped into a sneer, surprising him so that he nearly took a step back.

"I could have sent those pictures to your bishop. Have you thought of that, Joseph?"

"And I would have repented," he realized aloud. "And the community would have accepted me."

"Listen," she hissed. "You owe me. Your silence. Your pleasure. Your money . . . Now when can I expect payment?"

He was opening his mouth, longing to deny her but still feeling shaken inside, when a clear whistling broke the moment. Joseph turned to see Dan Kauffman, Ben's eldest boy, come striding to the garden with the ease of a regular visitor.

The tall lad lifted a hand in greeting and Amanda called out in return, using a sweet voice. Joseph watched the *buwe* for a moment and a shiver passed through him as the scene played out with strange familiarity. Dan took off his shirt and started to rake the ground. A pulse beat like a violent drum through Joseph's head as truth finally won the moment with disturbing clarity. *Dan is sixteen . . . sixteen . . .*

Joseph spun on Amanda and she took a wary step back. "Witch," he said low. "You would do this to an innocent *buwe*? Dan is a *gut* lad."

She pursed her lips and nodded. "Indeed he will be."

Joseph had never felt like striking a woman, but the compulsion now was so great that he had to fist his hands at his sides and grit his teeth. "You're through on this mountain, Amanda. If I have to drag you by your hair to the nearest authorities and see you locked up—I will do it."

She laughed. "For what? Giving pleasure to a willing partner?"

"No partner, no equal. A lad . . ." He felt his throat tighten. "An innocent *buwe*."

"Oh, Joseph, you really have fooled yourself over the years."

He stared into her sharklike eyes and nodded. "*Jah*, I have, but no more. You will be gone from here by tomorrow and never return, or I will find justice that knows no mercy for your—crime."

"You can try," she said, but he could tell by the quiver in her shoulders that his words had found their mark.

He turned and walked down the steps of the cabin and out into the garden. He laid his hand on Dan's shoulder and looked the *buwe* square in the face. "Dan, Amanda—Ms. Stearn—no longer needs you here. I want you to put your shirt on and *geh* . . . Ride Ned home and stable him. I'd like to offer you a job apprenticing at carpentry and the like. I've plenty of money to pay you well."

"*Jah*, Joseph, *danki*." Dan nodded, but his eyes strayed to the porch. "Did I—do something wrong?"

"*Nee, sohn*. Nothing at all."

Dan nodded and shrugged into his shirt, walking off and beginning to whistle again. Joseph watched him go, a ghost of himself, free now of Amanda's talons of abuse.

Joseph didn't turn around as he walked off the property; he didn't need to look back. Priscilla had been right in what she'd tried to say about the abuse, and he'd cut her off. He wanted nothing more now than the peace of her presence and the chance to start things right for the first time in years.

Chapter Nineteen

Priscilla was surprised to see a young, slender *Amisch* woman bent near the open fireplace when she entered Grossmudder May's cabin. She had thought the old woman lived alone.

"My new apprentice in the healing arts." Grossmudder May gestured to the girl. "Sarah Mast."

Priscilla smiled, noting that Mary seemed surprised by the introduction.

"Sarah," Mary said slowly. "I didn't know you were working here. Is everything well with you, Grossmudder?"

"*Jah*, sweet Mary. Except that I grow *aulder* by the month and we must have someone to help with the ills of the community. Young Sarah shows the right spirit."

Mary smiled at Priscilla as she moved to press Sarah's hand. "Priscilla, Sarah is my brother Edward's girl. They were courting before he left for the rigs to make money so that they might marry sooner."

"Oh." Priscilla struggled to contain her surprise.

From what she'd briefly seen of Joseph's brother, Sarah seemed a quiet and unlikely match for the handsome, quick-talking Edward.

"You've met Edward, *jah*?" Sarah asked softly. "How is he?"

Priscilla hesitated, unsure what Sarah knew about the Texas job, but the girl hastened to reassure her.

"I get two letters a week from him," Sarah revealed, a flush mounting on her cheeks. "I know he's moving on to Texas for a bit."

"I thought he was very kind and seemed to be doing well," Priscilla said with relief.

Sarah nodded her thanks, then held aside a curtain that led to an adjacent bedroom. "Mary, if you'd like to *kumme* and lie down a moment, Grossmudder will see how you and the *boppli* are doing."

Priscilla ducked her head beneath some hanging dried herbs and sat down at the small kitchen table while Mary followed Sarah. Grossmudder May placed a cup of tea in a delicate cup and saucer in front of Priscilla. "Rose tea, child. Drink while I see to Mary. She is weary with the news of her *fater*, I know."

Priscilla was only too glad to obey, hoping the aged healer could lift Mary's spirits. The tea before her was fragrant and a beautiful color of pale pink. She sipped slowly and soon Sarah came out from behind the curtain.

"I've got to get home. Grossmudder says her knees tell her that a storm is coming in this afternoon. My *fater* worries if I'm away too long." She picked up a wicker basket and looped it over her arm. "*Danki* for telling me of Edward."

"It was my pleasure. Nice to meet you, Sarah."

The girl slipped from the cabin door and Priscilla soon abandoned her tea and rose to go and check on Hollie.

"She's fine, Priscilla," Grossmudder May assured her as she came from the room. "I saw her out the back window."

Mary soon joined them, straightening her apron. "Priscilla, I thought I'd head home to get Jude's lunch. I could take Hollie with me. Grossmudder would like to talk with you for a bit."

Priscilla hesitated. "Will you be all right walking back with only Hollie for company? How are you feeling?" *And I'm not sure I want to have an intimate talk with this knowing woman alone . . .*

"Everything is as it should be," Grossmudder May said in satisfaction. "Derr Herr be praised."

Priscilla received Mary's quick hug with pleasure. "It'll be fine, Priscilla. I'll go call for Hollie. We'll see you at home later."

When Mary had gone, Priscilla felt strange being alone with the healer. But she sat back down with determination to finish her tea, and Grossmudder May joined her with her own cup.

The quiet in the cabin, save for the gentle fall of embers in the fire and the slight breeze stirring the drying herbs above, was peaceful, and Priscilla found herself beginning to relax.

"That's better, child," Grossmudder May said after a moment. "There is nothing to fear here."

Priscilla smiled a bit sadly, thinking of her previous constant fear of Heath. "No . . . I suppose not."

"I would tell you something of my past, Priscilla Allen. If you care to listen . . ."

"Of course," Priscilla said politely.

"I have not always been Grossmudder May of Ice Mountain. Once, I was May Miller of Elk Valley, a sheltered *Amisch* girl and the youngest of six *kinner*. I was blessed by the love of my family and believed that all would have that same kind of love for me—especially the man I chose to marry—Elias Stolfus." The old woman paused to sigh, her eyes focused on long-ago memories. "In any case, I was wrong. Elias was a brutal man. He sought to control through violence and harsh words. He crushed me for a time; physically, mentally, spiritually."

"How did you escape?" Priscilla asked with her heart beating in her throat.

"How did you?" the old woman returned softly, and Priscilla's gaze lifted to hers in both wonder and alarm.

"Bishop Umble told you my story?"

"*Nee*, child. Derr Herr revealed it to me. So, I wonder again . . . how did you escape?"

Priscilla swallowed hard, thinking of her darkest fears. "I—I haven't escaped. Not even here, in this beautiful place. Sooner or later, he'll find us—take Hollie and perhaps—leave me to die."

"Do you believe that is the plan that Gott has for your life?"

"I don't know . . . why has He let all of this happen to me?" *To Joseph . . .*

"We might spend a lifetime asking those questions, child. And never know the answers this side of Heaven. But I believe He allows things that hurt for a time, to turn them ultimately for *gut* . . . to make us stronger, deeper people who can then go on to help others."

Priscilla swallowed a hasty response, part of her wanting to protest at the simplicity of the answer, part of her finding the resonance of truth from another woman who had walked her path. "I guess," she began slowly. "I guess that we cannot live every day in fear. That we have to believe that God wants better for us."

"But you've never heard talk of Derr Herr like this before . . . except, maybe with . . ."

"Joseph," Priscilla confirmed with a faint sob.

"*Ach*, yes . . . Joseph. Tell me, Priscilla Allen. What was your mother's favorite flower?"

Priscilla was surprised by the turn of the conversation and tilted her head. "Lilacs. Purple ones. She told me once that heaven would smell like lilacs. But why?"

Grossmudder May lifted a large bentwood basket from the floor and passed it across the table to Priscilla. "Go behind the cabin here, child, and walk a ways 'til you *kumme* to the hollow below the cemetery. You'll find many lilac bushes there. Their fragrance will renew you."

Priscilla took the basket and rose from the table, prepared, for some reason, to do exactly as she was instructed, even if it was strange and fanciful.

Joseph looked to the sky as he passed by the *Amisch* cemetery. A storm was coming in by the looks of the clouds, but he lingered, feeling compelled to pick a bunch of deep purple lilacs and take them to his *mamm*'s grave. *Soon my* fater *will lie here too . . . but I must go on and build my own life, find my own way.*

He looked up as the sound of delicate humming drifted to him. He stood and gazed down into the hollow and saw a slender *Amisch* woman, dancing among the lilac bushes. He didn't recognize her at first and then she turned to face him. He caught his breath at the vision of Priscilla dressed in *Amisch* clothes and slowly walked down the hill toward her. She had frozen to the spot when she'd seen him, and now he felt his throat tighten with all that he wished to share with her.

"Priscilla, you look—beautiful." *Have I told her that before?*

Her cheeks took on a rosy hue and she curtsied a bit. "*Danki*, Herr King."

He smiled in pleasure and reached out a gentle finger to her burgundy sleeve. "May I touch?"

She twirled a stem of lilac in her right hand and extended her left to him. "You may."

He thumbed his way across the delicate veins of her wrist, finding the place where her pulse point beat near the hem of her sleeve. He longed to press his mouth to the spot but knew it wasn't proper behavior for someone who was supposed to be an *Amisch* prayer partner. But when she made a soft, feminine sound of approval at his touch, and looked so full of happiness for the moment, he took a step nearer her. He liked the way her lashes swept downward in a demure fall, emphasizing her ivory skin and the smattering of freckles that had developed on her cheeks.

He wanted to tell her everything that had happened with Amanda, but he couldn't get to the words when she leaned in to him. He reached up to brush a stray tendril of red hair from her brow, then bent forward to press his mouth to a place behind her ear. "May I kiss?" he whispered, his heart hard in his throat.

"You may," she said after a quick moment. Her voice was a bit hoarse but there was no misunderstanding the tremble of desire that passed through her as she pressed her small hands to the breadth of his chest.

He smiled as the stem of lilacs in her hand bumped his chin. He couldn't resist the sensory delight of the flower and pressed his lips to the purple blossoms. "Watch," he said softly. "This is what I would do to you, Priscilla."

He heard her shallow intake of breath and it fueled the excitement that caused his belly to tighten and his cheeks to flood with heat. He played his lips across the delicate blossoms, slanting his head, tasting, dampening, and then trailing the tip of his tongue over each petal.

"Joseph . . ." Her voice came out in a breathless sigh. "Please."

He heard the urgency of her plea and quickly transferred his attentions to her mouth.

Even his drugging kisses in the ER didn't match the nuanced dance his lips and tongue performed against her mouth. She wanted him to hold still, to hurry up, and somehow do both at the same time. She'd never been kissed with such staggering intent, such visible savoring of each of her breaths.

"Mmm," he whispered. "You taste like lilacs and roses . . ."

Her lips curved in a soft smile as she gazed into his green-gold eyes, which had darkened with their kissing. "Joseph . . . I feel—I feel like there's something different about you—more free, more alive."

She shivered under the intensity of his gaze. "How do you know me so well?" he asked, his tone full of wonder.

"I don't know for sure." She ran her hands down his broad shoulders. "It seems so natural."

"Well, you're right. I do feel—free, for the first time in years. I went to see Amanda . . . the woman who—took advantage of me when I was sixteen."

"What?" Priscilla blinked in amazement.

"Are you surprised that I saw her or that I finally see what you were trying to tell me about being . . . abused?"

"Both."

She watched him close his eyes for a moment, as if struggling to organize his thoughts. Then he looked at her. "I told you I was sixteen . . . it was my birthday."

He's going to tell me about it . . . Oh, dear Lord, give me the right words to say to him. She prayed silently without thinking twice.

"I was—so happy earlier that day," he went on. "I felt so *gut* inside, like everything was right with the world. Anyway, I went to Amanda's garden to work as I had all summer. I had my shirt off, and she said she'd made a cake for me. She led me inside and touched my chest. I'd never had a girl touch me before, not even hold my hand, and I froze. I think she took my reaction to mean . . . that I wanted—" He broke off for a moment.

"It's all right, Joseph," Priscilla whispered with tenderness. "Tell me. You'll feel better after."

"Again, it's hard not to say that it was my fault, but I—I saw Ben Kauffman's eldest *buwe* there when I went today and I knew the cycle was continuing, that she was going to do it again to an innocent lad."

"And you were an innocent boy, Joseph," she said gently, but he shook his head and swiped with sudden fury at his eyes.

"*Nee* . . . I knew it was wrong, what I did to her. *Ach*, Gott, help me. I knew it was wrong but I enjoyed it too." He began to cry in earnest then and she moved to put her arms around him, holding him close, making soothing sounds from the back of her throat.

"Joseph, you were a boy. Underage. That's what we call it in my world. What she did was not only a sin; it was a crime."

He laughed bitterly. "A crime? Not to the older *Englisch* boys in the mountain cabins. They—teased me. I didn't fully understand half of it then. But they said I was lucky to be working for such a fine woman, that she must pay me well. If they only knew . . ."

If they only knew . . . The words echoed in Priscilla's mind. *How many times have I thought exactly the same thing about Heath?* She realized that one of the main connections she had with the *Amisch* man in her arms was the fact that he would

162

understand, that she could trust him with her past as he trusted her. It was an amazing revelation to both her heart and mind. There had never been anyone she could trust, and now, here, in the middle of nowhere, God had seen fit to give her a friend, a true friend . . . and maybe so much more.

Chapter Twenty

A loud crack of thunder signaled to Joseph the imminent downpour and he quickly grabbed up Priscilla's basketful of lilacs and caught her hand.

"*Kumme* on, or we'll be drenched. Let's go to Grossmudder May's."

He heard Priscilla's laughter as they ran in the now pattering rain, which quickly turned into huge drops. He glanced at her by his side; her *kapp* askew, her beautiful face upturned to the heavens, and her small bare feet slapping in the growing mud. He felt he'd remember her for always in that moment of freedom.

They reached the porch of Grossmudder May's cabin, wet but still laughing, and would have entered but for the sight of Jude Lyons suddenly appearing over the rise on his brown horse. Joseph immediately sobered.

"Something's wrong," he said to Priscilla through the downpour as Jude flung the reins over a bush and frantically climbed the steps to them.

"It's Mary," Jude shouted. "She dropped Hollie off at the schoolhouse and I thought she looked pale, but when I got home for lunch, she was lying on the bed in terrible pain . . . there was blood." He moved to brush past them. "I need Grossmudder May."

Joseph looked down into Priscilla's worried blue eyes. "The *boppli* . . ." he said, not even able to name the fear he felt for his sister.

"Grossmudder May will help." Priscilla pressed his arm in support, but Jude emerged from the cabin, his handsome face pale.

"She's not here! I've got to go down the mountain for a doctor."

"In this storm, on a horse? You'll break your neck." Joseph caught his *bruder*-in-law's arm, but Jude shook him off.

"Go stay with her, please. I've got to try!" Jude ran down the steps and mounted the horse, setting off at a dangerous pace.

Joseph grabbed Priscilla's hand and they began to run as fast as the rain would allow. *Dear Gott . . . help my sister. Have mercy on her and the babe . . .* His prayers beat a tattoo in time with the sloshing pound of his footsteps and he knew by the way that Priscilla's lips were moving that she was praying too.

They passed the school *haus* in another clap of thunder and Bishop Umble's wife waved them on.

"She'll be watching the *kinner* and Hollie,"

Joseph called as Priscilla slipped. He paused only a moment to help her up and then they continued on, the quarter mile feeling like a path of eternity.

Finally they came to Mary and Jude's cabin and Joseph was surprised when Priscilla's wet hand clamped onto his at the door latch. He looked down into her soaked, mud-splotched face and saw her lift her chin.

"I can help, Joseph. I know what to do. I delivered Hollie by myself."

Priscilla ignored the look of shock on Joseph's face and pushed open the door. She immediately went to the kitchen to wash her hands over and over with the homemade lye soap she found under the sink. Then she went to the master bedroom. Joseph was kneeling by the bed, holding Mary's hand.

Priscilla's heart leapt in her throat when she saw the dreadful paleness on Mary's face, but she squared her shoulders and pushed at Joseph, using her elbow. "Go and wash your hands. I'll need your help."

Thankfully, he rose and did as she asked, allowing her to gently lift Mary's dress. Mary moaned and didn't open her eyes as Priscilla began to talk to her. "Okay . . . okay . . . there's a lot of blood or else there just looks like there's a lot. These things can be deceptive. We're going to get through this, Mary. Your *boppli* is going to live." *Please, dear God, let this baby live . . .*

"*Jah*," Mary whispered weakly.

Priscilla laid a hand on Mary's brow and found her to be hot with fever. "Colonized strep B can produce a high fever at birth . . ."

"What?" Joseph asked, returning, soft-footed, into the room.

"It's a type of strep that can be present at birth. It technically needs antibiotics, but if we can get the baby delivered, we can limit the potential damage." Priscilla pressed gently on Mary's swollen abdomen.

"You sound like a doctor," Joseph murmured.

"Heath told me I'd have no help when Hollie was due and I . . . well, I read everything I could about what can go wrong with a pregnancy and birth."

"Why didn't you leave such a man?" he asked, his frantic eyes on Mary.

Priscilla rounded on him with something like a primitive cry. "How dare you ask me that?" she whispered. "Do you think I didn't want to . . ." She swallowed hard and turned back to his sister, regaining composure. "We have to focus on Mary now."

"You're right. I—I'm sorry," he said.

She nodded but then became too absorbed in what was happening before her to notice Joseph beyond giving him brief instructions for the next hour and a half.

She had gotten Mary into a sitting position and

was encouraging her to make an effort to push when a strong contraction seized all control of the moment. Mary arched her back, gave a brief scream, and the baby was born.

Priscilla caught the slippery, tiny body with surprise and wonder. "It's a girl," she exclaimed, hastily bundling the baby in the warmed blankets Joseph had prepared.

Mary smiled feebly. "A *maedel*? Joseph, where's Jude?"

"Here," a voice rang out as Jude and Dr. McCully, as well as a helicopter transport team, crowded into the room.

Priscilla met Joseph's eyes and wanted to duck her head at the shining pride she saw there. *He's proud—of me.* But she couldn't forget his earlier words as they clouded her mind with sudden remorse. *Why didn't I leave?*

Joseph saw the moment that Priscilla's eyes darkened with grief, and he cursed himself silently for what he'd asked earlier without thinking. Even the doctor's assurance that all would be well for both *mamm* and babe only relieved his anxiety for the brief moments when he touched his sister's hand and felt Jude's tears fall on his neck.

Soon both Joseph and Priscilla stood on the periphery of the room as the support team bundled Mary onto a stretcher and put the *boppli* in a portable incubator. Then there was only the sound of the front door being closed and the *haus* stood in palpable quiet, as if breathing again after a long run.

Joseph sat down in a chair in the master bedroom only to rise quickly when Priscilla began to strip the bed in silence. He moved to help her, not knowing what to say until their eyes met across the spread of a quilt.

"You were alone?" he asked, barely able to get the words out at the thought.

"You should go and tell your *fater* about Mary. He will want to go back down the mountain, you know. And you should go too—to make sure everything is as well as the doctor thinks." Priscilla grasped a top sheet and pulled it to her in a protective stance.

"My *fater* and the rest of the mountain already know, without a doubt, and I saw the life in my sister's eyes because of your quick thinking. I'm concerned about you right now."

"Well, don't be. I'm fine." She bustled past him, carrying bedding out to the back porch, where a large tub and winding press arm served as the washing machine.

He followed, watching until she'd piled the sheets inside the tub, then caught her hand. "*Jah*," he whispered. "You are fine indeed, as fine a woman as I've ever met. I have told you much. Will you not share your secrets with me also?"

He saw her blue eyes well with tears, waver in

indecision, but then she returned his grasp and he led her back into the *haus* to sit in the quiet of the living area on the comfortable couch. He stroked her hand with his fingers in a slow, soothing motion, waiting until she was ready to speak— willing to wait for all time, if necessary.

Priscilla drew a shaky breath. "I was nearly three months along before I told Heath about the pregnancy. He was furious, of course . . . not that I didn't tell him right off, but because of the baby. He said I did it to hold him at a distance, to keep him away from me. But he also said that I wouldn't be able to use the pregnancy as an excuse for him to stop controlling me, managing me, as he should."

"So he was still—hitting you while you carried his babe?" Joseph knew a savage and distinctly un-*Amisch* desire to seek out this man and end Priscilla's troubles once and for all. But he continued to stroke her hand and remembered that *Derr Herr* said "Vengeance is mine."

"He hit me, but he was more careful about where, so marks wouldn't show . . . And then, for the last months of the pregnancy, he was strangely calm. I thought that the baby's coming might have changed him, but then, about two weeks before I was due, he locked me in a room. He told me that he'd let my father know that I'd gone to a special birthing facility, a luxury place, to have the baby —that it was his gift to me. He left books on pregnancy and delivery in the room, and when I realized he wasn't going to let me out, I read them. Then, I think because I was so stressed, I started labor early. I begged him to help me, but he never came in . . . Not until I called out it was a girl and that I thought she might not be breathing. Then he unlocked the door. He said if I told anyone at the hospital that I'd never see the baby again, and I was so—so stupidly afraid that I believed him." She choked on a breath and Joseph drew her within the circle of his arms.

He rocked her gently, trying to regulate his own breathing after hearing the incredible horror of her story. "And then you named her Hollie?" he asked in soft tones.

Priscilla nodded and sniffed against his chest. "It was Christmas Eve when I delivered her."

Joseph rested his chin on top of her damp head. "Priscilla . . . will you marry me?"

Chapter Twenty-One

Priscilla struggled to draw back in his arms, wanting to see his face, wondering if he'd had a temporary lapse in mind or judgment. But when she looked into his eyes, she saw only level sincerity and calm respect.

"Why—why would you ask me that? Because you feel sorry for me?"

He shook his head and kissed her forehead. "Because you've found a place in my heart that only you can fill, but I know that you'll need some time to accept that. So, I ask you to marry me . . . in name only for now. And, perhaps in time . . ." He shrugged. "You may begin to feel something for me in return."

She lifted shaking fingers to her wilted prayer *kapp*. "But Joseph, I'm *Englisch*."

He smiled, a rakish look that caught at her heart. "So, you look *Amisch* to me. Besides, your mother was *Amisch* . . . and this is a *gut* place for you and Hollie to be safe from that—Heath."

I don't know if I can ever be safe from him. "Oh, Joseph, I don't know. What will the bishop say?"

"Bishop Umble married Jude to my sister. I'll tell him the truth. Priscilla, you deserve a chance to be nurtured, to heal . . . Let me give you a taste of that. Let Derr Herr give you peace and show you how to love yourself here on Ice Mountain."

Peace . . . what is that? But after all, what do I have to lose—except my heart?

She looked up at him solemnly. "Yes, Joseph, I'll marry you."

"*Gut.*"

"I don't want to get married," Bishop Umble intoned with mockery, and Joseph resisted the urge to roll his eyes.

"*Jah*, I admit that I said something along those

171

lines." Joseph shifted on the wooden bench. He was tired and still had to take his *daed* and Priscilla down the mountain to see Jude and Mary and the new baby.

"Uh-huh . . . well, you see what good comes from being a woman's prayer partner—unwilling bachelors turned to the solid life of family. I should partner more couples in prayer."

Joseph waited, not rising to the bait.

Bishop Umble sighed. "It seems your family has a penchant for marrying *Englischers*. You know she's going to have to ask to join the church, and that the community will have to be in agreement about her place before you can marry."

Joseph looked down into the coffee mug the bishop's wife had filled before she'd left the room. Although he'd told Priscilla that he'd tell the bishop the truth, he couldn't keep himself from wanting to hurry things on a little. "Do you remember why you married Jude to my sister?"

"*Jah*, because your *fater* forced me out of bed and dragged me to do it. I remember there was an accusation about some dalliance in a blueberry patch." The older man peered at him with suspicion. "Why?"

Joseph shrugged and found it wasn't too hard to look uncomfortable. "Priscilla has no *fater* here to speak up for her, so I'll do it on her behalf. I admit to a bit of a . . . dalliance in a lilac grove."

"You've dishonored her and yourself?"

Ach, if you only knew about my dishonor . . . but that's over. It wasn't my fault . . . it wasn't . . . "A *gut fater* might say so," he admitted roughly, dropping his gaze.

The bishop slapped his hands on the tabletop and got to his feet. "Well then, I'll marry you now."

"Uh . . . right now?"

"*Jah*, right now. There's no sense waiting to put things to rights, though I tell you again that Priscilla will have to seek community afterwards. There's service tomorrow."

"I'm not even cleaned up." Joseph indicated his mud-splotched clothes from the earlier rain.

"Better that your soul be clean first. Now, *kumme*. We will go to Jude and Mary's *haus*."

Joseph rose with reluctance, hoping that Priscilla had had enough time to bathe and dress after the difficult morning.

Priscilla lifted one leg and gently scrubbed it with the rose-scented soap that Mary had made. *Dear God, be with Mary and the baby. Bless them both with long life . . .* She swallowed and tried to concentrate on the water. The bath was heavenly after the tumult of the morning and she allowed herself a few moments to relax back in the brass tub, luxuriating in the warmth of the water that she had heated on the stove.

A sudden loud knocking on the front door sent her splashing though, despite the bathing screen.

And she had to resist the urge to duck her head under the water when she heard Joseph's deep voice.

"Uh, Bishop Umble—perhaps you might wait on the porch here a moment. Priscilla's a bit— um—disheveled and I would tell her of your wish that we marry now."

Marry! Now? Priscilla hastily bound her hair in a knot on top of her head and submerged herself to a decent level as she recognized Joseph's footfalls across the wooden floor.

"Now this is an interesting situation." His voice was low and she caught a note of laughter in it that made her fume.

"Joseph King—I am in the bathtub," she hissed, though she knew her situation needed no explanation.

His large shadow loomed from the other side of the screen and she froze.

"Do you need a towel, my sweet? Or would you rather I remove all doubt from the *gut* bishop's mind that we should marry immediately by drying you myself?"

"Joseph!"

"All right, all right, little spitfire, I'll leave you to dry and dress, but I must beg you to hurry as the bishop is impatient to redeem our souls through marriage."

"What? What did you tell him?"

"That I dallied with a *maedel* in a lilac grove . . .

that's all," he stated airily, and she didn't know whether to catch her breath or hold it as she heard his footsteps recede.

She listened as the door opened and closed with a quick click and then she scrambled from the bath, thankful that she'd had the foresight to place towels down around the tub. *The bishop must think me a wanton Englisch woman.* Then she recalled her response to Joseph's kisses with a sigh. *And maybe I am . . .*

Joseph had to suppress a smile of pleasure as Priscilla finally flung open the front door and stood, barefooted but properly garbed and *kapp*ed, to let them enter. She wore a light blue blouse beneath her dress and apron and damp tendrils of red hair clung to the nape of her neck. She smelled of sweet roses when he passed by her, and then he did smile, unable to suppress a passing *narrisch* thought: the desire to be the soap that bathed her.

He cleared his throat to ward off such meanderings and looked to the bishop, who was paging through his Bible.

"Bishop Umble, don't we need two witnesses?" Joseph asked.

"Hmm? Why, *jah*! I forgot, and now we'll have to go back and . . ." The bishop paused as a knock sounded on the door. "Providence!" the old man exclaimed and opened the door to reveal his wife and Hollie.

Joseph watched Priscilla hold out her arms to Hollie, and the little girl went running.

"Excellent," the bishop said. "We have our witnesses."

"May a child be a witness?" Priscilla asked.

Joseph saw the bishop give her a keen look. "It is my thought that children witness much in this world, both *gut* and bad. To witness the marriage of her mother is no doubt a blessing which she will long remember and treasure."

"Mommy—you're getting married? To Joseph? Yay!" But then the child's face took on a look of confusion. "But what about Daddy?"

Joseph couldn't mistake the beseeching look that Priscilla gave him and he looked to Bishop Umble, who nodded and gestured to one of the bedroom doors. "Take all the time you need—Priscilla and Joseph."

Joseph walked with heavy steps, his face grim. *However could I have forgotten the* kind *in all of this?* Then he recalled what Hollie had said about fairy tales, that her mother did not believe in them but that she did. He turned and faced Priscilla and Hollie and stood solemnly, staring down at the little girl. Priscilla started to speak, but he waved her silent with a gentle motion. Then he dropped to one knee in front of Hollie and bowed his head.

"Forgive me, Princess Hollie. You see, I asked the wrong girl about this wedding. I should have asked your permission first and I did not. I beg for your forgiveness and ask now instead . . . will both you and your *mamm* marry me?"

There was an infinitesimal pause and then he felt small fingers thread through his hair and come to rest on his head. "Arise, Mr. Knight. I give my permission. You can kiss my hand."

Joseph felt tears prick the backs of his eyes as he got to his feet and took the small hand into his own. He bent to brush his lips carefully over the tiny knuckles. Then he saw another hand extended in his direction and glanced at Priscilla, who had tears in her own eyes.

"*Jah*," she whispered. "*Gut* Sir Knight, you may kiss my hand as well."

It was an admission, Joseph realized as he caught her hand. An admission that some part of hope and fanciful notion still existed for her, and the kiss he placed on her hand meant more to him than any other they'd shared. Then he caught both mother and daughter together in a great hug, spinning them round until they were all laughing.

"Now," Joseph suggested when he'd finally let them go. "Shall we have a wedding, my dears?"

Chapter Twenty-Two

Priscilla was grateful for the strength of Joseph's large hand when she peered into the NICU window at the tiny baby girl she'd helped to deliver only that morning. The tubes and machines and deliberate movements of the nurses all worked to produce what seemed like a strange scene in a play. *But God is in control . . .* Priscilla blinked as the thought riveted, unbidden.

"*Kumme*," Joseph said after a few minutes. "Let's go and see Mary and Jude. It does no good to stand here."

Priscilla obeyed the husky timbre of his voice and walked with him down the hospital hall. Hollie had reluctantly agreed to stay back on the mountain with the bishop's wife, while Mr. Ellis had driven Priscilla and Joseph, as well as the bishop and Mr. King, to Coudersport. Priscilla had sat next to Joseph, hardly able to believe that she was now his wife.

But now, she could tell, his thoughts were wholly of his sister and her little family. She was about to try and speak to him when Dr. McCully walked toward them.

"Ah, the heroes of the hour, or so I hear from Mary Lyons. You two did an amazing job with

Mary and the baby—saved both their lives without a doubt. Congratulations!"

Priscilla felt herself color hotly when she felt the weight of Joseph's gaze. "It was Priscilla, *dochter*. My wife now, in fact."

"Well, well . . . even more congratulations then." Dr. McCully smiled. "I've got to get up to the NICU and see that little wonder of humanity. We're lucky to have the facilities to care for her here—a grand donation from a local family years ago. All right . . . see you both soon . . ." The doctor's cheery voice drifted to them from down the hall.

"It sounds like everything will be all right," Priscilla ventured, looking at Joseph's solemn face.

"*Jah*, and I meant what I said, Priscilla. You saved my sister and my niece."

A moment of insecurity pierced her heart at his words. "Joseph, is—was that the real reason you wanted to marry me?"

He smiled then, a flash of even, white teeth in the dreary hall, and casually stepped nearer until she had no choice but to back against a closed wooden door.

"Joseph," she squeaked. "We're in the hall."

"And, little spitfire, what are you expecting me to do, hmm?" He lifted a hand to gently twine a loose tendril of her hair around his finger. "The *Amisch* are renowned to the *Englischers* for keeping their—um—public displays of affection under lock and key." His lips brushed close to her right ear and she shivered, half closing her eyes and forgetting where they were as his voice continued to lull her.

"So, former *Englischer*, tell me about the Mountain *Amisch* . . . do we not touch?" He moved his hand from her hair to brush his fingers down her cheek, and she caught her breath. "Do we not kiss?" He placed a single hard kiss upon her lips, then drew back only to rock his hips forward again. "Do we not want?" His voice dropped to a whisper and she could not help but feel the heat and pulse of him through her dress.

"Joseph," she whimpered, needing something she could not explain, right there, right then.

"I promised to give you time to be nurtured, and I will keep my word." He drew back from her and she knew he was caught in his own game as his dark hair fell forward to cover his heated cheeks and brush at the darkened emerald-gold of his eyes. "But don't waste any more time on notions about why I married you, Priscilla King." He smiled as he said her new name, lazing it out, as if he savored a sweet. And she could not help but smile in return.

Joseph held Priscilla's hand tighter as they neared his sister's room to discover his *daed*, Bishop Umble, and Mr. Ellis, all gathered outside in a waiting area. His *fater* held a handful of cellophane-encased roses that he'd obviously purchased at the gift store, but he looked grim and was using one of his inhaler medicines.

"What's wrong?" Joseph asked, his eyes sweeping the group. "Is it Mary?"

Bishop Umble cleared his throat. "Nothing's wrong, lad, that we know of—only a doctor wanting some time alone with your sister. Your *daed*'s had a bit of a coughing spell."

Abner got to his feet, thrusting his inhaler into the pocket of his black pants, and held out the roses to Priscilla. "It's pleased I am to have another daughter . . . and another grand-*boppli*— your Hollie. I—I can't thank you enough for what you did for Mary . . . and for bringing this stubborn *sohn* of mine to marry as Bishop Umble has told us."

Joseph was pleased with his *fater*'s speech and swallowed as his *daed* whipped out a large red hankie and blew his nose loudly before sitting back down. Joseph looked down at Priscilla and found her clutching the roses with a tremulous smile on her red lips.

"*Danki*," she whispered. "If—if Joseph agrees, I hope you won't mind us taking up living with you, Herr King . . ."

"Daed," Abner corrected. "Call me Daed."

"All right . . . Daed."

Joseph heard the tremor in her voice and understood. *What was it like to have the offer of another earthly* fater*, when one had already failed you so badly?* He clutched his wife's hand a bit tighter and nodded to his *daed.* "*Jah,* Priscilla is right. We would stay with you at the cabin, if it's all right."

Abner snorted. "It's your home, even though I know you can build as fancy a *haus* as any an *Englischer* could dream of. Just ask him, Priscilla. He's a master builder and carpenter but won't admit it."

Joseph colored as Priscilla gave an indulgent laugh. "I know—Mary's told me."

He looked down at her in surprise, then was distracted by the female doctor emerging from Mary's room.

"You may go in now, but no more than two at a time, please," the woman said pleasantly. "She's doing well but is tired."

The doctor nodded and walked away, and Abner pointed toward Joseph. "You and Priscilla go—we've already been for a bit."

"All right." Joseph smiled down at Priscilla, who suddenly seemed reticent.

He stopped her right outside the large door. "Is everything okay?"

"I—I don't want Jude and Mary to think I've come seeking praise or something."

Joseph considered the implication of her words. *How wounded she is inside . . . Gott, let me help her in her brokenness. You help her,* sei se gut,

Derr Herr. He slid a hand to the small of her back. "They won't think any such thing, Priscilla. Now let's go tell them we're married."

He swung the door open and ushered her inside the pleasant room. His sister was lying in a hospital bed, her hair bundled beneath a kerchief, her beautiful face tired but holding so much more color than when they'd seen her last.

Jude got up from her bedside and came to embrace Joseph, then fervently shook Priscilla's hand. "*Danki*," he muttered, bright-eyed but clearly exhausted. "Thank you both so much."

Joseph clapped him on the shoulder, then led Priscilla to the bed. He took his sister's outstretched hand and squeezed it, the minutes during the birth passing rapidly through his mind. Then he blinked and pulled Priscilla close with his other hand.

"I don't know what to say," Mary whispered. "Have you seen her?"

Joseph watched Priscilla nod, a quick, humble motion of her *kapp*ed head, and he had to swallow hard.

"Priscilla," Mary asked. "Could you please tell us your middle name?"

Joseph looked at his sister in surprise, then suppressed a quick grin, guessing where the question was leading.

"Um, it's Rose," Priscilla said. "It was my mother's name."

Mary gave a brief clap of delight. "*Ach*, I love it . . . don't you love it, Jude?"

Jude nodded. "I do." He lifted Mary's hand and pressed it to his lips, then smiled. "And, if you don't mind, we'd like to name our little *maedel* Rose, in your honor, Priscilla."

Joseph hugged Priscilla close to his side as she let out a gasp of surprise. "What? You don't have to do that . . . I don't . . . I don't know what to say."

"Say yes, my sweet," Joseph murmured and caught his sister's eye.

"What did you call her?" Mary demanded.

"Nothing that isn't appropriate for one's *frau*, I promise." Joseph enjoyed the looks he got, then smiled at the resulting exclamations of pleasure as Priscilla was welcomed warmly into the family.

Chapter Twenty-Three

Priscilla watched with a tired smile as Hollie wrestled on the floor with the great black dog. They'd returned from the hospital to settle in at Abner's cabin, and Hollie had found a true friend and companion in Bear.

Joseph was outside doing evening chores, and Abner gave a belly laugh occasionally at the antics of the wolf dog and the little girl.

"Hey, Mommy? Are you watching? It's getting

dark out . . . Where's my bedroom gonna be? And you're going to sleep in Joseph's bed, right?"

Priscilla was startled out of her tired mood and glanced at Abner, who had abruptly taken to coughing. She rose, moving for his inhalers, glad of the diversion, when she turned and saw the merriment in the old man's eyes. He waved her back with the medicine.

"It's sorry I am, Priscilla, but the child gets to the heart of things, doesn't she?"

"Well, Mommy?" Hollie persisted.

"I . . ." Priscilla broke off as her heart began to beat faster. She hadn't gotten to the actual logistics of where she would sleep with a marriage "in name only." *Wasn't that how Joseph had put it? But what will Abner think if I don't share Joseph's bed? And, oh mercy, what would it be like to lie close to him, to have him near enough to touch and . . .*

She was puzzling all of this out, with a rapidly increasing pulse, when Joseph entered. She launched herself across the room to grab his arm. "Uh . . . Joseph. Hollie here was wondering where she would sleep? I think she might be getting tired."

She watched his intelligent green-gold eyes sweep the room and take in her urgent words with barely a pause.

"Hollie shall have Mary's room, of course. And

you and I, Priscilla . . . we'll sleep in the room Edward and I used to share. It'll all be fine." She gazed up into his face, unsure whether the soothing note in his voice was meant for her or himself but grateful for it nonetheless.

She released his arm and he went to the sink while Hollie plucked at Bear's ears with a joyful cry. "Yay! My own room. Can we paint it pink, Mommy? And maybe have some white roses on the walls, can we?"

Again Priscilla was at a loss, not sure how Abner would tolerate change in his household. But the old man laughed and swiped at his eyes. "You may do anything you like, *kind*. It's your room, your home too."

Hollie jumped to her feet to run and hug Abner, who returned her embrace with obvious enthusiasm.

Priscilla bit her lip, feeling again the wash of unexpected tenderness that these people extended to her—to her daughter. She prayed then that they might continue to abide on Ice Mountain without harm for as long as possible. And meeting her husband's eyes, she saw the echo of that hope reflected there.

Joseph paced the confines of his *auld* room like a caged mountain lion. Priscilla had lain down with Hollie for a bit to settle the *kind*'s excitement at being in a new place, and his *daed* had long since retired. Joseph knew he had only a few more minutes to make a decision about whether or not he should sleep on the floor. He didn't want to appear as though he was rejecting Priscilla in any way, but he also couldn't decide how much he could trust himself not to touch her in his sleep. *I could stay awake at night . . . take naps during the day.* He abandoned the foolishness of the thought, then turned as Priscilla quietly entered the room and closed the door behind her.

She looked at him, her blue eyes wide with questioning and something else—was it a hint of fear? He had a sudden pounding intuition that it might have been like this her first night with Heath . . . uncertainty and then violence . . .

He stepped toward her and she lifted her chin. He'd come to recognize the gesture as her preparing to face something difficult, and he felt both admiration and despair in his heart. He backed off and sank into his old reading chair between the bookshelf and the window, praying about how to proceed.

"Priscilla," he whispered finally. "I don't want anything from you, expect anything. You don't owe me and never will."

He saw her shoulders slump a bit and felt confused.

"I was afraid of this," she said.

"Afraid of tonight?"

She shook her head. "Afraid that you'd find

me . . . well, unclean or not worthy or some-thing . . . because I feel so—sullied—by what I went through with Heath."

Joseph gripped the arms of the *auld* chair, forcing himself not to go to her, to give her a chance to talk.

"And was—Heath—brutal during your time together in the bedroom?"

Her eyes took on a haunted, faraway look and he cursed himself for asking the question, but any kind of real intimacy between them had to be wrought in truth . . . and he knew that secrets hurt when they were left unspoken.

"He was horrific," she said suddenly, simply, then put her face in her hands, and he saw her shoulders shake with silent sobs.

He was out of the chair before he could think and gathered her close against his chest. "Dear Gott, Priscilla, I wish I could take this from you —all of it. The pain, the memories . . ."

She lifted her tearstained face and looped her arms around his neck. "You can," she half sobbed. "Kiss me. Please. When you kiss me, I can't think of anything else."

He was caught by the franticness in her voice and lost all sense of finesse as he urgently bent to kiss her mouth. He slanted his head and heard a roaring in his ears as she arched on tiptoe and fit her small frame against his body. Then he lifted her easily and carried her to sit in his lap on the chair he'd abandoned moments before, never breaking contact with her soft lips.

Finally, he had to gasp for breath and drew air harshly into his lungs. He stared down in the moonlight at her swollen and reddened mouth, then met her eyes. She lifted her hands to touch his face and he turned his head to bite gently at the juncture of her thumb and forefinger when she stroked back his hair. He watched her reaction through narrowed eyes, unsure of how far she'd be willing for him to extend the kiss. But she seemed to stare in abject fascination at his teeth on her skin, and her beautiful mouth formed a soft O of surprise and pleasure.

Then he shivered, knowing suddenly that there were a hundred things he could teach her to make her feel *gut,* and he knew he'd love to spend his life in the process. But suddenly, she'd wriggled her soft bottom back from his thighs and had risen to her feet before he even knew what she was about.

She stood before him, her hand over her mouth. Then she dropped her shaking fingers to clutch at her apron.

He leaned forward, his voice urgent. "Priscilla, what's wrong?"

"I never even thought about how you might feel when I asked you to kiss me—maybe it was selfish. I mean—did it make you think about when you were sixteen?"

He leaned back in the chair, thoughts thrumming through his mind at her question. Then he sighed and passed a hand over his eyes before he looked up at her once more. "Maybe . . . but not in the way you might think, my sweet *frau*."

Priscilla's lips stung sweetly from the heat and pressure of Joseph's mouth, but she could not allow herself to fully enjoy the tender pleasure of the burn until she heard what he had to say.

"Priscilla, I want to talk to you in truth, find freedom there, but I worry that it is you who might find me lacking if I were to—" He broke off as an urgent knock sounded on the door and then Hollie burst in, followed by the black tumult of Bear.

"Hollie," Priscilla gasped as she took in her daughter's distraught face. "What's wrong?"

"I thought I saw Daddy's face at the window," Hollie sobbed.

Priscilla immediately caught her daughter close and looked with frantic eyes to the window next to where Joseph now stood. She felt the impulse to run, somewhere, anywhere, but didn't know how she could when she was already in the middle of nowhere. She started to shake and sob and pressed Hollie against her chest.

"Priscilla," Joseph said softly. "He's not here."

"Hollie saw him!"

"The child's in a new place, a new room. She was dreaming. No one or no thing could get within a hundred feet of this cabin with Bear here. He'd tear them apart and howl like a wolf in the process."

Priscilla still sobbed, unable to stop as she shook her head fiercely and looked again to the unadorned, open window. She nearly jumped when Joseph touched her shoulder, then slid his arms around both her and Hollie.

"*Kumme*, my *maedels*, let's lie down in the bed and get some sleep. If it makes you feel better, Priscilla, I'll go have a look round with Bear and then stay up to watch tonight."

"No, don't leave us, please." Priscilla felt her teeth begin to chatter and was grateful when Joseph walked them to the bed and helped tuck in first Hollie, then herself. He piled quilts from an old chest on top of them and Hollie was soon fast asleep in Priscilla's arms with Bear taking up the other side of the bed.

Priscilla watched as Joseph stood by the window, his broad shoulders silhouetted by moonlight, his stance relaxed and comforting. She closed her eyes and almost drifted off, only to wake with a start. Joseph came to bend over her and gently kissed her forehead. "Happy wedding *nacht*, my beauty, my spitfire. Sweet dreams." And then she slept.

Chapter Twenty-Four

Joseph caught himself twice during the three-hour church service nearly falling asleep and probably would have done so had Ben Kauffman not elbowed him discreetly. He'd stayed awake all *nacht* as promised . . . his wedding night. But he had the extreme satisfaction of seeing Priscilla sleep, even if she did toss a bit—which, of course, led his already heated mind and body into secret places not suitable for guard duty. In the end, he'd resigned himself to studying the moon, and dawn had *kumme* steady and sure.

Now, he tried to focus as Bishop Umble began the usual announcements that followed the service. He wondered if Priscilla was nervous, but had already arranged with the bishop that he would go and stand with her when she asked for a place in the community. But first, he knew, Bishop Umble would speak in the strange way that he had of making a person feel both frustrated and alive.

The *auld* man was speaking now, stroking his gray beard, as he paced before the rows of backless benches filled with both old and young of the Mountain *Amisch*.

"There are times, my friends, when Derr Herr demands from us more than we think we have to give—our dreams, our fears, our lives. But it is

He Who gives us the power to make the necessary surrendering of these and much more. This morning I ask the new *frau* of Joseph King, Priscilla King, to *kumme* before you with her husband and present to you a question of surrender."

That's all, Joseph thought ruefully. *We could have used a bit more of an introduction.* But he stood and met Priscilla's eyes across the sea of interested faces, ignoring the faint murmurs of those who had somehow missed the news of yesterday's impromptu wedding.

He eased out of the row to take Priscilla's hand as she came forward, but he paused to wink at Hollie, who was now ensconced on Frau Umble's ample lap.

Then he led his wife to the front of the pews laid out in the Kauffmans' clean barn. He glanced down at Priscilla and hid a smile when she lifted her chin. It was appropriate to let her speak first without him, and she was apparently prepared as much as he was ultimately unprepared for what she began to say.

"What is a husband? Many of you may have heard some of my story or mine and Joseph's story, and I want to tell you that there is much more to know. A husband treats a child with tenderness, with laughter and affection. A husband treats a wife with gentleness and honor. A husband . . . stays awake all of his wedding night to keep watch against anything that may plague a wife's mind and heart . . ."

Joseph choked on a laugh as she'd no doubt shocked some of those present with her details of their wedding *nacht*, but it felt *gut* at the same time. He pressed her hand hard as she went on.

"I had the pleasure of meeting Grossmudder May yesterday and found her to be a woman of my own heart. When I asked her how Mary Lyons's *boppli* was, she said 'Everything is as it should be.' I realize now that she was speaking from Gott's sight and with the truth, knowing that Mary would deliver that very day and without her help. It was—my honor to be part of that help instead. And I know, as I stand before you, that everything is truly as it should be, as I have found sisters and brothers among you, fathers and mothers, and grandparents for my—our—daughter. So I beg you, *sei se gut*, for the gift of community as I study to learn and grow and understand your ways, to become part of you and wife to Joseph King, forever."

Joseph waited, filling his heart with his wife's words, knowing they were right and spoken in truth. *She wasn't going to run again . . .*

Bishop Umble came to stand beside them. "You have heard Priscilla King's words, her confession of love for you. What do you say to her plea for community? Her lifetime with Joseph?" A joyous chorus of *jah*s broke out and

Joseph smiled down into Priscilla's bright eyes until a lone, strident voice cried out.

"No!"

Priscilla jumped at the cry that silenced the voices of acceptance. The barn door had opened and she blinked into the bright sunlight of the morning as a lone figure came forward. It was a woman, attired in *Englisch* dress and holding her head high. Without knowing how, Priscilla understood that this was Joseph's abuser, daring so very much to come before a people to whom she did not belong.

Priscilla was aware of many things happening at once—Joseph's hand fisting inside her own, his big body tensing, Bishop Umble moving to face the woman, and then the woman locking eyes with her, a smile of vengeance on her lips.

"What right have you to interrupt this service?" Bishop Umble demanded.

The woman spun to face those gathered. "You joyfully welcome a woman into this community without asking about the fitness—of her husband. What do you really know of Joseph King? Of his past?"

"Enough!" Abner King rose and pointed a shaking finger at the *Englischer.* "You will not speak against my *sohn*. You have no right."

"Even when it is the truth? Don't your people live by the truth?" the woman cried.

"What truth do you speak of?" Bishop Umble

asked sternly. "Say your piece and be gone from here."

The woman pointed a finger at Joseph. "This man . . . assaulted me in the most intimate way. He was at my cabin yesterday to try and quiet me about it. He even sent one of your young men away so he could be alone to threaten me. And then"—she sniffed—"he said you'd all forgive him anyway—I'm only a widowed *Englischer.* I have no one but myself to speak for me."

Priscilla knew a fury in her chest that bubbled up from reserves suppressed for years. She clawed past Joseph and the bishop to grab the woman by the arm and shook her hard enough to rattle her teeth. "Liar!"

"Of course you'd want to defend him—you're his wife now. I am so sorry for you." The woman now sobbed with effective anguish and the crowd of *Amisch* murmured among themselves.

"She lies, I tell you!" Priscilla screamed, then spun to the bishop, still not letting go of the other woman.

Bishop Umble met Priscilla's stare and something in his eyes made her drop her hands from the intruder. Then the old man turned in profile to Joseph, giving him a fierce look. "Joseph King, what do you say to these accusations?"

Everything moved in time to the play of his senses. Joseph could smell Amanda's familiar perfume from where he stood and a sick feeling roiled in his stomach, forcing him to swallow. He felt the wood of the barn floor beneath his feet, the crack in the timbers reminding him of the rift between heaven and hell, and he saw his beautiful wife wild with fury. He knew his delay in speaking caused concern among the onlookers, but he wasn't sure how to begin. Thoughts pounded in his brain, images he'd long tried to suppress—him kissing Amanda, stroking her white thighs, dipping his head according to her direction. *My fault . . . my fault . . .*

Then, somehow, he focused on Dan Kauffman, standing with the other youths at the back of the barn. Dan's face was stricken and centered on Joseph almost immediately. He remembered the bishop's words at the end of the service: *Derr Herr helps you to give.* Maybe he could give truth here and be free at last . . .

"What she says is false." He heard his own voice from far away and had the strange feeling that he was standing outside himself, watching everything from a distance. "I did not assault her . . . she assaulted me."

He realized the barn had grown dead quiet and briefly saw Frau Umble and some of the mothers slip outside with the younger children, including Hollie. Then he went on. "I was sixteen—seven years ago. I had—never known a woman. I gave in to temptation, true, but it was never at my seeking. I did—wrong things with her, but my wife knows of this. Priscilla—she convinced me that what had happened when I was young was not purely my fault. I give you the truth today and will answer any particulars that the bishop or deacons would care to ask. I was at her cabin yesterday, but I believe that Derr Herr allowed me to be there to prevent such an event as happened to me from reoccurring with another young *buwe*. I ask you to forgive me as I've asked Gott for forgiveness in not confessing before you all . . ." He was about to stop when he saw Amanda's face—older, broken, her makeup running in a ghastly mask to a gaping red mouth. He cleared his throat and felt a cool breeze touch the back of his neck. "And I ask you to forgive Amanda too—as I forgive her, through the power of Derr Herr."

Joseph stared at Priscilla as people began to come forward. She quickly moved to his side and he caught her close. He didn't know what to expect, but he knew that Priscilla would stand with him through it, and it was the first time he hadn't felt alone in a long time.

He watched as Bishop Umble gently touched Amanda's arm and bent to murmur something to her, but she threw up her arms and ran shrieking from the barn. "You Amish are crazy . . . Forgiveness! Ha! You're all fools. There is no forgiveness . . . not ever!"

Joseph felt Priscilla reach to stroke his arm as

he shook his head with regret over Amanda's decision, but he knew now that he'd seen the last of the woman this side of Judgment Day.

Ben Kauffman approached him, his hat in his hands, then pulled Joseph close in a bone-jarring hug. "*Danki, bruder.* I know my *sohn* was working for her—but I never would have thought . . ." Ben swallowed and broke off before moving away.

Grossmudder May stepped up, leaning heavily on her carved cane. "Now, see, my *kinner,* all is as it should be."

Joseph felt his heart swell with emotion as Priscilla embraced the *auld* woman and Grossmudder May laid a hand on the red hair escaping Priscilla's white *kapp.* "Fair blessings on you, child. May your lap be filled with *kinner.*"

Joseph flushed at the *auld Amisch* blessing, especially when Grossmudder May tapped him on the knee with her cane. She leaned in and he bent low. "And may you both have pleasure in the making of those *kinner*—you can see to that, I imagine, young Joseph."

He could barely nod and was glad when the next friend came forward.

Finally, all had received them into the community, and Bishop Umble approached.

"Well, *sohn* . . . how does freedom taste? I'd wager you've carried that burden far too long. And I cannot help but wonder if you'd do me a favor, perhaps . . . seeing that you're right with the community and all."

"Of course," Joseph replied, seeing Priscilla's nod of agreement.

"*Gut . . . gut. Kumme* by and see me next week and we'll talk about it."

"*Jah*, sir. *Danki.*"

"All right, then. I've a mind to sample Frau Kauffman's honey ham. Will you two join us?"

Joseph smiled. "It'll be the most blessed meal we've eaten in a very long time."

And Priscilla squeezed his hand in agreement.

They sat on the high ridge of a hill on a large blanket. Priscilla leaned back against a sheltering oak tree with its green, gracious branches while Hollie turned somersaults down the hill with the other children. Joseph lay with his head in Priscilla's lap, sound asleep.

She was so grateful for the heavy weight of him pressed against her thighs, and she looked with pleasure from the children back to Joseph's handsome face, unable to decide which gave her more satisfaction in the moment.

She studied Joseph objectively and knew he could have had his choice of any woman, *Englisch* or *Amisch*, but he'd chosen her. And now she wondered how to tell him that she didn't need time to wait and learn to nurture herself, that he'd been teaching her right along, and that she was more than willing to accept his feelings for her. Though he hadn't mentioned love—at least not outright—but respect was a great start to build upon.

Joseph stirred in her arms and she looked down in surprise to see his sleep-drugged, green-gold eyes open and watching her as if she were a dream.

"Hello," he breathed.

"Hello," she whispered back, feeling herself blush at the lazy heat in his gaze.

"I can see the swell of your breasts from this vantage point," he murmured, turning toward her a bit.

"Joseph . . . everybody can see us." But she could not control the contracting thrill his words gave her, making her unconsciously arch her back against the tree so that he smiled.

"And now twin points of interest are pressing through your dress, my sweet."

She caught her breath and snatched her arm across her front.

He laughed lazily. "*Ach*, you can wall up the garden, little spitfire, but you cannot take away the scent of the flowers—or the images in a man's mind."

"You're overtired." She tried to admonish him but he merely closed his eyes, a smile on his perfectly shaped lips.

"And you cannot think about anything else

when I kiss you—shall we test that theory here?"

"Now I think you really are sleep-deprived. Bishop Umble would have a heart attack," she burst out.

He laughed, a rich, throaty sound that echoed back against her stomach and made her feel hot all over.

Then the bell rang, signaling Sunday dinner was ready.

"*Ach*, well—" He lifted his head. "Time to eat." But he gave her a wicked glance as he sat up, his dark hair ruffled. "Though I think I've already had my dessert . . ."

She flushed and swatted him on the arm.

Chapter Twenty-Five

Later that night, Joseph hurried through evening chores, anxious to kiss his wife, and pleased with her responsiveness to his teasing that afternoon. He whistled to himself as he walked back toward the *haus*, enjoying the play of lightning bugs in the open field. Then he passed the toolshed and stopped in his tracks—realizing he had one more thing to do to make the day complete.

He entered the dark building, holding his lantern high, and saw his toolbox beneath the workbench. He bent low and slid the metal box out, no longer feeling the impulse to shudder as he glanced at the images staring up at him. He calmly took a match and flint from his pocket and struck a purging flame as he dropped the match into the box. The photos caught and burned in minutes and then he dumped spring water from a jug onto the ashes and closed the toolbox, sliding it back beneath the workbench.

He picked his lantern back up, glad there was only a slight breeze so his *fater* would not be troubled by the smoke, and carefully fanned the shed door back and forth until the scent of smoke had dissipated freely into the night air. Then he closed the door and made for the *haus*, glad to be able to tell Priscilla that he was free of the photographs now forever.

"But, Mommy," Hollie wailed softly. "Why can't I sleep with you again? Joseph didn't seem to mind the chair."

Priscilla shook her head and put her finger to her lips. "Please, Hollie, Abner's gone to bed. We mustn't wake him; he's sick, remember?"

"I couldn't help but overhear," Joseph said softly from the doorway to Hollie's bedroom.

Priscilla looked up with an apologetic smile. "She's afraid again tonight."

"*Ach*, I see . . ." Joseph entered with Bear in attendance. "Well then, I must tell you, *kind*, that you have a protector that will always keep you safe. In fact, I'd bet that Bear would defend you with his very life if necessary. Do you know he killed a wounded bear—that's how he lost his eye and why he limps so."

"A real bear?" Hollie's eyes were now diverted to Joseph and wide with interest. Priscilla had to smile.

"*Jah*, a big bruiser too, much bigger than Bear the wolf dog, but he fought and protected us all."

"Wow!" Hollie exclaimed, reaching to scratch Bear, and then yawning widely.

"So," Priscilla asked softly, "will you try your own room again tonight, sweetheart?"

Hollie nestled down among the quilts. "Yeah . . . with Bear."

Priscilla bent and kissed her and Joseph leaned over the bed to kiss Hollie's cheek as well. Priscilla's heart was caught as she watched with tenderness as Hollie's thin arms looped around Joseph's neck. "You're different from Daddy, Joseph. I think you won't hurt Mommy ever."

"*Nee, kind*," he whispered softly. "I give you my word."

Hollie snuggled deeper next to Bear and murmured as she drifted off to sleep. "I wish . . . I wish Daddy would never scare me again . . ."

Priscilla's eyes welled with tears, knowing in her heart that the child had been exposed to far more violence than any child should be. Yet her daughter was willing to trust, to build new relationships and accept new experiences. How could she do any less? Priscilla looked directly into Joseph's eyes and knew what she had to tell him.

Joseph watched his wife as she sat on the edge of the bed, idly pulling pins from her hair and removing her *kapp*. She had no idea what an alluring image she presented in her disheveled state and he paused at his dresser to clear his throat.

"You no doubt know that it is only a husband's right to see an *Amisch* woman's hair unbound?"

She looked at him thoughtfully. "You've seen my hair down a hundred times."

Not in my bedroom, I haven't . . . "True." He tried to sound casual. "But there's something about being in your boyhood room with a girl that makes it all different."

"I have to talk to you, but I'm not sure how to begin," she said, immediately diverting his wandering thoughts.

"Okaay." *She doesn't want me, won't ever be able to be with another man after Heath, she—*

"Joseph?"

"*Jah*," he said, straightening to attention.

She clasped her hands tightly together in her lap and looked him in the eye. "I think, in the bedroom, that you know too much and I know too little."

He blinked, then put a hand to his temple,

rubbing hard, puzzling out her words. "You mean because of what happened with Amanda—you think . . . and you . . ."

"I never experienced any pleasure with Heath. There. I've said it." Her small shoulders seemed to sag with relief and her words hit him hard.

Say something, you idiot . . . she's telling you she's never had . . . "*Ach*," he said finally, then went to sit down next to her on the bed. "Well, my *frau*, I can promise that I shall do everything possible to make sure you find pleasure in our marriage bed."

"And you understand pleasure. Do you—do you think it's all the same, no matter what woman you're with . . . ?" She twisted a length of hair about her fingers tightly and he caught her hand in his.

"Are you asking me about Amanda—if it's going to be the same, feel the same for me, with us?"

She shrugged rather helplessly. "I know it's not my business, but I feel so unsure sometimes."

He slid his hand away from hers to put his arm around her shoulders and draw her close. "Everything about me is your business, Priscilla. You're my wife . . . and do I have images in my head of being with Amanda? Well, yes . . . but I wish they'd go away, that Gott would take them away and replace all of that with all of you."

"I might not be enough of a replacement."

Joseph sighed. "You are weary and worn and so heart-wrenchingly beautiful that I can't stand to look at you sometimes, because I want until it hurts, and I feel out of control and wonderful at the same time." He turned and pulled her closer, into the crux of his thighs. "Priscilla, trust me. Let me have time to court you, to get to know you better, so that you might trust me more."

"Court me?" She looked at him with puzzled eyes.

He leaned forward and kissed her once hard on the mouth then drew back. "*Jah*, court you. And more than that, give you some control. You never had any with Heath. Part of you must feel like that's the way it's supposed to be between a man and a woman. But I love the little spitfire you are . . . the tempest and the storm." He reached to cradle her face in his hands. "So why don't you be in control for a while—ask me what you want, tell me what you need. I'll answer; I'll do whatever you like."

She stared at him and he felt as if he could drown in the vivid blue twin pools of her eyes.

"But if I . . . take control, won't that be like with Amanda?"

He shook his head. "She took from the *buwe* I was; I give to you from the man I am." He half laughed. "It might not seem like much, but it's all I can offer. Just as I made an offering to Derr Herr of those pictures Amanda sent. I burned them

207

tonight. I want to start fresh. I want a new beginning with you, Priscilla."

She covered his hands with her own and he smiled faintly as she lifted her chin. "All right, Joseph. I accept what you give. You can take your shirt off. I want—I want to see your shoulders and chest before you sleep."

Chapter Twenty-Six

Nine days later, Mary and Jude were to return to the mountain with their new baby, Rose. Priscilla had spent many joyful hours in the interim getting their home spic and span and ready for the new baby. She'd even coaxed from Ben Kauffman every bit of his skill at mixing paint, and managed to walk away with an old rose color that she painted the guest room in the Lyons' home. She now stood in the middle of the beautiful baby room with a handful of the community's women as they admired their own handiwork in free-painting roses and rich vines and leaves about the walls at Priscilla's urging.

Sarah King, Edward's girl, was particularly adept with the paintbrush, but she chewed on a fingertip worriedly as she surveyed the décor.

"What's wrong?" Priscilla asked in an undertone.

"Although we Mountain *Amisch* are more

liberal about arts and crafts—I don't know if the bishop would approve such paintings—they might be graven images."

Priscilla opened her mouth to soothe the girl when a buoyant male voice broke into the conversation.

"Well, I say it all looks great!"

Priscilla blinked in surprise as Edward King strode through the door, followed amazingly by an ebullient Mama Mary Malizza, from the Bear Claw Inn.

Edward gave Sarah a quick hug, then turned to catch Priscilla close. "Sister-in-law," he murmured in her ear, "remind me that I owe you a dance in Joseph's presence."

Priscilla watched Sarah's plain cheeks flame a rosy red as she spoke to her intended. "But, Edward, I thought you were in Texas . . ."

"So I was, sweet Sarah. But the King family seems to have taken several hits recently, as well as several blessings. So, I swung by my old job to pick up some gear and convinced Mama Malizza that this mountain air would aid her asthma." He gestured in introduction to Mary Malizza, who laughed in return.

"Just call me Mama, everyone, as it might get confusing with Joseph and Edward's sister being Mary too. I brought a thermal blanket for the new baby. Where is she?"

"Here," said a quiet voice, and everyone turned

in unison to see Mary Lyons standing in the circle of Jude's arm, her tiny baby nestled close.

Edward pulled Priscilla to the back of the room as everyone else gently moved forward to make much of the newborn.

"What's wrong?" Priscilla asked, sensing some pent-up energy in Edward's electric blue eyes that reminded her forcefully of Joseph.

"Nothing . . . Where's Joe?"

"You answered too quickly, and I suppose you have no intention of telling me, but Joseph went to bring your *daed* over."

Edward's handsome face clouded. "How is Dat?"

Priscilla shook her head sadly. "I don't know . . . At times, his breathing eases but then . . . I can't tell you for sure."

"All right, *danki* for the truth. I'll go and catch up with Joe on his way over."

Priscilla lifted her eyes to where Sarah stood, looking at the baby. "Perhaps Sarah would like to walk with you."

Edward followed her gaze, then shook his head. "Later, maybe . . ."

Priscilla watched as he excused himself with easy finesse from the room and wondered how two brothers could be so different—Joseph was all purpose and plan in movement while Edward had the casual lithe grace of a big cat. *But*—she smiled to herself as she went to hug Mama

Malizza—*there were definite benefits to purposeful movements* . . .

Mary Malizza moved among the *Amisch* women in somewhat of a daze. She felt out of place in her loud floral top and blue jeans, and the hike up the mountain had aggravated her asthma. She'd had to use her inhaler, which always made her feel jittery afterwards. But she knew that it was the pervasive sense of peace and order that hung over the house that made her feel the most nervous. Back at the Bear Claw, things were always hopping, and there wasn't a lot of time to think. Here, everyone moved with quiet purposefulness and Mary could hear her own thoughts like raindrops on a tin roof.

"Hi ya, I'm Martha Umble."

Mary looked down at the elderly *Amisch* woman. She was gray-haired and slightly bent at the shoulders, but there was strength of purpose about her stance and a keen look in her faded brown eyes.

"I'm Mama Malizza . . . but you can call me Mary."

"Can you make homemade spaghetti sauce?" the older woman asked bluntly.

"Yeah . . ." She grinned. "You think because my name is Italian that I can cook good? Isn't that what you'd call prejudice?"

Martha shrugged. "Not if you can cook."

"I can cook." Mary laughed, suddenly feeling more at ease.

"*Gut* . . . I get sick and tired of cooking. You can *kumme* home with me, and if you'll cook a few days, I'll show you a swell time on the mountain."

"Sounds fair, but what about your man? Won't he mind?"

"Hmm? The bishop . . . *nee*, he eats what's put in front of him."

Mary raised her brows. "The bishop, you say? Well, ain't he important?"

Martha smiled wryly. "He thinks he is, but then, so do most men."

Mary laughed out loud and knew she'd made a friend.

Joseph finished giving his *daed* his medicines and was ready to start out the door when a brisk knocking sounded.

"Anybody home?"

Joseph recognized his *bruder*'s voice and opened the door in amazement. He caught Edward close in a back-slapping hug. "What are you doing here?"

"*Ach*, I thought there were enough things to *kumme* home for, so I—"

"You came because you think I'm dyin'," their *daed* said quietly. "Well, I guess maybe I am."

Joseph watched his *bruder* take in the shrunken frame of their *fater* and met Edward's worried gaze with a faint nod.

Edward bent and hugged their *dat* then stood

back with his hands on his hips. "Daed, you're not dying as long as I've got breath to pray for you, and that's a fact. Now, let's take you and old married Joe over to meet Rose Lyons . . . and she's a beauty, I promise."

"You've seen her already?" Joseph asked.

"Yep . . . they're all home. And you'll be surprised to see who I brought with me, Joe. Now, let's go."

Joseph followed, grateful for his *bruder*'s presence and strength. It was *gut* to have family to lean on when things were changing and Edward, despite his wild behavior on the rigs, now appeared to be every inch a well-dressed *Amisch* man.

Priscilla trailed her fingers in the warm tub water she had prepared after a busy day of visiting and good cheer. Edward was to stay with Mary and Jude and the baby, and the bishop's wife had taken an inexplicable liking to Mama Malizza and had taken the woman home with her to extend hospitality for the impromptu visit.

Priscilla had started preparing the bath as soon as Joseph headed out for chores and now, as she heard his footsteps at the door, her heart began to pound in her throat. She'd loosed her hair and wore a simple, breezy nightgown that she'd cut down a bit from one of Mary's generous gifts so that it almost resembled a long slip.

There was no doubt that she was enjoying the so-called control that Joseph allowed her in their bedroom relationship. But, so far, she'd only worked up enough courage to ask for random kisses and having him take off his shirt. She wanted tonight to be different, though, and had discovered the delicious pastime of fantasizing about her husband in her plans for the evening.

Joseph stopped short when he came into the bedroom and looked at the filled, steaming tub. She'd added some orange slices and a few sticks of cinnamon so that the whole room had taken on the air of a scented sauna as the night air through the window screen mixed with the bathwater's heat.

"What's all this?" he asked softly.

She smiled at him. "Your bath."

"My bath?"

Was it her imagination or had his handsome face flushed a bit in the shadowed light of the single kerosene lantern?

"Yes, yours. Do you remember the first time I ever saw you? I think you'd just left the bath . . . you had a single hand towel . . . well, you know."

"I do indeed." He cleared his throat a bit. "So . . . you want me to undress?"

She nodded, managing to keep her composure. "*Jah*. But slowly, please."

"All right."

Priscilla screwed her hands into the light top

quilt on the bed and leaned back a bit. She felt the need to appear casual, but she really wanted to hide her eyes with embarrassment at her bold request.

But Joseph seemed perfectly composed as he lowered his suspenders and began to slide pins from his shirt front. He looked straight at her while he did it, his long fingers working with grace and ease in the half light. The pins made tiny pattering sounds on the dresser as he dropped each one, and she restlessly tightened her grip on the quilt as he eased his blue shirt off.

I can do this, she told herself. *He's my husband . . . the husband of my heart.*

He dropped his shirt on the floor and then reached for the hooks and eyes in his black pants. She felt pinned by his gaze, like a butterfly on a golden shaft, and she forced herself to focus on his eyes as he finished undressing. He stood before her—large, beautiful, so completely male, and she found she had to start twice to speak her next request.

"Please get in the tub, if you would." She wished she didn't sound so breathless, but he obeyed without comment, sloshing water over the sides as he eased his big frame inside the metal tub. She was glad now that she'd chosen to drag the larger tub instead of the hip bath to their bedroom, because it meant that he was probably more comfortable, able to stretch out his legs.

He lifted an orange slice from the water and arched a dark brow.

"Scent matters to me," she said simply and he nodded, dropping the slice back in the water. He watched as she moved from the bed to slide to her knees beside the tub. She took a sponge from the pile of items she'd assembled beforehand and drew a deep breath. "I want you dripping wet, Joseph King, so that you have to lick at the water running down your face like you did that day at the hotel."

He smiled and she suppressed a surprised shriek when he suddenly arched his back and dunked his head backwards into the water, splashing her in the process. He came up seconds later, his dark hair clinging to the nape of his neck and the sides of his face. He held her gaze as he put out his tongue and caught the water that ran past his cheekbone. Then he dropped his eyes to her damp gown and she had to resist the urge to cover her breasts with the sponge. But instead, she motioned for him to lean forward and started to diligently scrub the broad expanse of his back, wondering vaguely what she'd got herself into . . .

Joseph was doing sums in his head—triple digits and more—anything to keep from thinking about the languorous feel of the water, the ache of his mouth, and his wife's purposeful touch down the length of his spine. He closed his eyes when she'd finished and leaned back in the tub. *Now what? More gentle kisses when what I really want is* . . . He thought for a moment. *When what I really want is to do whatever she likes* . . . He opened his eyes to look at her, attentive and willing to wait and see what she asked for next.

"Put your arms behind your head," she said, inadvertently dampening her gown more with the sponge she tightly held.

"All right." He pillowed his head on his bent arms, resting on the back rim of the tub, and waited, feeling wonderfully vulnerable and intrigued.

She leaned forward, unknowingly giving him a rich display of full, rosy breasts, and then she used her hand instead of the sponge to cup a handful of the water up around his throat and another across his chest. He shivered at the satiny feel of her hand and the heated water and held his breath when she bit her lip and trailed her hand across his belly.

"Does it hurt?" she asked faintly.

"What?"

"The—the swelling. I've no idea how you must feel when your body . . . well, does that."

"It feels *gut* but there's an edge to it," he said after a moment, marveling at her innocence and wanting to curse Heath once more from the face of the earth.

"An edge?"

He nodded. He longed to touch her but kept his

arms in place. "When my body reacts like this—
it's because I want you, to be with you—
sometimes it can become painful if there's no
release for a long time." He stared at her hard,
wondering if he was making sense to her.

"And do you . . . do you need that release now?"

Dear Gott, jah, *right now. Simply pull her in the
tub, slide together and . . .* "I'm all right," he
managed. *Liar.*

She seemed to consider and he held his breath
in the sweet abeyance; then she tilted her head to
one side. "Will you show me, Joseph? How you
like to touch yourself when you need that release
. . . I mean, assuming that you, that you have
to . . ." She blew out a breath in frustration and
he did move then, to gently catch her hand and
stroke it down his cheek, turning his mouth into
her palm.

"Mmm, Priscilla, of course I touch myself. It's a
perfectly natural thing to do, and I can show
you . . . but you could help me, if you wanted,
my sweet *frau.*"

"How?" she asked, and he didn't miss the wide-
eyed look of mingled curiosity and wariness in
her eyes.

*Matter-of-fact. Be matter-of-fact and she'll
respond . . .* He nodded to the damp sponge in
her lap. "Any kind of friction can make it feel
better. That sponge will do nicely."

"Oh . . . here." She plopped the sponge into the

water in obvious embarrassment and a drop of water hit him in the eye.

He blinked rapidly.

"Oh, Joseph, I'm sorry."

He smiled. "Don't be . . . Here, you take the sponge and I'll put my hand over yours and sort of—guide you."

"Okaaay."

Her fingers were stiff around the sponge as he cupped them in his much larger hand. "Relax," he whispered.

She nodded, clearly concentrating. He led her small hand with the barrier of the sponge to the swollen part of him that pulsed beneath the surface of the warm water. He gritted his teeth when the sponge found its mark and he squeezed her fingers tighter.

"Oh," she gasped.

He managed a nod of encouragement. "Now," he instructed softly, "glide upwards and down with my hand. You won't hurt me, I promise. The tightness feels *gut*."

"Really?" she asked, clearly dubious.

"Really . . ." He couldn't resist a gasp of pleasure when her fingers convulsed inside of his. "That's . . . right." He let his head fall backwards and arched his back against the friction and pressure and then it was all over too fast and he sobbed aloud, part pleasure, still wanting.

"Joseph? Was that—all right?"

He laughed breathlessly. "That was perfect."

"Your face is red and you're sweating," she noted.

He smiled. "I'm lucky I'm alive after that, sweetheart. I felt like I was dying there for a moment."

"And it was still good?" she demanded.

"*Wunderbar*, my *frau*. *Wunderbar*."

Chapter Twenty-Seven

Priscilla watched Joseph from the corner of her eye as he worked busily with Jude and Edward, setting up a medium-sized quilting frame in the Lyons' front room. It was a week after Mary had come home from the hospital and she was feeling well enough to have the baby quilting that had been planned for some time. But as much as Priscilla delighted in the thought of trying out her quilting skills, the subtle bend and turn of her husband's body was all the more intriguing.

"I can see that I need not bless the marriage bed," Grossmudder May said aloud as she poked at Priscilla's skirt with her cane. "The way you're looking at him, the *kinner* will *kumme* fast and fine."

Priscilla jumped and flushed. She bent her head and hoped no one had overheard. "Grossmudder May . . ." She couldn't keep the reproach from her tone, though she smiled down into the wizened face.

"*Ach*, don't mind an *auld* woman, Priscilla King. It's one of my delights to speak both the truth and my mind. Now, where has Sarah gotten off to?"

Priscilla watched with true affection as Grossmudder May hobbled off toward the kitchen. She turned back to find the quilting frame in place and her husband right behind her.

"I'm off to see the bishop, as he asked me to," Joseph said.

Priscilla nodded, wondering how the simple sound of his husky voice could make her thoughts shimmer with delight. "All right."

But he didn't move and she knew instinctively what he was waiting for . . . What would she want tonight? Ask of him? She dropped her lashes and lifted them quickly, then stretched to whisper in his ear. "Tonight I want what you want, Joseph."

She wanted to giggle at the look of surprise on his handsome face and knew with joy that if they hadn't been standing in a roomful of people, he would have probably kissed her long and hard. As it was, he looked at her mouth with a none-too-subtle longing, then turned and left as if the room had grown too hot in a matter of seconds.

The other men soon left too, bent on meeting at Ben Kauffman's store for some talk and a round of cheese and crackers, leaving many of the women of the community to gather at Mary's door.

Frau Umble brought Mama Malizza and the two chattered on together like young girls, but Priscilla barely had time to visit with them as she found herself hurriedly making more sandwiches in the kitchen. Even though many had brought a dish to share, the finger sandwiches were disappearing at an alarming rate, and Priscilla learned quickly how to make *Amisch* egg salad. She was surprised at the amount of fresh celery and spicy mustard that went into the mixture, but after having a quick spoon taste, she found it to be delicious.

The little girls had their own tea too, but they mostly darted through the kitchen and other rooms and Priscilla had to content herself with the knowledge that Hollie was surely among those playing while her fingers flew at the sandwich board.

Finally, she had the opportunity to take one of the newly opened seats at the quilt frame, and sat down with a sigh of pleasure. She bent to glance beneath the spread of the quilting, wondering if Hollie was scrambling to fetch the women's needles that fell through, as she didn't seem to be running about. When she didn't see her daughter, Priscilla abandoned her seat and set about to casually look for the little girl, not wanting to raise an alarm and ruin Mary's day.

• • •

Joseph saw the little girl curled up in the shelter of some mossy rocks, her small shoulders shaking with silent sobs.

He walked up slowly, not wanting to startle the child, and then looked more closely at the golden hair sliding free of its braid.

"Hollie?"

She turned and gazed up at him, then burst into loud, renewed sobs.

He immediately went to her and sat down on the ground, tenderly feeling her arms and legs, searching for possible injury. "Hollie, are you hurt, *kind*? Tell me quickly, please."

"My . . . my heart hurts, Joseph."

"Your heart?" He pulled the little girl into the circle of his arms, feeling a faint relief, but not understanding at the same time.

"Yeah, I think it's broke—broken."

"*Ach*," he whispered. "I'm *gut* at fixing things, *kind*. Will you give me a chance with your heart?"

She shook her head. "No, I can't."

"Why not, sweetling?"

"Because you're why it's broken," she choked.

If she had struck him full in the face, it couldn't have shaken him more. He drew up his knees and cradled her closer. "What did I do?"

"Suzanne Mast said . . . she said that you're my daddy now, but you never told me that. And I have one other daddy, but he scares me and hurts Mommy, so maybe . . . I don't know—I don't know what I have."

Joseph felt his throat grow thick with tears and he leaned back against the rocks, murmuring soothing sounds to the child while his own heart pounded with uncertainty. *If I tell her I'm her father, what will it take from her? And why, Gott, did she have to see such ugliness with her real* daed? And then, as he eased his straw hat back, he felt a cool breeze spring up from the mountain as it so often did, soothing him. Bringing him clarity in heart and mind.

"Hollie, what you have are many people to love you and care for you now. Your *mamm*, my *daed*, Jude and Mary and little Rose, Edward and Grossmudder May, and on and on . . . too many to count. You have a whole community now. And nobody is asking you to stop loving your daddy . . ."

"But what about you?" she sniffed. "Are you . . . ? What are you?"

He smiled then and bumped his forehead against hers. "I'm whatever you want, *kind*. Whatever you need."

She reached up with soft hands to touch his face, then smiled slowly. "Will you be my daddy, Joseph?"

"*Jah*, sweet. I will."

"Oh, thank you." She placed her small lips

against his forehead and to him it felt right, like a seal of hope.

"You're very welcome, Hollie. Now why don't you run back to the quilting before your *mamm* misses you, hmm?"

She rose and he helped her brush off her dress. Then she turned and blew him a kiss. "All right, good-bye . . . Daddy."

He caught her kiss and made a show of putting it in his shirt pocket, then watched her skip off along the path. He leaned back and stared up at the blue sky above the pine tops, his eyes filled with wonder and prayer. *Daddy* . . .

"Mommy! Joseph said he'll be my daddy—isn't that great, huh?"

Priscilla barely had time to glimpse her daughter's smiling face as Hollie darted past her on the path, headed back toward Mary and Jude's house. "Hollie! Yes . . . that's wonderful, but . . ." She was about to turn and follow the little girl when something made her turn instead to the path ahead. She peered round the bend and saw Joseph, sitting and smiling, leaning against some rocks.

"Joseph?"

She walked to him slowly, liking the way his eyes narrowed in thought as he watched her approach. She felt like blushing at his obvious attention but kept her composure; she needed to thank him for whatever he had said to Hollie.

She dropped to her knees in front of him and he pulled her to him in a deep hug.

"What happened?" she murmured against the sunshine freshness of his burgundy shirt.

"Nothing . . . everything. Hollie asked me if I'd be her father. I don't even know how to explain how much it means to me . . . if I can do a *gut* job."

Priscilla smiled at him. "Do you think I'd let you do anything but a *gut* job . . . and that . . . that God would let you do anything less with His help?"

He shook his head. "*Nee.*"

She brushed his hair back from his face tenderly, so grateful to have a man like him in her life, in her daughter's life. She bent forward and kissed him boldly, using her tongue, deepening the kiss until he groaned against her mouth.

"Priscilla . . . what . . ."

"Joseph, all the women are at Mary's and all the men are at the store."

"*Jah*?" he breathed.

"We could—we could go home or somewhere, anywhere, and maybe . . . do what you'd like for a change."

"I like what we do," he said hoarsely.

"I know, but . . ." She let her gaze drop suggestively, amazed that she could be so open with him, but the days he'd spent giving her control had somehow built up her confidence, her desire for him.

She watched him accept her words and then he pulled her to her feet as he rose. "Priscilla, if you'll trust me, I know the perfect place to go."

"Anywhere, Joseph," she whispered. "Anywhere with you."

Joseph held back the curtain of pine branches and lifted a hand to the hidden pool of water that formed in the creek bed. The place breathed of secret intimacy, in its moss-covered rocks, tender pine-strewn forest floor, and the distant song of a lark adding just the right music to the moment.

He watched his wife's face brighten in the play of sunshine that shafted through the trees and he swung her up in his arms with ease and abandon.

"Oh, Joseph, it's beautiful here. How did you find it?"

"I didn't. Jude did on one of his rambles over the mountain before he wed Mary. He gave me the general directions, and I've always remembered —not knowing why, of course . . . until now." He lowered his mouth to hers, then walked to the edge of the pool, not breaking the kiss.

Then he slid her to the ground, letting her feel his body, his longing, and she gasped softly against his mouth.

"I want to undress you," he said, unable to keep the urgency out of his voice.

"I want you to." She dropped her arms to her sides and he recognized the posture as one almost of submission—not what he wanted. He didn't need her to think in years to *kumme* of their first lovemaking as even a vague reminder of what had surely happened with Heath.

He dropped to his knees and lifted one bare foot into the palm of his hand, running his mouth over the small bones on top and the gentle curve from heel to ankle. Then he rested his hands on his thighs and stared up at her petite frame. *Dear Gott, let me do this right . . .*

He ran a questing hand upwards beneath her skirt, skimming over clearly defined calves and soft knees and then found her right thigh and let his quest stop there for the moment. She leaned forward to put her hands on his shoulders, her slender limbs shaking, and he pulled his hand back down only to quickly work at the apron pins so near his chin. He knew they'd have to search the moss for the tiny glittering silver things later, but right now, he was past caring. He verged on the edge of franticness and decided with some vestige of control that he needed to cool down, take his time.

He glanced at the pool round the curve of her hip and stared up into her wide blue eyes, eyes that competed in beauty with the skies above.

"Priscilla, let's swim for a bit first."

She stood up, taking her hands from his shoulders. "You mean skinny-dipping?"

"Skinny—what?"

She laughed, a free, easy sound that he took to heart and treasured. "It's an *Englisch* expression but it means—well, swimming naked."

"Mmm, I like the sound of that better. So, will you swim . . . naked with me?"

She nodded. "I've never done that before."

"*Gut.* Neither have I."

She seemed pleased by his admission and he watched for a moment as she laid shaking fingers on the first pin near her hip. Then he brushed her hands aside. "Let me, sweet spitfire, if you can stand my ministrations for a moment."

"Take your time," she urged and he laughed, finding pins here and there. Then he reached to lift off her dress, leaving her in only a shift bottom and light blue blouse. He was quicker than he'd intended, anxious to see her in the state of undress she'd had him in so many times over the past days, but also inspired by the soft, slight beauty of her as he removed the remainder of her clothing and her *kapp*.

"*Ach*, Priscilla," he whispered, letting his eyes rove over her body and wondering for the first time if she might be too small for his big frame. But she clung to him, hiding her body against his blackpants and shirt, letting him feel the press of her against every inch she could seemingly reach, standing on his boots and arching her back to kiss him.

He ran his fingers through the long red fall of her hair and let his hands slide downward to cup her soft bottom, closing his eyes on the wash of sensation. He felt alive, restless, yet riveted to the moment in a way he'd never been.

"Is the water cold, do you think?" she asked, pulling back to gaze down into the pool.

"Ice-cold." He laughed, then reached to squeeze her hand. "But I'll be glad to keep you warm."

"Then undress," she suggested lightly, watching him.

"As you wish." He obeyed her in what had to be record time, then took her hand again and pulled her to perch on the edge of the pool. "Ready?" he asked.

"I don't know . . ." She dipped a toe in hesitantly then drew back with a shiver.

He smiled. "The best way to do it, I think, is fast. *Kumme* on." He gave her a brief tug and pulled them both into the deep, swirling water.

They both screamed as their heads emerged.

"I am soooo cold." Priscilla laughed, her teeth chattering. "Was this your way to cool my desire, my husband?" she teased, grabbing for his arms.

Joseph was shivering too, but he had to laugh at the exhilarating feel of being alive and with someone he loved . . . *I love* . . .

"I love you," he said.

"What?" she asked, flipping back her hair.

"I said I love you." He raised his voice and it felt so *gut*. He watched as her eyes darkened and she pressed the hard tips of her breasts against his bare chest.

"I love you too," she murmured, then put her mouth close to his ear. "I love you," she said again. And he swept her up in his arms, holding her against the rushing cold, feeling renewed in his heart and mind in a way only ice water can bring about refreshment of the spirit.

Chapter Twenty-Eight

At his insistence, Priscilla let him lie on his back on the mossy bank.

"I don't want to hurt you—in any way, this first time," he admitted.

"You won't," she chided with confidence, biting her lip and still shivering from their cold dip in the creek.

"I'm not taking any chances. You be in control —have . . . uh . . . as much or as little of me as you want."

She looked down at him, calm, steady, waiting, except for the heat in his gold-green eyes. "I don't think there's anything little about you, Joseph," she quipped, half-embarrassed, but she saw the shallow rise and fall of his chest and knew he was holding back. She'd seen him in enough postures of abandon over the past days to know that it was the calm before the storm, and part of her badly wanted that storm. She loved to see him aroused and the drowsy look that followed when she'd helped him find release. But now he was encouraging her to take for herself and she wasn't sure exactly that she knew how.

"What's wrong, my sweet?" he asked when she paused.

"I don't—I don't want to disappoint you by not finding pleasure with you. I told you I've never . . ."

He steadied her with a sure smile as she straddled his hips. "Did you ever stop and think, Priscilla King, that violence is no way to produce arousal?"

"No-o," she gasped while he helped her, held her, even when she squirmed against his hands, wanting more.

"Be careful, *sei se gut.*"

"I don't want careful, Joseph. I want you. All of you . . . wild, big . . . ooh . . . out of control."

And he gave, fitting his movements to her words, arching his neck, arching his back, making hoarse sounds of pleasure between his teeth, until she knew that whatever Amanda had taken from him, she'd never had him like this . . .

And then she found sweet release with him, a dazzling, breathless chain reaction of a thousand suns bursting behind her eyes. She stared down with amazement into the tender emerald gaze locked with her own.

She collapsed on his chest, hearing his wild heartbeat, feeling it mingle with her own, until she sobbed for joy in the aftermath and he cradled her close.

After a few minutes, she lifted her head and moved, with a luxurious intimate ache that she hoped would last for hours. Her secret—their pleasure.

He helped her dress quietly, searching the moss for the proper pins and finally having to give her some of his own.

"I'll go see the bishop now, though I'll have to tuck my shirt in far enough so that it doesn't open." He made a show of adjusting his clothes and she giggled, feeling young and carefree.

"And I'll go back to the quilting. How do I look?"

He gave her a wicked, sidelong glance. "Like you've been ravished and took some pleasure during the process."

"Joseph!"

He gathered her close. "You look beautiful as always and neat as a pin. I make a pretty *gut* lady's maid, if I do say so myself."

She stretched to kiss his lips with confidence. "You may say so—anytime."

And she left him by the secret pool to walk

through the trees, feeling special and loved, and a bit more magical than flesh and blood.

"I wrote a letter to Priscilla's *fater*," Bishop Umble said casually as he finished his lunch of deviled eggs and cheese sandwiches.

"What did you say?" Joseph asked.

"What's wrong with your hearing, *buwe*? I said I wrote a letter to Priscilla's *fater*—wanted to let him know she's safe. I used the address from the flyer you showed me. You said he knew her former husband and I thought he might talk some sense into—what's wrong?"

Joseph clenched both sides of his head and shook it slowly. *How stupid am I not to have told him that Priscilla's* fater *led Heath on, encouraged him to . . . Dear Gott, he'll tell Heath where she is.*

"Priscilla's *fater* is not—well. He's the one who told her ex-husband to subdue her, control her, and he'll tell that freak where she is . . ."

"Hmm," Bishop Umble grunted. "This is a pickle."

Joseph's temper was quickly reaching the boiling point as the *auld* man pushed aside his plate and picked up a molasses cookie, munching thoughtfully. "Well, *buwe*. I did what I thought was right before Derr Herr. I expect He'll turn things around."

"Turn things . . . You were wrong! That's what! Dead wrong. *Ach*, Gott, what am I going to do to protect them?"

"It's not your job to yell at me, Joseph King, or to protect anyone from what plans Gott has for them. That's part of love, real love. You risk things every day but love anyway!"

"And you cannot admit you're wrong. I'm leaving; I've got to tell Priscilla." Joseph pushed back from the table and got to his feet.

"So you think that telling Priscilla will bring her peace?"

Joseph stopped as the bishop's words rang through his mind. He sat back down slowly. "All right . . . I can't tell her. She'll be looking over her shoulder all the time, but what about Hollie? She runs wild with the other *kinner.* Heath could—"

"There you go again, trying to act as an amateur providence. It'll only bring you grief, *sohn.*"

Joseph blew out an exasperated breath. "Then what am I supposed to do?"

"Pray."

"What?"

"You can pray—" The bishop chewed. "For the ex-husband."

"You really are batty, do you know that?" Joseph asked ruefully.

Bishop Umble shrugged. "It goes with the job. Now . . . let's talk about that favor I asked for . . ."

Priscilla found a space once more at the baby quilt and began to stitch with a pale pink thread on the rose petal nearest her. The quilt was an amazing design of flowers and stems and tiny embroidered pastel animals; she had never seen such a pattern before and remarked on it to the table at large.

"We do much free-hand design up here in the mountains, Priscilla," Grossmudder May pointed out. "We aren't so rigid as some of the other *Amisch* communities."

"Well, I can tell that, by the way you all took me and Hollie in like friends. I truly appreciate it."

There were gentle, matter-of-fact murmurs of acceptance from around the quilt frame, and Priscilla bent her head in attention to her work. She knew that many *Amisch* girls could stitch five stitches for every quarter inch of fabric, but she was not so adept. Still, the quilting soothed her and she loved the moment when Mary passed by, carrying Rose.

"Priscilla, would you like to hold the baby?"

Priscilla stuck her needle into the quilt and turned eagerly.

She took the tiny bundle to her breast and breathed in the amazing scent of newness and baby and grace, and she couldn't help but think of when Hollie was young—all the fear she had felt trying to protect her from Heath's rages. She drew a deep breath. *That's all over now; we're safe at last . . .*

She handed the baby back after a few minutes,

then hugged to herself the thought of what it might be like to have a child of Joseph's—it could even be possible that she'd already conceived. The idea made her blush and she rose from the quilting to get herself a glass of cold spring water, feeling more than content with her life for the first time in years.

"So, a promise, young Joseph, if you don't mind?"

Joseph regarded the bishop with a wry expression. "Why not?" he asked dryly.

"*Gut!*" Bishop Umble slapped his hands on the table top. "I want you to consider teaching a group of our young men, leading them in—study, shall we say, that they may not fall victim to the same abuse that you did."

Joseph leaned an elbow on the table. "Me? Why not Jude? I'm not qualified to teach."

"Derr Herr has revealed to me that you would be the perfect teacher, having gone through the experience yourself. You know that the Bible commands, 'What I tell you in darkness, proclaim in the light.' "

"*Jah*, but—"

"*Gut*, then it's settled. You can start on Wednesday nights. Let's say about six p.m. You can meet here on the front porch during the pleasant weather."

"I didn't say I would—"

"And perhaps, in time, Priscilla might meet with

the young *maedels* and give them insight on healthy relationships as well."

Joseph's shoulders slumped in defeat; he knew Bishop Umble too well to protest, but Priscilla would have to make her own decision. Yet, in the end, he had to admit both ideas to protect the local youth sounded *gut*.

"All right. I'm going home." Joseph rose once more and the bishop waved a cookie at him.

"What's your hurry, *buwe*? Your wife's at the quilting—your *daed* and *bruder* are at the store."

Joseph suppressed a baleful glare and made for the back door. "I need a bit of time alone."

"Ahhh . . . *gut* man! Good for the spirit I always say and—"

Joseph closed the door.

Chapter Twenty-Nine

Priscilla shifted restlessly beneath the cool linen sheets, wearing only the wispiest of night dresses, which she'd cut down with heavy shears. Joseph seemed to be taking an extra-long time with chores, though of course Edward was around, and maybe they wanted to talk. Still, she couldn't wait for Joseph to come in, hoping that they might relive some of the moments from the secret pool that day.

She jumped when he entered, and she thought

he looked weary—weary but tense. *Perhaps he's regretting what happened today . . . that he said he loved me . . .*

"I can hear the proverbial wheels turning in your head from here," he said with a faint smile, leaning against the dresser.

"Can you?" she sniffed. "Then what am I thinking?"

He came near and sat down atop the turned-down quilts. "That I have regrets—about today—about what I've said or done."

She was amazed at his accuracy and he half laughed.

"How do you know?" she sputtered.

He bent and kissed the edge of her throat where it met the top of the gown. "Because I love you," he murmured. "Mmmm . . . I love you and you smell so *gut*."

"Joseph?"

"Mmm-hmm?"

"I want to answer a question you asked me."

He drew back a bit, studying her face with his mysterious eyes. "*Ach* . . . I sense that this might not have been a *gut* question on my part."

"Nooo, it's not that. I—well, the day Rose was born and you asked me why I didn't leave Heath . . ."

His lashes lowered and he rubbed the back of his neck. "Priscilla, forget that. I was wrong and—"

"No, it was a fair question. I couldn't answer then but I can now."

"What's changed?" he asked, almost warily.

"Everything, especially how you made me feel today—safe and loved and like there were no more secrets between us. And I—I wanted to tell you that I didn't leave because I was too afraid. I know it sounds silly, that I should have thought of Hollie, but I really believed on some level that my life was in danger. I can also cite the curious truth that desperate people do desperate things, and I was desperate to stay alive and now I know why—because of you."

"Priscilla . . ."

"Yes?" She waited anxiously for his response.

"I—I love you, remember that, will you? For always and ever? And Gott loves you too."

"You sound so serious." She reached out and touched his arm.

"Do I?"

"Yes . . ."

"Well, forget me. Forget how I sound. Let's think only of us." He bent and began kissing her fast and hard so that she could barely catch her breath. Then she laughed in giddy freedom and relaxed into his embrace, reaching with eager fingers to help him loosen his shirt.

Joseph lay spent, listening to Priscilla's soft breathing. The bishop said he should pray, but for the life of him, no prayers seemed to come for the man who had been her first husband. And worse than that, he was lying to her by omission, keeping the secret of Bishop Umble's letter to her *fater* from her, when she had been so honest tonight with him. He half turned, considering waking her and telling her about the letter, but then she sighed deeply in her sleep and he drew back.

He passed a hand over his eyes, knowing he couldn't sleep, not with the thought that Heath might be out there in the dark. And if not tonight, then what night? What day might he show up and seek vengeance on Priscilla and possibly Hollie? Joseph actually considered for a brief moment calling the *Englisch* authorities, but he knew that even the *Englisch* law usually left the *Amisch* to deal with matters in their own way. *And what was the bishop's way of dealing? Prayer!* Joseph sighed aloud and Priscilla stirred. He gently cradled her closer, loving the softness of her small body, wanting desperately to keep her safe . . .

He saw by the wind-up clock that it was past four a.m., and he knew he had to sleep a little. He reluctantly closed his eyes and fell into a deep slumber, fraught with vivid dreams . . .

He couldn't reach her. A dangerous crevasse seemed to fill the space at his feet but he could not suppress the desperate need he felt to get to her, as if something watched from the shadows. He cried her name, once, twice, but she did not answer, could not answer. And then he was struck by frigid cold, a consuming cold that shook him from inside out, torturous turmoil and pressure with no way to gain a foothold. He crumbled, lost without her, until a mocking voice seemed to compel him to rise and find his feet, to go on. He followed the mockery, down one dark road to another until tree limbs grabbed him, stinging with welting purpose as they slapped against his face and chest. He could see her now, right within reach, her hair flowing long and unbound. If he could only catch her, touch her, then things might be right again, but her hair slipped through his fingertips and she was lost, gone, into a dark abyss . . .

"Joseph?"

He awoke with a harsh indrawn breath to discover sunlight pouring in through the window and Priscilla standing over the bed, fully dressed.

"Joseph, were you dreaming? It's all right . . ." She leaned down to touch him and he caught her in his arms, pulling her to the bed and then moving atop her.

He felt frantically through her skirts, desperate to touch her skin, to banish the nightmare. "Priscilla," he gasped. "Let me make love to you, *sei se gut* . . . please . . ."

He didn't care that he begged. He wanted her right then, right there, and felt driven by a need so frantic, his own breath seemed to roar in his ears.

"Yes," she whispered. "Oh yes . . ."

He was moving, deliberate, hard, fast motions that caused a sob from the back of his throat on each stroke until she cried with him and he finally found what he sought so desperately.

His body was soaked with sweat as he clung to her. "Priscilla," he groaned. "I love you. I love you so much."

"And I love you too . . . Are you all right? You seem . . . distraught."

He forced himself to smile then and stroked her *kapp* strings back from the tangle of her dress. "I'm fine, my *frau* . . . I needed you, that's all."

"And that's more than enough," she murmured against his mouth. "Anytime."

It was almost summer and Priscilla relished the feel of the fresh earth of the kitchen garden between her toes. She still tingled inside from Joseph's passionate lovemaking that morning and smiled as she overturned the dirt with a spade, sparing a fat worm and making room for the pepper plants Edward had brought over from Mary's seedlings.

Hollie scampered about until they both heard the echo of the school bell, and then Priscilla kissed her and sent her on her way with an old-fashioned lunch pail. She returned gaily to her planting, imagining what it would be like to have fresh vegetables and fruits from the garden that she might cook with. It was true, she thought, that human life began in a garden. No wonder the Lord was often thought of as the Gardener. She realized that her feelings toward her faith had softened during her time with the *Amisch* and she knew she was working on developing that relationship with God that Joseph had spoken about in the hospital chapel.

"Hey there, pretty girl!"

Priscilla looked up in surprise to see Mama Malizza picking her way across the rows of plants. The older woman was dressed in jeans and a pretty blouse that became her large figure. She looked younger somehow, too, and more relaxed than usual.

"Hello. Time with Frau Umble must be good for you—you seem happy." Priscilla leaned on her spade and gave her a hug of greeting.

"Well, I've got to say that we stay up yakking longer than the bishop. He shakes a hand at us and goes to bed—gives up. Can I help you plant? I've got to get my own little patch of tomatoes going when I leave. I make homemade spaghetti sauce and can it for the restaurant."

"Oh, I hope you don't have to go soon," Priscilla said, meaning it. She'd grown very fond of the woman who'd given her the break that led to meeting Joseph.

"Leave this mountain in a hurry? No . . . You remember Dan, my assistant manager? He's been pestering me for more responsibility, and I was thinking of buying a summer cottage somewhere nearby here so I could come every year."

Priscilla smiled widely. "That would be wonderful. You know I have to thank you for giving me that waitress job. I wouldn't have my husband without it."

Mama shrugged her hefty shoulders. "I was doing what I felt led to do, I guess, though I thought you'd never last—you still look young enough to be seventeen. And I guess you were telling the truth when you said you had no man. You got one now though, and a fine-looking one at that."

Priscilla blushed. "Thank you, Mama. And what about you? Are you married? I've never asked."

Mama gently lifted a celery seedling. "Me? Naw . . . tried two times to stick with a marriage but the men ended up being jerks . . . and probably I was a bit of a fool, too, when I was younger."

"The *Amisch* have a saying—'to call no man a fool.' So I can't let you say that about yourself," Priscilla said, bending close to Mama.

"Well, we all make bad decisions now and then, but I guess that don't mean life's over. I do get lonesome sometimes, even at the inn."

Priscilla had a sudden inspiration. "Well then, I'm going to pray for you, Mama, that God brings a man into your life, a good man, not a jerk, who you'll stay with and love forever this time."

Mary considered the open words of the girl as a hundred images seemed to flash through her mind—what would God say if He could see the dirt in her past? The broken-down houses, sometimes littered with booze and drugs, the puppy she'd tried to keep alive but couldn't afford for the vet to see . . . She swallowed hard. *Jake said he'd do me a favor and shoot the dog . . . I can still hear that gunshot. And what about trying to go to church and finding out that I wasn't dressed right, that I'd never fit in with all them women with their heavy wedding bands and confident smiles . . . Lord have mercy, I don't even have half my teeth . . .*

"Well," Mary said slowly, "I guess I'll thank you for your prayers, not that I think God will hear them about somebody like me."

Priscilla stopped her work and Mary felt the weight of the girl's stare. "What do you mean, somebody like you, Mary?"

Oh, gosh, here I go, offendin' some kid who doesn't even know what she's doin' in her own life. "Aww, forget me, Priscilla. I'm jest talkin'. I've made it this far alone, so I expect I'll make it the rest of the way without no God."

"But you haven't been alone," Priscilla persisted. "I mean—I'm not very good at talking about God, but Joseph told me something about how everyone can have a relationship with Him. And He's not—not a jerk like the men in your life who've let you down and left you alone or who've hurt you."

Mary watched Priscilla's throat work and she regretted having said anything . . . *though the kid does seem to be real serious about this idea of a relationship.* She stepped over some plants and gave Priscilla a hearty hug.

"I'm sorry, kid. I'll listen to what you have to say as long as I'm here, okay?"

Priscilla nodded against her chest and Mary released her to clear her throat hastily. "All right . . . guess I'll walk back to Martha's. We're supposed to go look for herbs or some darn thing today."

Mary was glad to see Priscilla's smile return and set off with the girl's words echoing in her mind.

Chapter Thirty

"I cannot believe it's nearly summer and you've got a beautiful wife, yet you're sitting in this hot shed, reading the Bible!" Edward put his hands on his hips and Joseph almost smiled at his *bruder*'s exasperated expression.

"Why the mention of the beautiful wife?" Joseph raised a brow at him.

"Darn it, Joe, you know what I mean . . . I think I'd be doing something else if I was married." The last word came out a little thin, and Joseph put his finger in the Bible and closed it slowly.

"What's wrong, Edward?"

His brother kicked idly at a stand of hoes and shrugged his broad shoulders. "Nothing and everything, I guess. Sarah is . . . and I'm . . ."

Joseph sat up straighter on the workbench stool. "You're not saying that you're breaking your intentions, are you? I thought—you told me everything was fine before I left the rig."

"It is, I guess." Edward glanced at him warily. "Can I tell you something?"

"Am I going to lecture you about it?"

"Joseph, *kumme* on . . ."

"All right. I'll listen. What?"

Edward drew a deep breath. "One night I was drinking a little bit, maybe a bit too much, but anyway . . . there was this *Englisch* girl . . ."

"Oh Gott."

"Joseph—it was only one kiss."

"Uh-huh."

"It was. I'm serious."

"All right, what do you want me to say?"

"That you get it. I mean—I heard about what happened when you were sixteen . . ."

"Don't compare those two things, Edward. I

didn't seek it out and you drink far too much."

"I haven't had a drop since I came home. And I'm sorry for that shot about when you were young. I . . ."

"Are you going to tell Sarah?" Joseph asked, wondering if it would be a *gut* idea in the end.

"Are you *narrisch*? Her *fater* would kill me—and she'd probably poison me with some herbal concoction."

"Maybe you'd deserve that," Joseph mused.

"Look, I regret it, all right? I wanted to get it off my chest, that's all."

"Okay." Joseph nodded.

"Well, aren't you going to read me a sermon or go find the bishop or something?"

"*Nee.*"

"Why not?" Edward demanded.

"Because you're my little *bruder* . . . and because you're going to sit down here with me in this hot shed and help me work on a surprise for Priscilla."

"I knew there must be a catch. What are you doing?"

"Well, if you think it won't upset Daed too much for a day or two . . . I wanted to put an addition on the cabin. You know everyone in the community will probably help, so it'll go fast. I wanted you to have a place to sleep when you're at home and then have a little extra room for—well—other *kinner*, should Gott allow that."

"Now who's flushing red? Good ol' Joe, the *kinner* maker."

"Shut up."

"All right, let's see your drawings, though I know they'll be within an inch to scale."

"*Danki*, Edward."

"Back at you, Joe."

Joseph rolled his eyes. "You, little *bruder*, have got to unlearn your *Englisch* ways or I'll make you an herbal concoction that you'll never forget."

Edward thumped him good-naturedly on the shoulder and Joseph gave him an elbow dig back; and all seemed better with the world for the moment.

Priscilla looked up from her teacup as she visited with Mary. Jude had come home for lunch and, as usual, went to kiss his wife immediately. Then he caught up a mug and glanced at Priscilla.

"Is Hollie lying down here?"

"What?" Priscilla asked with a smile.

"Hollie . . . she was absent this morning. I assumed she was sick."

Priscilla placed her cup in her saucer with a hand that shook slightly. "She's not sick. I kissed her good-bye when we heard the bell."

"Oh." Jude turned slowly from the sink. "Priscilla, I'm sure she only stopped to play or got caught up doing something . . . I bet she's at Frau Umble's right now."

"The Umbles' house is past the school gate. She wouldn't have stopped. I have to find Joseph." Priscilla clenched her hands together to stop their shaking.

"I'll go with her, Mary," Jude said.

Priscilla heard his mug clatter in the sink as if from a long way away. Then she was out the door, running, running to Joseph with Jude hard on her heels.

Joseph was about to pour his *fater* some soup when Priscilla tore through the front door. Bear began to bark in alarm as Jude followed her. Joseph watched as Priscilla yelled Hollie's name, then stopped dead in front of him. He put down the soup.

"What's wrong?" he asked, already knowing the answer as his heart began to thump.

"Hollie's missing."

"*Ach*, dear Gott . . . how do you know?" Joseph caught her stiff frame in his arms and looked at Jude.

"She wasn't at school even though Priscilla sent her."

"Perhaps she's playing somewhere," Abner suggested. "Let Bear loose; he'll find her any-where on this mountain."

"She may not be on the mountain," Joseph said slowly.

"What?" Priscilla cried. "Do you think he's had

time to get her away so fast? Surely, with the hike and all . . ."

Joseph swallowed hard. "Priscilla . . ."

"What? What is it?"

"Bishop Umble told me that he wrote to your father a while back to let him know you were all right. He didn't know that your *daed* might tell Heath where you were."

"And you didn't tell me?" she whispered, her face pale, her eyes haunted.

"I didn't want you to worry and I thought it best to—"

"You thought it best?" She slammed her hands into his chest. "How dare you? How dare you?" She pummeled her hands against him and he kept his arms around her.

"I'm sorry. So sorry."

She drew a long, agonizing sob and collapsed into him. He held her close, rocking her gently.

"All right, enough of this," Edward said decisively from the doorway. "We search the mountain first. Get every man out there. And we should call the police."

"No," Priscilla gasped. "Don't let him, Joseph. Heath will hurt her. I know he will."

Joseph met Edward's gaze over her head.

"Okay," Edward snapped. "We handle this alone. Let Bear loose."

The wolf dog took off at a run once let out-

252

doors. "I'll follow him," Edward called. "Joseph, you and Jude round up the men."

"I want to come," Priscilla said.

"Of course you'll *kumme.* Daed, can you stay here and make some coffee? And don't get all upset." Joseph was picking up lanterns, and other odds and ends that he stuffed in his pants pockets.

"I wish I could go with you. I can't do anything," Abner said, aggrieved.

Joseph put a hand on his *fater*'s shoulder. "*Jah,* you can do something, Daed. Pray." *Like I should have done when the bishop told me to . . . Dear Gott, let it not be too late. Forgive my foolish pride. Have mercy on Heath, on Hollie . . . And give Priscilla strength beyond strength . . .*

He caught his wife's hand and together they ran with Jude to Ben Kauffman's to ring the large bell over the store, signaling that there was important information for the community and that everyone should gather.

Priscilla was grateful that Ben Kauffman had insisted she slip on a pair of moccasins from the store because she knew her feet would have been torn by now from all of the briars. She pushed aside the thought that Hollie had been barefoot when she left for school that morning and focused on keeping up with Joseph.

They passed an area where she thought the secret pool was located and caught up with her

253

husband. "Joseph . . . I never thought, but should we check the water? What if a bear . . ." She couldn't finish the sentence and he squeezed her fingers briefly.

"Some of the men already checked the creek, Priscilla. And we would have heard the dog if there was a bear involved." His voice was sober and she shuddered, thanking God that it hadn't been the creek, but what would Heath do? *What will he do if my father has told him I married Joseph? What will he do . . .*

She tried to abandon the fretful thoughts when a gunshot rang out from a distance. Priscilla stopped as if she'd been shot herself, but Joseph grabbed her arm.

"*Kumme* on. One of the men has found something. That's the signal."

Chapter Thirty-One

Joseph led Priscilla in the direction of the gun signal and soon they crossed the meadow and emerged at the treeline that led to the path down the mountain.

Bear was panting and Edward pointed to a pine tree branch. "The dog found it." He backed up to join the other *Amisch* men standing silent.

Joseph turned and stared at the bright paper with Priscilla's picture on top, exactly like the one from the hospital bulletin board. The photo had been stabbed through by a short limb and there was a note in black marker written over the language of the flyer.

Dear Daddy Joseph,
    If you want to see your new little girl, bring me my wife. Come alone with Priscilla. If you know where I am.

Joseph frowned after he read the note aloud.
"What does he mean, if you know where he is?" Edward growled. "How are you supposed to know that? And there's no way you're going alone to face some psychopath—sorry, Priscilla."
Joseph watched his wife shrug and reach her fingers out to trace the written words, as if she might touch Hollie through the paper, like she was in a dream . . . *A dream.*
Joseph remembered his nightmare. "He's at the ice mine."
Priscilla stared at him. "How do you know?"
"I . . . know. The rest of you stay up here. Priscilla and I will go alone."
"*Nee.*" Mahlon Mast, Edward's future *fater*-in-law, a tough, grumpy *auld* man, spoke. "We won't have you go alone, as Edward says. You can approach the mine from behind and we'll wait on the ridge back there. That way we can *kumme* down from the top should we hear anything that doesn't sound *gut.*"

255

"Agreed," Joseph said after considering. "Let's move."

The trek down the mountain was fraught with palpable tension, and Priscilla stifled a gasp when one of the men shooed a six-foot-long black snake off the trail with the butt of his rifle. It seemed a bad omen to some of the *Amisch*, who Priscilla knew were superstitious at heart given their Appalachian tendencies. She ignored their mutterings until Joseph turned and spoke harshly to the group.

"It was a black snake, not a rattler. It's not poisonous. It means nothing—but if you must think on it, think of it as a sign there will be no poison spread today." He turned and continued on, holding back overgrown limbs from Priscilla's face.

The trail finally broke and bright light could be seen up ahead, but here the search party veered off to the right, tramping through forest where there was no path, sinking sometimes ankle deep in leaf falls and the occasional hidden animal hole. It was treacherous going, but soon they all stood on a rock outcropping.

"The mine's directly below us," Joseph whispered in Priscilla's ear and she nodded. "We'll go down the side here while the men wait."

Priscilla saw Edward move forward to grasp

his brother's arm and then turn to give her a quick hug. "Be safe, little sister-in-law."

She followed Joseph past the men, one of whom hesitantly held out a rifle to her husband. Joseph shook his head and she knew he would not take the weapon, both because he was *Amisch* and because there was no telling what Heath would do.

They made their way down to the right of the entrance to the mine and Priscilla saw with disappointment that the boards stood in place. She almost turned away in despair when Joseph squeezed her hand and pointed to the play of light at the base of the entrance. Someone had lit the kerosene lantern inside. Priscilla understood. Heath had put the boards up from the inside so that he could be aware of anyone approaching. It gave him a distinct advantage, but she knew Joseph was smarter than Heath and waited for her husband's cue.

Joseph decided to opt for the obvious, seeing no way to undo the boards without making a racket. His hands were sweating but he moved and knocked on the middle board, as plainly as if he were knocking on a *haus* door.

"Heath, it's Joseph King. We've *kumme* as you asked."

There was a shuffling sound inside and Hollie suddenly cried out. "His ankle's hurt, real bad . . . He fell down the mountain."

There was a frantic hiss of words and Joseph saw Priscilla clench her hands in her apron as they both heard Heath grind out, "Shut up, Hollie."

"If you're hurt, Heath, we can help," Joseph said, keeping his voice level.

The top board was ripped off from inside with such fury that the wood splintered. Joseph caught a glimpse of blood-shot blue eyes, filled with vengeance and something beyond sanity, and he almost recoiled out of instinct.

Another board came off and Joseph caught Priscilla's hand in his, finding her palm surprisingly cool, despite the monster slowly revealing himself. Joseph glanced down at his wife and saw her lips moving. *She's praying . . . she's not afraid now . . .*

Her posture heartened him and he didn't move when the third board was thrust outward, broken in two, by a blood-streaked hand. Joseph caught the hand automatically, not exactly sure what he was doing but understanding that he needed to follow his instincts.

He let go of Priscilla and grasped Heath's hand in both of his, holding on against the incredible pull in the opposite direction. "I've got your hand, Heath. It's going to be all right."

An inhuman, ragged sound followed and Joseph had to jump back, releasing contact, as Heath crashed his leg through the remaining boards. Joseph gazed at the man, who stood as tall as he was, but thinner, more gangly . . . Yet his limbs seemed swollen by some unholy power as he stood, panting, with teeth gnashing, in the doorway of the mine. His strange, fiery gaze shifted to Priscilla and he lunged, but Joseph was faster.

He put his hands on the other man's chest and held him back, but only barely. *Dear Gott, he's strong . . . and completely out of his mind.*

Priscilla spoke from behind him, sounding calm and cool. "Heath, where's Hollie? Can you get her? Then I'll come with you."

Joseph blinked. *What is she saying? She's not going anywhere with this—thing . . .*

But amazingly, Heath seemed to respond. He stepped backwards, clinging to the shattered boards for a moment. Then Joseph saw that his ankle was bent at an unnatural angle and was bleeding profusely.

"Heath, you're hurt," Joseph said, mimicking Priscilla's calm, but obviously not having the same effect. The other man growled at him and struck out an effective blow to Joseph's right shoulder. Joseph staggered for a second but then made a dive for Heath's ankle.

Joseph gritted his teeth against the pain he knew he was inflicting but he hung on, forcing the broken bones into an even more improbable alignment as Heath screamed. Joseph twisted his body, concentrating everything he had on torturing the broken ankle, and he finally brought Heath down, half in and half out of the mine. Relief surged through him until he heard a familiar voice cry out.

"Joseph . . . Let him go. The rope is almost worn through and I'm going to—fall."

Joseph recognized Mr. Ellis's voice, the voice of the trustworthy and loyal *Englisch* friend to his community, from inside the mine, and slackened his hold long enough for Heath to kick him hard in the chin.

"Choose!" Heath commanded. "Let me go or save your friend. Which is it?"

Joseph saw Priscilla bolt past them and scamper into the mine. Then he heard her sharp cry and knew she must have slid on the icy floor.

"Priscilla, dear Gott, the mine is almost solid ice now. Are you all right?" he cried.

"Yes . . . Hollie's on the far side of the cave and Mr. Ellis is tied by some unraveling rope over the shaft, but I can't lift him, Joseph. Help me!"

He opened his mouth to call for help, but Heath jammed his fist against Joseph's teeth, pushing with a stranglehold back against his throat. Joseph bit automatically, feeling sick as the metallic taste of blood filled his mouth.

Then Heath let go and Joseph drew in a ragged breath, only to find himself beneath the other man. Heath lifted Joseph's head and banged it against the pine-needle-laden ground. Joseph saw stars for a moment but quickly refocused. He focused all of his energy on getting Heath off of him and finally reached for his throat, pushing upward. Heath gagged and Joseph used that moment to let out a yell for help.

"Edward!"

Immediately, like a black-and-white blur, *Amisch* men scrambled down the outer sides of the mine. Edward was first to reach them and jumped over Joseph and Heath to rush inside the mine. Soon other men followed, while some bent to try and subdue Heath's frantic thrashing and screaming.

Joseph held on gamely but his hands had grown slippery with blood, and somehow Heath wrenched himself free of his grasp and got to his feet. Joseph watched the other man's eyes dart upward and then Heath was off, scrambling up the rocks that protruded from the side of the mine entrance like an enraged animal, his ankle trailing dark blood. But then Joseph heard the sound of rocks cracking and Heath fell backwards, fast and hard, to land on the ground with a strangled groan.

Joseph staggered to his feet and looked at Mahlon Mast. "Go down to Mr. Ellis's *haus* and call an ambulance."

Joseph dragged himself to the large inert figure on the ground and stared down at Heath. The unearthly fury seemed to have left him and his blue eyes stared up at the sky. He twitched and Joseph dropped to his knees beside him.

"Heath, it's Joseph. Look, I'll take good care of Priscilla for you. It's going to be all right."

A faint shake of the head and Heath drew a long breath. "No . . . it's . . . hell for me."

Joseph opened his mouth to try to answer, but a soft voice spoke first from over his shoulder.

"I forgive you, Heath. I forgive you. No hell," Priscilla said clearly.

"I . . . can't . . . breathe."

"Relax," Priscilla said and Joseph watched her touch Heath's large, bloodstained hand. Joseph put his own hand over hers and felt tears sting his eyes.

Joseph saw Heath struggle to focus, then a dwindling gray light filled the other man's eyes as if he was walking backward down a long, dark road . . . and then he was still and gone.

Chapter Thirty-Two

Two weeks after Heath's death, summer came in its full glory to Ice Mountain and Priscilla found herself beginning to take a faint interest in life around her again. Dr. McCully had told her that she was suffering from shock, on various levels, and needed time to process the fact that she was now free in the world and no longer the prey of an angry man. Mr. Ellis, too, had suffered some shock at being taken hostage from his own home, and the *Amisch* community spent much time with the man, visiting and ministering to him.

The authorities had taken statements and transported Heath's body south to his home church for proper burial. Priscilla dreamed the day of the funeral that she could hear the dirt clods strike the coffin and awoke, knowing some part of her would always be wary, haunted even.

Mercifully though, Edward had had the foresight to sweep Hollie away from the scene of the accident and Priscilla had done her best to explain to her daughter that Heath was gone and could never hurt them again. But Hollie, too, suffered nightmares and finally had ended up sleeping between Priscilla and Joseph with Bear in attendance for the last several nights.

Now Priscilla sat in a bentwood chair and watched Joseph work in the garden and felt the earth call to her. The pepper plants she'd put in the day of Hollie's kidnapping were now strong and sturdy, and Priscilla felt Joseph's gaze as she rose from the chair then bent to begin weeding around the small stalks.

"Are you all right?" he asked tentatively. She knew he'd been worried sick for her and Hollie. She reached out and grabbed his nearest boot around the ankle and squinted up at him in the sun.

"I feel better today."

"*Ach*, thank Gott." He dropped to his knees

beside her and encircled her with his strong arms. She could feel the warmth of his body through his green shirt and noticed how tanned his forearms had grown from working outdoors.

"I think—I think I'd like to forget things for a while," she said, wondering if he'd understand.

He apparently did because he laughed, an exultant, grateful sound and turned her to face him. He kissed the hollows in her cheeks and the circles beneath her eyes, then fell to tasting her mouth in long, luxurious, drawing sips that made her clasp his shoulders and savor everything about the moment: the smell of the garden, the fall of bright sunshine across her face. *I'm alive . . . praise God . . . I'm alive!* Her spirit seemed to ring with the words as she returned his kisses eagerly, wantonly.

"Well, now, this is a pretty picture," Edward drawled with a faint smile from where he'd taken up residence in Priscilla's abandoned chair.

Priscilla hid her face in Joseph's shirt and felt his muscles tense, though she wanted to laugh even when her husband was losing his temper.

"Edward, what do you want?" Joseph ground out.

"Nothing. To help with the garden, or Daed, or maybe a certain surprise for the lady hidden in your shirt there. It's fine weather we've been having."

Priscilla peered at her brother-in-law, who was merrily eating an apple while baiting Joseph.

"A surprise?" she asked, growing excitement in her veins.

Joseph looked down at her, a reluctant smile pulling at his lips. "I thought we'd expand the cabin, Priscilla. Daed's said it's all right, and I could show you the plans . . ."

"Oh, *jah*," she almost purred. "Do show me your plans."

His golden green eyes widened in surprise and then he laughed and bent to nuzzle her neck, making her giggle.

"Okay, clearly I'm not wanted here," she heard Edward say from far off.

Then she relished the feeling of her husband's gentle affections in the heat of the summer's day and knew inside that she was growing stronger, like the plants that surrounded them.

Joseph walked in the cool evening air to the bishop's *haus*, his Bible under his arm, and his throat tight. He wished Edward or somebody would be here for his meeting with the youth of the community—*nee*, the *buwes*. *What* en der weldt *am I going to say to them about sexual temptation?* Then he remembered his wife's parting words—that they were probably going to be more nervous than he. So, he sucked in a breath. *I suppose it'll turn out all right . . .*

He passed the overflowing flower pots dotted with lightning bugs and mounted the stone steps to the bishop's front porch. Thankfully, the place was screened in so the mosquitoes wouldn't be a distraction.

"Hiya, Joseph King." Bishop Umble bade him enter and extended a plate of teaberry cookies. "Have one—it'll calm your nerves. Mary Malizza made them."

Joseph took a cookie and sank down at the table bench. "Where are the womenfolk?" he asked idly.

"Off to wash their hair in the creek, and me with nothing to say about it. Martha's found more of her girlhood with that kind *Englisch* woman than I can even figure."

"That's *gut*."

"Listen, *sohn*, the *gut* Gott will give you the words you need to minister to these *buwes*. Trust me."

"I suppose," Joseph agreed, then nearly jumped when a knock sounded on the screen door.

"All right, I'm going to have a lie-down in the bedroom while you do your group. I've got a *gut* book going . . . so . . . go answer the door, Joseph." The bishop grabbed the plate of cookies and Joseph glared at him, then rose to answer the door.

It was Dan Kauffman, and Mahlon Mast's *sohn*, Ernest. Dan was the older but Ernest was only a year behind. Joseph opened the door and the *buwes* entered rather solemnly. They were dressed

266

formally, including their black hats, and Joseph had to smile as their gangly legs tried to find comfort in the porch chairs.

"Next time, don't dress up," Joseph said with a grin.

Dan nodded, wetting his lips. "Are we really going to talk about sex, Joseph?"

Joseph read the anxiety and eagerness in the face of the sixteen-year-old and suddenly realized how important this group could be to prepare young men for future life. He knew other more conservative *Amisch* groups would never dream of such a meeting, but Bishop Umble was an original, for sure.

He cleared his throat and found his voice came out normally. "*Jah*, Dan . . . we are. Who else is *kumming*?"

"John Byler and Jay Smucker."

Great . . . I've seen those two jokesters in church service, but maybe they need ministering to as well.

He waited another ten minutes for John and Jay, and they, too, showed up formally dressed but full of suppressed mirth.

Joseph sighed to himself. *I might as well get started . . .*

"Let's begin with prayer." *And so help me, if that Smucker kid giggles, I'll wring his neck.* "Holy Gott, we pray that You'd bless this time together and that You would give us wisdom and discernment on this difficult subject and that You would equip us with knowledge for both today and the future. Amen."

Joseph opened his Bible, then closed it again. "You know, I wasn't sure until this moment how to go about teaching all of you what you might need to know. But I think I'll start with what I didn't know and how it got me into trouble. For example, some women find it within them to try and beguile a man—I'm not talking about husband and wife, *Amisch* or *Englisch*, but in general, be wary of a woman who uses sex to gain something she may want."

Dan shrugged, then spoke up uncertainly. "Well . . . what else would she want besides sex?"

Joseph nodded. "Fair question. Some women want to have an unhealthy balance of power in a relationship, the same way some men do. And these people use sex as a weapon almost, either to trap you with desire or to humiliate you or degrade you as a person."

"I don't get it," Jay spoke up. "I wouldn't be humiliated if I could actually find a *maedel* who wanted to do it with me."

Joseph thought hard. Clearly, beating around the proverbial bush with abstract thought wasn't going to work here. At least Jay was putting things bluntly, which was closer to the truth in any case. "All right, let's talk about doing it—as you put it. What does that look like to you all?"

"Aren't you married, Joseph?" John asked with a smirk, and Jay laughed.

Laugh with them, some instinct prompted. *Relax . . .* So Joseph smiled good-naturedly.

"No talking about my wife here," he ordered. "Back to you men—what does it look like? Feel like? Make you want or not want? You see, we keep it such a mystery that most *buwes* your age are absolutely broadsided the first time it happens and can't think straight, so you might find your-self in a situation like I was . . ."

"Should you get married just because you want to have sex?" Dan asked.

"*Nee*, that is not a way to build a life. You need respect and friendship and love; and yes, sexual attraction, but not as the sole basis for a marriage."

"So you should have sex without getting married?" Jay demanded while John shifted violently in his chair.

"*Nee*, I mean . . ." Joseph swallowed. *This is not going well . . .*

"Who's having sex without getting married?" a brusque female voice demanded, and Joseph jumped a bit along with the *buwes* as two dripping-haired, nightgowned female figures appeared on the doorstep.

Dear Gott . . . it's the bishop's wife, Joseph thought, appalled.

Frau Umble and Mary Malizza came barefooted onto the porch and Joseph saw Dan eye the door.

He thought escape might not be a bad idea. But Mary gaily pressed her question, then looked at Joseph.

"What are you teaching these men, Joseph?"

"I—I don't know, really." He avoided Frau Umble's gaze.

"Well," Mama Malizza said, "I say we make cookies and talk things over. You boys hungry?"

There was a chorus of relieved *jahs*—not the least of which was Joseph's own affirmation.

The kids followed Frau Umble into the kitchen and Mary Malizza bent near Joseph. "I got your back, Joe. We'll get a good start talkin'."

He nodded his thanks gravely, having a sudden headache but grateful for the smell of coffee and the clatter of mixing bowls.

Mary Malizza poured fresh oats into a bowl and added cocoa powder. "We'll make ice-box cookies," she announced to the kitchen at large. "Quick and easy, and no need to take time baking."

She stirred meditatively and caught the nearest boy's eye. "What's your name, honey?"

"Dan," the good-looking youth answered politely.

Mary wondered what it was like to be able to say your name with quiet confidence, based on years of love and a good upbringing. *But the world eats up the Dans and spits them out . . .*

She gripped the spoon tighter. "You got a girl, Dan?"

The boy appeared petrified and shook his head. "*Nee*, I only now can start *rumspringa* or decide to join the church."

Mary nodded. "Oh, that running-around thing you all do. I seen that on the TV . . . a bunch of you run off to the city and wear regular clothes and smoke and drink. Don't look like as much fun as it is right here making cookies."

Dan looked surprised. "*Nee*, I'm not going anywhere. My *daed* said I could start full-time at the store, or Joseph promised me an apprenticeship in carpentry and such. I think I like Joseph's offer best though."

Mary watched Joe give the boy an affirming nod while the others looked longingly at Joseph, though he didn't appear to notice.

"Hey, Joe, I'm thinkin' maybe yer teachin' ought to extend further than the old bishop's porch. I say you got a group of boys right here who'd all like to be apprenticed to ya."

Joseph looked up, clearly startled. "*Ach . . . jah.* Well, sure, fellas, if you want . . ."

Mary smiled to herself.

"They were in their nightgowns . . ." Joseph pillowed his head on his hands, facedown on his side of the bed.

Priscilla leaned over him. "Was it that bad, really?"

He groaned, not wanting to rouse Hollie but

unable to keep quiet. "And now I've got to teach that Smucker kid to build . . ."

She stroked the back of his neck and he shivered involuntarily.

"You can do it, Joseph. I know you can." She kissed his right ear and then his thoughts were sliding to other areas of life.

"I wish we could do it," he muttered, and she giggled against him, and he loved the press of her softness on his back.

"We will soon," she promised in a whisper.

And he fell asleep with her cuddled close, forgetting his failed attempt at teaching, but as sure as her warmth that he could always try again . . .

Chapter Thirty-Three

"Why are all these people here?" Hollie asked sleepily as she eyed the crowd of folks arriving outside the window.

Priscilla smiled. "They're coming to help build the new part of our house, Hollie. It's a surprise I've been keeping for you—Now you'll definitely get your pink room!"

"Oh boy!" The little girl clapped and Priscilla breathed a sigh of relief. It was as much healthy enthusiasm as Hollie had shown over anything in the past weeks. Priscilla had been beginning to worry that Hollie might need professional help getting over the time with Heath. But now the little girl scampered out of the big bed, rolling over Bear in the process.

"Help me get dressed, Mommy. Hurry."

Priscilla went to the makeshift drawer where she kept Hollie's things in the big bedroom and hesitated as her hand hovered over the yellow dress—the one Hollie had been wearing when Heath kidnapped her.

Suddenly Hollie was at her elbow, her small fingers touching the yellow fabric. "I remember Daddy—that other Daddy."

"Oh," Priscilla exclaimed softly. "You don't have to wear this, Hollie. We can give it away or put it somewhere and—"

Hollie touched her arm. "Mommy, I want to wear it 'cause it helps me remember."

Priscilla felt her eyes well with tears as she knelt down next to her daughter. "Hollie, what do you want to remember about that day?"

"I want to remember the angel in the ice mine," Hollie said slowly, as if Priscilla herself was the child.

"You mean the man Daddy tied up—Mr. Ellis?"

"No, the angel beside me when my back was against the ice. He stood by me and kept me safe. Can we go back there and see him again sometime?" Hollie grabbed the yellow dress and wriggled it over her golden head while Priscilla sat still, watching her.

"Hollie, I—an angel?" Priscilla felt a tear slip down her cheek. *Was the child losing her mind?*

"Yeah, Mom. Can I go out and see everybody now?"

"Sure . . . sure you can."

"Bye, Mommy."

Priscilla didn't move, one hand still in the clean clothes as she struggled over what to do with what Hollie had shared. She looked up when Joseph entered the room, a work apron and tools hanging from his large frame.

"What's wrong? Are you not feeling well? If this is too much for you today, sweetheart, we can send everybody home and . . ."

"Joseph?"

"What?" He knelt down on the floor beside her, cupping her chin in his large hand.

"Do you believe in angels?"

Joseph held the frame of the window casement in place while others nailed it from inside. The smell of the fresh cut lumber and the sound of hammering and sawing were vitally renewing to him, and he needed the revitalization after his talk with Priscilla. He knew angels were in the Bible, but he didn't know if Hollie believed something false merely to comfort herself or if what the *kind* said could possibly be real . . .

274

He shook off his musings, knowing that a lack of paying attention was the cause of most accidents on a work site. Just then Dan Kauffman came hurrying up to him. The *buwe* looked *gut* outfitted in his carpenter's belt—more mature—and Joseph had to smile. Then he saw the other three would-be sex- and cookie-makers lagging behind Dan, and his smile became a bit forced. He sighed, realizing he'd made a commitment and needed to follow through. *Maybe an angel will help me . . .*

"Joseph," Dan said eagerly, holding out a sketch on a torn piece of paper, "we were all thinking and we wondered if we could make your daughter a dower chest today to go in the new room."

Joseph smiled easily now, taking the paper. *I wish I'd thought of this.* Dower or hope chests were common among the Mountain *Amisch* and were usually built by an *aulder bruder* for a younger sister or were passed down from one woman to another, like a mother to a daughter.

"I think it's a *wunderbar* idea, Dan . . . and uh . . . *buwes* . . . *danki*." He bent to study the drawing of the chest. "Did you do this, Dan?"

"I did the scaling and the wood measurements, but the drawings on the chest front and sides— Jay did those. We thought we could paint them, and Ernest knows the *auld* German lettering, so we could put 'Hollie King' on the front. And John's real *gut* at mixing paint and doing strap work, like for the hinges."

Joseph could tell that Dan was waiting rather breathlessly for his response and Joseph had to marvel at the combined talents of the four.

"I'd say you *buwes* could help me run a real carpentry shop one day. Not that we'd do cabinetry—Luke Lapp's got the corner on that up here. But we could build other things to market . . . things like hope chests. Great idea, men! I'm so glad you showed me this. Go on ahead and start work. If you need help, don't be afraid to ask—either me or any other builder." Joseph watched them scurry off, tripping over their own feet in their hurry, and shook his head in disbelief. *Was teaching those* buwes *going to be easier than he'd expected?*

He turned back to work, then saw his *daed* through one of the partition frames, wielding a hammer and coughing furiously at the same time.

Joseph walked through the site quickly to get to his *fater*. "Daed, what are you doing?" he asked low, not wanting to cause any embarrassment. It wasn't right that a *sohn* should dishonor a parent by questioning his actions, but Joseph didn't like the pallor of his father's skin or the fact that his cough didn't seem to respond to the inhaler he was sucking on.

"Daed?"

"I—built this cabin—for your *mamm* and me. Want to give now to you and—yours." His father

276

leaned against a doorjamb and looked like he was going to pass out.

Joseph put out his hands to steady him. "Daed? Daed, you do give, every day. And now that you've hammered a bit, you did your part."

"Not . . . enough," his *fater* wheezed. Then he collapsed in a shaky heap at Joseph's feet.

"*Ach*, dear Gott . . . Help!" Joseph called, then leaned back over his *dat*'s ashen face. "Daed? *Sei se gut*, it's all right. You're going to be all right. We'll get you to Dr. McCully . . ."

Joseph saw a blur of motion around him as friends gathered and began to pray. Edward was at his side in an instant and both of them struggled to try to will breath through their *fater*'s bluish lips. Then Joseph felt a pull on his elbow and he turned to see the earnest face of Sarah Mast. He remembered that Sarah was working with Grossmudder May and hastily moved away.

"Send everyone out, Joseph," she said quietly.

Joseph got to his feet. "Will you all, please, go outside and keep praying so Sarah has space to work?" There was a shuffling behind him and then he met Priscilla's eyes through the crowd. She ran to him and he caught her close. They turned and knelt down near his *fater*'s side.

Joseph watched Sarah run calming hands down his *dat*'s arms and then across his shrunken chest. "It's not the cancer. I think he's had a heart attack," she said softly, almost to herself.

"A heart attack?" Edward groaned aloud. "*Ach*, Gott. Where's Mary? She should be here."

"There's no time," Sarah said, then lifted her gray eyes and looked at Joseph. "Do you want your *fater* to be well?"

"*Jah*," Joseph gasped, squeezing Priscilla's hand. "Please."

He watched Sarah rustle in a pouch at her waist then nod. She leaned over his *fater*'s face, slipping a dried leaf under his tongue. "Abner, it's Sarah Mast. I want to tell you that Derr Herr is the same—yesterday, today, and forever, and He Who healed many heals you now too. You touch the hem of His robe and you are made whole. Believe."

And that was all. Joseph held his breath and watched, amazed, as his *fater*'s face was suddenly suffused with color and he drew a deep, full breath, chewing at the herb Sarah had placed in his mouth. He opened his eyes and reached to stroke his beard. Then he looked up at Sarah. "*Danki*," he whispered.

Joseph watched her nod, with a humble bow. "Gott be praised," she said. "Now, have something to eat and drink and be still for today."

She got up, nodded to Edward, and slipped from their midst.

"What just happened?" Joseph asked Priscilla in wonderment.

"I don't—I don't know."

"I feel a whole lot better, that's what," his *daed* muttered. "Now help me up."

"Fine," Joseph said shakily. "But tomorrow, you're going for a checkup with Dr. McCully."

"If I feel like it." His *daed* grinned and Joseph could only shake his head.

Mary Malizza was in her element. A bunch of people to cook for and spaghetti on the menu. It seemed that her friend, Martha Umble, had let it get round the mountain that there was no better food than Mary's spaghetti, and the house raising—or frolic, as Martha called it—seemed the best place to showcase the very nontraditional *Amisch* dish.

Mary baked her spaghetti in a rich sauce and added meatballs the size of small snowballs. She'd also prepared, the night before, many loaves of fresh Italian bread, which were now being busily sliced by the womenfolk. Mary put her hands on her broad hips and smiled to herself. *I could use some of these girls back at the inn— they're hard, fast workers . . . and pleasant to boot.*

Priscilla came into the kitchen, looking happy but a bit dazed, and held out an envelope to Mary.

"What's this?"

"Something you gave me once. I only remembered it this morning when we were moving things, but it made a huge difference at the time."

Mary pulled down her glasses from her hair and peered into the envelope.

"Five hundred dollars," Priscilla said softly.

"Awww, I forgot about this too, girlie. You keep it." Mary thrust the envelope back, but Priscilla took a step away.

"I have everything that I could possibly need, Mary Malizza, and you had a hand in it. I want you to take that money and use it as part of a down payment for a cabin here on the mountain like you told me you wanted to do, because I don't think any of us could get along without you here at least part of the year."

She wants me . . . they want me. Mary lifted her apron to her eyes with one hand, waving a spaghetti spoon with the other.

"Oh, don't cry," Priscilla soothed, putting an arm around her shoulders.

Mary sobbed. "You don't know what it means to have come here, to have been accepted, only for me being me. I haven't had that much in life . . ."

Mary felt other hands join Priscilla's on her shoulders and glanced over to see Martha Umble hugging her too. Mary burst into renewed sobs and then, one by one, women came to surround her. Some she knew well, some she didn't, but they all displayed a love and caring that she'd never felt before.

Then Martha laughed and joked softly, "Don't let this go to your head, Mary Malizza. It's your spaghetti we're all really celebrating."

Mary had to laugh. "All right, but if you all want to taste it more than once a year, you'll have to come to the Bear Claw Inn and you're all more than welcome!"

Chapter Thirty-Four

"We are alone, in our own bed," Priscilla whispered late that night into Joseph's ear.

"Mmm-hmm," he sighed.

She knew he was exhausted after the day of overseeing the building, not to mention the strange but wonderful occurrence with his *daed* and Sarah, but she'd missed him, missed his body and his touch.

She bit her lip and leaned over him, studying his dear face in the light of the single kerosene lamp. His lashes were thick as they lay on his sunburned cheeks and his beautiful lips were parted slightly.

She was so grateful that he'd been matter-of-fact about Hollie's mention of an angel; it had made Priscilla feel infinitely better. And Hollie and Bear were in her very own pink bedroom tonight . . . which led Priscilla back to the issue at hand.

She experimentally swiped her tongue across his bottom lip and he turned his head in her direction, his dark hair rumpled against the white of the pillowcase.

She slid the crisp sheet down to his hips, glad that he was back to sleeping naked, now that Hollie and Bear were out of the bedroom. She bent her head and sucked gently on the male nipple nearest her, loving the erect nub in her mouth and the way he arched his neck, still half asleep.

She drew harder on him and she smiled against his skin when he moaned faintly. "Mmmm . . . Priscilla . . ."

"Yes, Joseph?"

"Kiss me," he murmured.

She complied gladly, slanting her head, using deft, artful strokes of her tongue, teasing his mouth, until he opened his emerald eyes and stared up at her, his pupils dark and dilated.

"Are you too tired?" she asked with a faint smile.

"Are you?"

He grabbed her with easy strength and pulled her beneath him, the sheet tangled between them. She loved the sight of him hovering over her, balancing on his elbows and forearms, his face intent.

"Put your fingers in my mouth," he commanded suddenly and she obeyed, surprised at the odd request until he drew two of her fingers into his mouth, sucking hard. The double sensation of his body and mouth working over hers was more than amazing and she felt herself begin to slip toward that edge of pleasure that blurred between the passionate and the surreal. But then he turned her again, so that she was atop him, her fingers still in his mouth, and she gasped aloud. "Joseph."

"Don't wake me up unless you really want to play," he murmured against her flesh.

"Oh, I'll remember that," she panted.

He released her hand from his lips. "*Gut*. Now suck your fingers like I was doing."

She hesitantly did as he asked, feeling slightly foolish, until she tasted his mouth on her hand and stared down into his eyes, seeing the faint look of male pride and satisfaction reflected there. She closed her eyes and found sweet release with him, then fell forward to collapse on his chest.

"How was that, my *frau*?" he asked, nudging her with his shoulder.

"You know exactly how it was, Joseph. Now be quiet . . . I'm sleeping."

"We'll understand if you don't want to drive us to Dr. McCully's," Joseph said to Mr. Ellis. "Priscilla can always drive her car, sir."

Joseph had chosen to *kumme* alone inside Mr. Ellis's home while Edward, Mary, Priscilla, and Jude stayed out on the porch with their *daed*. He knew that the community had been ministering to Mr. Ellis, that the older man had truly been shaken by what had happened with Heath. Now

Joseph was surprised to see the quick grin beneath Mr. Ellis's graying mustache.

"Joseph, I'll drive you anywhere you like. Don't be afraid that one crazy man is going to put me off a lifetime of loving your people. And . . . I can now honestly say that I've been almost every-where in that ice mine—including nearly inside the hole in it."

Joseph laughed and clapped the older man on the shoulder, so grateful that things had turned out the way they had. He debated telling Mr. Ellis about Hollie's angel, then decided he'd save that for another time as the man was jingling the car keys and looked ready to go.

"I don't understand," Dr. McCully said slowly to the family gathered in the waiting room.

The doctor had been past the waiting room nearly a dozen times in the last four hours and Joseph had begun to worry. Now the physician stood before them studying the pages of a chart and shaking his head.

"What's wrong?" Joseph asked finally.

"Wrong?" Dr. McCully shook his head. "There's nothing wrong. Nothing."

"What do you mean?" Edward asked.

The doctor sighed. "The chemical enzymes in your father's blood show that he had a massive heart attack within the last twenty-four hours, but his heart shows no damage . . .

and his cancer is apparently . . . in remission."

"What?" Joseph met Priscilla's wide eyes and tilted his head, wondering if he'd heard correctly.

"I mean what I say." Dr. McCully shrugged. "I have no logical explanation for it, but Abner King has turned a corner. I want to write up an article about his case and send it to a medical journal."

"Dr. McCully," Joseph said, "I don't mean to be rude, but could your tests have been wrong initially about the cancer?"

"No, I've double-checked and triple-checked every test, every image we have. Abner had stage four cancer—no doubt. But now he's in full remission. It's nothing short of a miracle. All right, well, he's raring to go, so I'll let him get dressed and send him out. I'll see you all in a month."

Joseph watched the white-coated gentleman leave the waiting room and looked at Edward and Mary then Priscilla. His heart was beating fast and he didn't know what to do except bow his head and thank Gott.

"Joseph, Daed had cancer . . . caaancerrrr," Edward hissed later that afternoon as they put the finishing touches on the new construction at the cabin.

"I know." Joseph shook his head for the tenth time that day.

"You know . . . What do you know? You're not as good as engaged to that—that girl."

"Sarah? What are you talking about? She healed Daed or Gott used her to heal him." Joseph squinted at a measurement and made a notch in a door frame.

"Yeah, and you don't think that's the tiniest bit weird?" Edward demanded.

"Weird? *Nee*—wonderful more like. Look, what is wrong with you? You have the chance to marry a very special person."

"Maybe I don't want to marry anybody," Edward admitted, slouching against a chair back.

"*Ach*, I've heard that before—used to say it all the time. And then I met Priscilla . . ."

"Yeah, I know." Edward smiled sourly. "The whole lousy, romantic story. But maybe it's not my story."

"You don't love Sarah?" Joseph asked.

"I don't know what I know anymore."

"Well then, maybe, little *bruder*, you don't know much at all, but that's okay . . . Our *fater* is well. And you'll figure things out. I'll give you a hand."

Edward's forlorn look didn't reassure him, but Joseph had faith that his *bruder* was both the *buwe* who'd brought home injured birds and nursed them back to health as well as the man who could stare down anyone—*Englisch* or *Amisch*. *A soft heart in a tough exterior, and all mixed up . . . but he'll be all right.*

Joseph went back to measuring and started to whistle, ignoring Edward's groan.

Chapter Thirty-Five

Priscilla walked solemnly with a handful of other women through the trees to the meadow at the top of the mountain. They were gathered to say good-bye to Mary Malizza, who was leaving that day to drive back to her other life at the inn. Edward was to escort her down the mountain to where her big SUV was parked at Mr. Ellis's house. Mary held up pretty well until they got to the top of the trail, then she turned and cleared her throat.

"I'm not much of a speech maker, but I'll say to you here and now that you all are real people— not what we see on TV or what we read about in them books but real . . . with real problems and heartaches and blessings. And you've all blessed me by letting me be a part of you. I thought I was comin' for a vacation, but what I found was a family. So let's not cry . . . even though I'm cryin'. Let's jest say good-bye . . ."

Priscilla saw that she might have gone on but Martha Umble suddenly caught her in a fierce hug. The two women clung together, a strange meeting of *Amisch* and *Englisch*, but that was only their clothes; aside from their dress they were just two people, two friends, and the image made Priscilla's eyes water. It was a picture of her and

Joseph too, the blending of their lives—and a reminder that Mary Malizza had been responsible in a way for their union. *But God had a good hand too . . .*

Priscilla smiled through her tears as she gave her good-bye hug, then stepped back for others to do the same. Edward was looking impatient with all the feminine outpouring, but Priscilla knew he'd never interrupt. Finally, Mary blew her nose and took Edward's arm as they started down the mountain.

"She'll be back," Priscilla said with confidence to Martha Umble.

"She'd better . . . I need a friend to wash my hair in the creek with . . ." Priscilla caught the older woman's speculative look and smiled even though she could think of a hundred other things she'd rather do. But Martha was the bishop's wife . . . and a real person.

"Anytime." Priscilla smiled. "Anytime at all."

"So what's eatin' you, Edward *Amisch*?" Mary Malizza asked, looking up at the set jaw of the young man beside her.

He helped her over some roots and shook his head. "Nothing."

"Want me to shut up and stop pryin'? Well, I owe yer people somethin' and if I can lend an ear to help some fella, I might do it."

She felt him look at her, and then he gave a wry

288

grin. "All right, Mary, I'll tell you. I don't know what I'm doing with my life here."

"You liked the rigs better?"

"Nooo . . . but there was freedom there, a—a bigness, a wideness, for a man to feel alive, like he could run and keep on running. Here, there's . . . peace."

Mary couldn't contain a brief laugh. "Peace, you say? And you'd rather be runnin'? Aww, but ye're young, that's what. But I can tell you that you can search the world over runnin' and never find peace, or satisfaction fer that restlessness inside. I know—I've tried. In a way, I've been runnin' since I was seventeen, and I've had a lot of regret, until now, until here."

"I know." He lifted a hand as if in defeat. "I know that I should be grateful for peace . . . that it is hard to find, but I'm also sort of promised to this girl . . ."

"Sarah?"

"How does everybody know that? I sure hope Mahlon Mast doesn't know. He'd kill me if he knew I'd been courting his daughter."

"Had been courting . . . but not since you've come back?" Mary brushed a ladybug off her arm with care.

"No."

"Well, why not? Because you come home and don't find some passive *Amisch* miss but a real woman, learnin' to be a healer and all that?"

He gave her a baleful look and was silent.

"So you loved the girl, but not the woman . . . That's a curious thing."

"Yeah, real curious."

"I'd say ye're scared to death fer some reason. What is it?"

She watched him consider as he held branches back out of her way with easy strength. "I don't know, honestly. If I knew, I'd do something about it. But . . . I see Sarah and then I think about how different she seems from when we . . . well . . . before, and I cannot seem to reach her."

"So it's her problem."

Edward groaned. "No, it's my doing. I thought when I came back that everything was going to be the same—then Daed's sick, and Mary has a baby, and Sarah's gonna be a healer woman in a cottage, handing out herbs . . ."

Mary smiled. "So you think you're marryin' Grossmudder May, in a way? That might scare me too. But you're not. Sarah's plain but pretty at the same time with those big gray eyes that look like a kitten's eyes. You could do far worse."

"But I don't want to settle."

They'd reached the bottom of the trail and Mary turned to him. "Love is never settling, boy—it's a decision you make. To stick together through all them good times and bad times, like a preacher says. You got that in you. I can tell. Remember that."

They turned and walked past the newly boarded-up entrance to the ice mine and on down to Mr. Ellis's house.

"Well, thank you, Edward, for bringin' me here and seein' me down."

"Thanks for listening." His voice was quiet.

"I hope it done some good."

He nodded and she stretched up to give his tall frame a brisk hug, which he returned.

"I'll go get your keys," he offered and she nodded.

When he'd gone into the house, she stood still in the strange quiet of the woods all around her, the mountain like a bulwark against the evil in the world, and she breathed in the rich, floral-scented air and knew she was truly alive. *I'm comin' back . . . I'm comin' back to you.* She swiped at her eyes and listened to a robin's song and knew she'd never be the same again because of Ice Mountain.

Joseph walked out to the woodshed, which had been cleverly enlarged as part of his *haus* plans and discovered all four of his *buwes* working on Hollie's hope chest, though it was still early morning.

"Hiya, men, when did you get here?"

"We've been working all night," Dan said, straightening proudly.

"All night?" Joseph exclaimed. "You didn't have to do that."

"We wanted to," Ernest said in his still squeaky voice. "Look how it's coming."

Joseph bent down to stare at the nearly completed softwood chest. There was an interior end compartment and several ingeniously concealed secret drawers, as well as a massive lock that looked like it belonged to a treasure chest.

John handed him a skeleton key and shrugged. "We thought she'd like the big lock and her own key—like in a fairy story."

"*Ach*, she will," Joseph said, still in awe of the workmanship before him. One of the lads had sketched out with pencil grand decorations to be painted on the front and sides. Tulips, daisies, stars, and angels vied with unicorns and cardinals, and Joseph could only imagine how it would look, fully painted and highly lacquered.

He shook his head, then rose to his feet. "Fellas, I owe you all an apology." He studied the face of each *buwe*, even Jay Smucker, whose nose was smudged with dust and whose shock of red hair was askew with sweat and effort. "I thought, when Bishop Umble asked me to teach you about sex and temptation, that it was a burden, that it would be too difficult. Our first Wednesday didn't go great, but what you're doing here, what you're showing me and giving me, is a hope for me also. I hope that we can become friends and that you can *kumme* to me when you have questions— about anything—or if there's something you need.

And we are going to make this carpentry shop, and I'm going to give each one of you all that I have in teaching and knowledge and wisdom—from my heart. *Sei se gut*, forgive me."

It was a long speech for him, Joseph realized, but he meant every word. He waited, looking each boy in the eye until Dan broke into a wide smile.

"*Danki*, Joseph. I think we all would appreciate your friendship."

The others murmured and nodded and Joseph looked once more at the pencil drawings on the chest front.

"An angel, hmm?" He smiled. "You don't know it, but that's actually most appropriate."

Chapter Thirty-Six

Priscilla looked up in surprise when Edward handed her a letter.

"What's this?" she asked as she laid aside some mending she was doing on Joseph's socks.

"Mr. Ellis had it . . . he gets the mail for us. I picked it up when I took Mary to get her vehicle." He sat down across from her, pulling the coffee-pot nearer him; then he looked at her. "Do you want me to leave while you open it?"

"Oh, no—I don't even know who it's from—there's no return address." Priscilla slipped her finger into the back of the envelope and pulled out the letter. She started to read aloud in an automatic voice.

Dear Daughter,

I want you to know that I know I have wronged you. I didn't understand the full extent of Heath's abuse until the details of his death came to me. He hurt you and I hurt you. I am now searching for what is next in my life.

Your father,
Marcus Allen

Priscilla stared at the page she held with shaking hands. Edward reached out to touch her arm.

"Are you all right, Priscilla? Do you want me to get Joseph?"

"I'm right here." Joseph walked into the kitchen. "What's wrong?"

"It's from my—father," Priscilla said hoarsely, handing him the letter.

He read briefly, then looked at her. "*Ach*, Priscilla —what do you need?"

She shook her head. "I don't know. How dare he write to me! He's despicable, and now I'm supposed to forgive him? Even though he doesn't say it, that's what he's looking for . . ." She half sobbed.

"And that's what you should give him," Edward said clearly.

"Edward." Joseph's tone was warning.

"What? She's not supposed to be *Amisch* about this? You forgive the sin; you hate the sin, but you love the sinner. Isn't that how it goes? Seriously?"

Priscilla stared at him, thinking hard.

"I think you should leave," Joseph said to his brother.

"No," Priscilla protested. "Let him stay. Let him say it—if it's true. Is it true, Joseph?"

She watched her husband swallow hard; his lashes swept downward then up as he nodded with visible reluctance. "*Jah*," he whispered.

Fresh tears filled Priscilla's eyes. "Oh . . ."

Then Edward leaned closer to her. "You can forgive him, Priscilla, but you don't have to respond to that letter or have any kind of a relationship with him . . . especially if he's poison to you."

"Is that true?" she asked.

Both brothers answered in unison. "*Jah.*"

She nodded. "Then I'll have to work on the forgiveness part—thank you, Edward. Thank you, my sweet Joseph." She hurried from the room, leaving behind a heavy silence.

Joseph sat down at the table with the letter and ran a gentle finger over the tip of the needle Priscilla had abandoned.

"You're a pain in the neck, do you know that?" he asked Edward in a matter-of-fact tone.

"Yeah, I know."

"Why did you talk like that to her?"

Edward shrugged and swiped a hand across his eyes. "I don't know. Maybe because I'm drunk."

"What?" Joseph asked, appalled. "Where did you find alcohol here?"

"I didn't, actually. I took a shortcut through the woods on the way back . . . ran into an *Englisch* still. Nobody was around, so I helped myself. Smooth, Joseph. So smooth for white lightning."

Joseph had to restrain himself from grabbing his *bruder* by the nape of the neck. "Edward, I know you're going through a tough time—"

"A helluva time, Joe . . . let's get it straight . . ."

"*Nee*, you're nowhere near hell. You're confused, hurting, I know . . . but drinking isn't going to fix that. Promise me you won't touch that stuff again."

Edward stroked the coffeepot with an idle finger. "I can't make that promise, Joe, because it feels so good and right when I drink—I think I can think more clearly. Look how I helped Priscilla just now. Don't worry about it, all right? I'm not going to make a fool of myself . . . I only want a nip now and then."

Joseph let out a long breath and ran his hands over his eyes in despair. "Edward, please . . ."

His *bruder* got to his feet, knocking over the wooden kitchen chair in the process. "I said forget it, Joe, and I mean it." He walked to the front door and left with a slam.

Joseph got up and lifted the chair from the floor, feeling as if he was moving in a fog.

Priscilla came back out and joined him. "What happened?"

"*Ach*, Priscilla . . . it's Edward."

"And?" She moved to slip into his arms, and he loved the feel of her against the length of him. "No secrets, remember?" she chided gently.

"*Nee*." He bent and kissed her. "Edward is drinking," he said softly.

"Drinking? He drinks?" Clearly, his wife was surprised.

Joseph nodded. "And he's as stubborn as a ram about it too. I can't seem to reach him. I'm not sure if anyone can, really. He's got to *kumme* to himself and to Gott and no one can force that *kumming*."

"No," Priscilla agreed against his chest. "That's true. I know it personally."

Joseph smiled down at her, unable to remain joyless with her so near. "*Ach*, but you, my love, are made of stronger stuff, I think . . . I know." He kissed her nose. "And sweeter stuff." He kissed her eyes. "And wiser stuff." He kissed her mouth hard. "And softer stuff." He reached his hand up her small frame to gently stroke her breast and she sighed aloud.

"Joseph, we're in the kitchen."

"*Jah*, and it's getting hot . . ."

Chapter Thirty-Seven

Priscilla awoke the next morning with the feeling that she was being watched intently. Her eyelids fluttered and she thought for a moment that it might be Joseph, but then she blinked and realized with a start that it was Bear's one baleful eye staring her in the face.

"Bear? What are you doing, boy?" She reached sleepily to scratch behind his ear and Hollie soon appeared over his broad back.

"Mommy?"

"Mmm-hmm?"

"I want to go back to the ice mine today."

"Mmm . . . not today, sweetheart. Joseph—Daddy's busy with work I think."

"Then you and me can go."

Priscilla came fully awake, hearing the urgency in her daughter's voice.

"Why do you want to go, Hollie?"

"I want to pick some flowers and I made a note for the angel. I wrote it in the night and wrapped it in tinfoil so it won't get wet."

Priscilla sat up in bed as Joseph came whistling into the room. "Now, there's my two girls," he said with an indulgent smile.

"And Bear, Daddy." Hollie pointed to the lumbering dog.

"And Bear, of course."

Priscilla felt his eyes upon her. "You shouldn't have let me sleep," she said.

He sat down on the edge of the bed and took her hand while Hollie jumped on his back and Bear snuggled closer.

"Whoa!" he yelled, dipping forward so that Hollie tilted and screamed with laughter. Priscilla had to smile. She felt surrounded by love and it was still too unfamiliar a feeling to take for granted.

"Hollie wants to go to the ice mine today," she said above the din.

"Does she, now? And . . . are we going?" Joseph asked, still tilting back and forth.

"Don't you have to work?"

"*Jah*, but it can wait."

Priscilla shook her head faintly with a laugh. *He'll spoil Hollie and me and everyone else who shows up for the party.* It was a delicious thought . . .

"All right, then I need to get dressed for the hike. Hollie, you'll have to wear shoes."

This brought a sudden halt to the horsing around as Hollie groaned. "Aww, Mom!"

"Listen to your *mamm*, *kind*. *Kumme*, I'll help you find your shoes." He winked at Priscilla, then scooped Hollie up off the bed, leaving the room with Bear in close attendance.

Priscilla sat for a moment in the sudden silence.

She found herself thanking God for Joseph and Hollie, and then her thoughts drifted wide to include all of those on Ice Mountain who had so influenced and changed her life for the better.

Joseph plopped Hollie down on her bed and started to hunt for her shoes. He poked around the corners of the freshly painted room and then looked at Hollie, who gave a deceptively innocent shrug. He smiled and went to sit next to her on the bed.

"You know where the shoes are, right?"

"Maybe." She lifted her pert little nose in the air and he had to suppress a laugh.

"Well," he said honestly, "one thing I do notice is your distinct lack of toys, *kind*."

"What does that mean?"

"You don't have many things to play with," he clarified.

"I've got Bear."

"I know, but let me see . . . You find your shoes while I go look for something up in the rafters." He got up and patted her head, then left the room.

"What are you crawlin' up there for?" Abner demanded as Joseph stood on a kitchen chair and poked around in the opening of the cabin's ceiling.

"Where's that farm *haus* you made us when we

were little? Seems like I can picture Mary playing with it at one time." He shifted his weight and the chair creaked alarmingly.

Abner snorted. "*Jah*, about fifteen years ago, and you're going to fall and break yer neck."

But Joseph kept reaching and finally let out a whoop of triumph. "Here we go." He jumped off the chair, holding a tall barn that folded in on itself. The paint was a bit faded but he still felt he'd found one of the best toys a *kind* could have.

"*Danki*, Daed." He held the barn close to his chest while his *fater* brushed his words away but still couldn't suppress a smile.

Joseph went whistling back to the bedroom.

Priscilla was fitting on Hollie's shocs when Joseph came in carrying the large red barn.

"What's that?" Hollie and Priscilla asked in unison.

He sat down easily on the floor and put the barn beside him, turning it to face the bed.

"My favorite toy when I was little." He lifted the latch on the barn and slowly spread open the two bottom doors. A sprawl of wooden figures tumbled out onto the floor and Priscilla thrilled to hear Joseph's rich laughter.

"Oooh boy!" Hollie cried in excitement, scrambling off the bed. "Come down and look, Mommy."

Priscilla joined them with a smile of gaiety. There was a vibrant energy about Joseph as he lovingly picked up a pink pig cleverly shaped out of wood.

"It's Pete," Joseph exclaimed with all the enjoyment of a young boy, and Priscilla gazed at him lovingly.

"Hello, Pete!" Hollie waved. "Daddy, who else is there?"

"Well, if you open the top of the barn . . ." He slid the loft's doors wide and a variety of hens and a black rooster burst forth. "We've got the Griddles." His long fingers lined up the hens. "Let's see. Wanda, Nellie, Martha, Esther, and Tabitha. Aaaand, Gray the rooster."

"Why Griddles?" Priscilla asked with interest.

Joseph shrugged and looked sheepish. "I used to like fried chicken—hot off the griddle."

She laughed and picked up a brown cow. "And who's this?"

"Cocoa . . . and my favorite sheep dog, Colt."

There were many more animals in addition to the farmer and his family, and Priscilla lost track of time as they laid out the carved toys and fences and set up an imaginary farm with Hollie's enthusiastic help. Abner even came to the door and stood and watched with a faint smile while he stroked his beard.

Then Hollie sighed and gently put down a gray barn cat that was made to perch on the fence. "Oh, Daddy, you have a *wunderbar* toy."

Priscilla saw Joseph's surprised look.

"But it's yours, *kind*. I want you to have it."

Hollie clasped the buxom farmer's wife tight in one hand, then threw her arms around Joseph. "Oh, Daddy, thank you, thank you so much."

He laughed and Priscilla saw him close his eyes, delighting in the hug of their daughter.

"What does your note to the angel say, Hollie?" Joseph asked in a soft voice that echoed against the crystalline stillness of the summer ice.

"Oh, it's for him, Daddy. He'll read it when he needs to . . ."

Joseph watched his daughter carefully lay a bouquet of fresh flowers and the tinfoiled note on the ground where she'd been huddled during the time with Heath. He grappled with the images of the fight himself and could only wonder how it must have been for Priscilla and Hollie.

"It is like a fairy palace here," Priscilla said finally, breaking the silence.

Joseph looked at her. "Really?"

"Yes. The first time I came here, I was scared and couldn't appreciate it. The second time was not good, of course, but now there's a calm, beautiful stillness in this place that seems to wrap around me."

"Like a hug, Mommy?" Hollie asked, wrapping her arms around her mother's hips.

"Yes, exactly like that . . ." Joseph watched her hug Hollie and felt a warmth in his heart that rivaled a furnace in winter. *I am so blessed . . . What I thought was going to be a lonely and lost life has been redeemed.* Danki, *Gott.*

"C'mere, Daddy," Hollie invited, holding out one small arm, and Joseph complied readily, gathering his girls close to his heart.

Chapter Thirty-Eight

Joseph had it in mind to love his wife to sleep. He wanted her exhausted, so there was no chance that she'd wake and find him gone in the night. He'd noticed the reflected light of the ill-concealed still on his way back up the mountain, and he intended to put an end to Edward's immediate access to alcohol once and for all.

"What are you thinking about?" Priscilla asked as he pressed her back against the pillows.

"You," he whispered.

"No secrets, Joseph, remember?"

"*Nee . . .*" He kissed her slowly, coming back to the moment. "No secrets." He trailed his lips down the line of her white throat and slipped an arm beneath her, feeling her shiver with pleasure.

He loved the sense of her slightness against him and bent to run his tongue over the soft warmth of her breast, dampening the gown that clung to her, until she shifted restlessly, arching against him.

"I think you're too anxious, my *frau*." He smiled down at her.

She clutched his arms, her eyes half-closed. "Please, Joseph . . ."

"Not yet, my sweet. Slow. There's heightened pleasure if you learn to go slow."

She whimpered when he turned his attention to her other breast, lavishing it with all the intentness of someone licking ice cream from the tip of a cone.

"Mmm . . . you make me feel delicious," she sighed.

"And so you are."

Priscilla loved the emerald gold glow of his eyes when he loved her. He looked like a big cat and moved with easy grace in their bed, turning her with lithe strength until they were both kneeling upright. She leaned her back against the oaken hardness of his chest while he ran his large, clever hands up and down her front until she wanted to beg him to stop . . . start . . . do something and anything. She felt so small near him but also confident, and reached behind her back to rub his thighs with questing fingers.

"Priscilla . . ." he choked.

"What?" She feigned innocence, then giggled when he gave her a sudden nip on the back of her neck. Then he turned once more, pulling her beneath him, his beautiful face taking on shadows from the light of the lamp as he moved above her.

She threaded her fingers through his dark hair, then arched to twine her arms around his neck, loving the forest and sunshine scent of him.

"I love you," he whispered, his eyes glowing and then closing in pleasure.

"And I love you too, Joseph King."

He could tell that he left Priscilla more than sated and quietly slipped from the bed once she'd fallen asleep, to dress and grab a lantern and a sledge-hammer. He left a mournful Bear behind at the cabin door and started through the woods.

It was a bright summer night and the moon's glow led him easily to the track down the mountain. Then he was in denser forest, but he knew the landmarks where he'd seen the still that afternoon. He passed a low grove of mountain laurel and turned off the path, working his way through the brush until he found the still. He turned up the lantern and set it on the ground near the old-fashioned copper coil, then raised the sledgehammer.

"Don't do it, Joe."

Joseph nearly jumped when he heard his *bruder*'s voice from the dark trees, outside the circle of the lantern's light.

"Edward! What are you doing? You scared me half to death."

"Put the hammer down, Joe."

Joseph tightened his grip and shook his head.

"*Nee*, Edward. This is wrong. You're not going to get moonshine from some *Englischer* while—"

"It's my still."

Joseph slowly lowered the hammer. "What?"

Edward stepped into the light and Joseph saw that his *bruder*'s face was flushed and he reeked of alcohol.

"I lied to you, Joe. You think I don't know how to build a still? We've both known since Grossdaddi . . . well . . . Just go home to your pretty wife."

Joseph thought fleetingly of the giant of a man who'd been their grandfather, their father's *fater*. In retrospect, Joseph knew that he'd died from "the drink," as the Mountain *Amisch* put it, and Joseph wasn't about to let Edward fall into the same pattern.

He hefted the sledgehammer and struck with easy force, smashing the coil and drum. He didn't expect the rushing blow of Edward's fist in his belly and stumbled backwards, staring at his *bruder*.

After a moment, Joseph spoke evenly. "Even as children, we never brawled, Edward. I'm not about to start now."

Edward stumbled forward and struck him hard in the mouth and Joseph tasted blood. "God, yes, the perfect *Amischer*, even with your teenage forays. Hit me!"

Edward punched him again. "I said hit me."

Joseph swiped the blood from his face and

shook his head. "I don't have to hit you, Edward. You're already beating yourself up enough inside as it is . . ."

Joseph dropped the hammer and turned to go, but when he bent for the lantern, Edward pummeled him from behind.

"Hit me, you stupid ox! Hit me . . ."

Joseph shook him off and started the long trek home while Edward's drunken cries echoed in his ears.

Priscilla sat in the rocking chair of the master bedroom, fuming. *How dare he love me to sleep, then sneak off somewhere?* She rocked harder in the dark, waiting for Joseph to return.

She didn't have long to wait. Joseph quietly entered and she could barely make out his features in the moonlight and low light of the lantern, but knew that he was taking extra care in undressing.

She waited for a long moment, then snapped, "No secrets, huh, Joseph?"

She felt gratified when he jumped and turned rapidly in her direction.

"Why are you up?" he asked, though his voice sounded thick for some reason.

"I was waiting for you. Where were you?"

No answer.

She turned up the lantern on the side table near the chair, then gasped when she saw her husband's face. He was bruised and bloodied and she automatically rushed to his side to touch his bare arm.

"Joseph, were you fighting?" She couldn't believe her eyes.

He shook his head with a half laugh that had the catch of a sob in it and she slipped into his arms, all anger forgotten.

"Joseph, what happened?"

"It was—Edward. He was drunk and I destroyed his still." He stopped and swiped angrily at his face. "He wanted me to hit him—my *bruder* . . ."

Priscilla reached her arms around his shoulders and he bent his head to her. She began to kiss him; tiny, quick butterfly swipes against each bruise and the swollen part of his mouth. She kissed his tears and whispered softly in his ear. Then he turned his mouth to her as she'd hoped he would, wanting him to forget for a moment.

He swept her up in his arms and crossed the room to the bed in two strides, and she did everything she knew how to comfort him until he at last fell into a deep sleep.

"I need to see Joe."

Priscilla eyed Edward as he stood in the kitchen, his blond hair rumpled and his jaw in bad need of a shave. But his blue eyes were clear and she tried to push back the shadowy images of Joseph's tears the previous night.

"He's still asleep," she said finally, truthfully.

Edward rubbed a hand behind his neck and avoided her steady gaze. "I suppose he told you —I don't really remember everything."

Well, you should see his face . . . She lifted her chin. "He told me."

Edward nodded and drew a deep breath, then startled visibly as the door to the master bedroom opened and Joseph came out. Priscilla winced when she looked at his face, though she'd thought she'd seen the worst of it in the light of dawn. But still, his right eye was swollen shut and his mouth twisted with obvious pain as he reached long fingers over a tender bruise on his high cheekbone.

"Dear Gott, Joseph," Edward exclaimed in horror.

Priscilla thought it best to get up and go, but Joseph waved her back down in her seat. "*Nee*, stay still, Priscilla, *sei se gut*. Edward and I will talk outside. I don't want to wake Daed."

She nodded, unable to resist her mingled feelings of sorrow and satisfaction at Edward's stricken look as he gazed at his brother.

"I—I don't know what to say," Edward mumbled.

Joseph squinted in the bright morning sunlight and shrugged. "Me neither."

"I don't remember much, Joe. I—you—I hit you and you just let me?"

Joseph smiled grimly. "Somehow that makes it sound like it's my fault."

"That's not what I meant—I mean why the hell didn't you kick my ass?"

"For what purpose, Edward?"

"Because I've had it coming."

Joseph shook his head though it hurt. "I don't know . . . something about grace and you being my little *bruder* and—"

"Come on, Joe, don't give me all that crap." Edward kicked the ground fitfully.

"Maybe it's not crap. Maybe I took a beating because I'm the one who's had it coming—at least from your viewpoint—perfect *Amischer* that I am . . ."

"I don't understand you."

Joseph felt his stomach gingerly. "Look, Edward, it's done. Just stay away from the drink, all right?"

Edward's nod wasn't overly convincing and Joseph sighed, deeply troubled. "Edward . . ."

"Yeah, yeah, I get it—don't drink. Be *gut* . . . I'm gonna take a walk before breakfast, all right? I'm sorry, Joe."

Joseph watched his *bruder* disappear into the forest and rubbed the side of his head in frustration. Then he noticed the sound of voices coming from the woodshed and decided to take a look.

Chapter Thirty-Nine

Priscilla set about getting breakfast, deciding on fresh blueberry biscuits with crisp honey bacon, and fried tomato slices as well as coffee and orange juice.

Abner came out of his room with his usual taciturn but booming greeting. "Good morning, *dochder* Priscilla. Where is everyone?" He sat down at the table.

Priscilla bought time by opening the thin towel covering the biscuits and sending the delicious scent wafting in his direction.

He sighed. "*Ach*, blueberry—my favorite."

"Why don't you start, Abner? Hollie's still sleeping and Joseph and Edward—went outside."

She slid a mug of coffee beneath his beard, then lifted her sewing basket and took her usual place at the opposite end of the table.

She smiled as he practically inhaled two biscuits, then looked down the table at her. "Heavenly biscuits, Priscilla."

"*Danki*," she murmured.

"What are you working on there?" he asked in the pleasant silence after a few more bites.

"Hand towels for Grossmudder May. I think I'll finish them today. I've embroidered lilacs on the bottoms—they're kind of a thank-you gift." She hoped he wouldn't notice the blush she felt stealing into her cheeks at the memory of Joseph's kisses in the lilac grove.

"*Ach*, well, that *gut* woman deserves a thank-you a thousand times over and then some for all that she's done for this community as a healer."

"*Jah*," Priscilla said softly. "She's helped me too."

Abner chewed on, looking thoughtful, as she drew the last of the green threads through for the stem and leaves of the miniature lilacs.

Joseph realized that it was his four *buwes* working in the enlarged woodshed, and then wondered how he'd explain his physical appearance to them. He finally gave up trying to decide on a suitable explanation and opened the door.

He didn't expect to make such a dramatic entrance, but all four of them froze in various poses when they saw his face.

"Good morning, lads," he said heartily.

Dan Kauffman straightened to his full height and slowly laid down a brush dripping with lacquer. "Joseph—what happened?"

Joseph tried to smile though the effort hurt. *If I look that bad, I'll give Daed another heart attack. Maybe I should go and see Grossmudder May for some poultices.*

"How bad does the other fella look, Joseph?" Jay Smucker tried to joke.

"You can all rest assured that I wasn't beating anyone up—I got into a bit of a tussle, but it's over now, so let's forget it." He walked slowly around the hope chest and whistled low in appreciation.

Ernest jumped up from where he was tinkering with the heavy latch. "I made the hinges as smooth as honey, Joseph, so your daughter can raise the lid easily."

"*Danki*, Ernest."

John Byler pointed to the fine painting and decoration on both the front and the sides of the chest. "I think the drawings really came to life with the colors."

Joseph nodded in agreement. "It's as fine a piece of furniture as I've seen done by hand, *buwes*—it can go easily into any room in the *haus* and be graceful in its setting. But Hollie—she'll love it, I know."

Dan smiled, and for a brief moment Joseph saw a younger version of himself. It was enough to remind him that he'd made a promise to the bishop to teach—and not simply furniture making. He eased down onto a work stool and rubbed his hand idly against his chin, testing the pain.

"I'd like to talk with you, men."

They all turned to him eagerly, attentively, and he realized that the building of the chest and his praise had made all the difference in forming the basis of a relationship between them.

"I need prayer, men, for someone close to me."

Joseph took a deep breath. "I can't give you all the details, and I want to ask that our prayer requests never go beyond the walls of this shop."

"Our prayer requests?" Dan questioned.

Joseph smiled at him. "*Jah*, Dan, how can I pray for you? What do you need?"

Dan shuffled uncomfortably but seemed to understand that Joseph was asking to build intimacy among the group. "Well, I—uh—I'm not going to do *rumspringa*. I plan on joining the church directly."

Jay half laughed in disbelief. "No running around? But then how will you really know that joining and staying is the right thing to do?"

Joseph held up a hand. "It's a fair question, Jay, but I don't think Dan made this decision lightly."

"*Nee*," Dan said quietly but with conviction. "I've thought and prayed a lot and I need prayer to be able to understand what it means to be part of the community, to serve others . . . That seems hard for me."

"That's hard for everyone," Joseph said, thinking wryly of Edward. "Well, next?"

John Byler moved restlessly, fooling with a piece of leather strapping as he visibly worked up the nerve to speak. "I'm going to Lancaster for three weeks—to try out how it'd be to work my *oom*'s dairy farm."

"Do you want to go, John?" Joseph asked in the sudden sober silence.

"*Nee*, I want to stay here and work at the carpentry shop with all of you, but my *daed* says I need to go from the mountain and see other things, other ways of work first."

"Three weeks isn't so long, John," Dan offered. "We can pray for you here."

"And I can talk with your *fater*," Joseph promised. John nodded, visibly moved.

"And what about you, Ernest?" Joseph asked.

"My dog died yesterday. Just a dumb ol' dog, but I—she used to sleep with me when I was afraid of the thunder—and I . . ." He broke off, raising a fist to his lips.

Joseph shifted on the stool. "Ernest, all creatures are gifts—gifts of companionship and comfort and love. I'm sorry about your dog. How do you want us to pray?"

Ernest shrugged and bowed his head while Dan slung an arm over his shoulders.

Joseph decided to move on. "And Jay Smucker, how about you?"

"I don't need anything."

"Ahh," Joseph murmured. *So like Edward . . . maybe there was a lot of pain hidden there, in both of them.*

"Why?" Joseph asked finally.

"What do you mean?" Jay shifted his weight with visible unease.

"Why don't you need anything?"

Jay blew out a breath of disgust. "Because

what I need, Gott ain't gonna give me. He never has and He never will."

"We could try," Dan said encouragingly.

Jay shook his head, then spoke, his voice so low, Joseph had to lean forward to catch the words. "I want my *daed* to stop hitting my *mamm*."

There was silence as palpable as the dust motes in the shaft of sunshine from the window as Joseph scrambled for something to say. *Dear Gott, Jay's fater, Red, is a giant of a man and his wife is as petite as—Priscilla.*

"Does the bishop know?" Dan asked, and Jay looked up in alarm at Joseph.

"You said everything stays within these walls."

Joseph nodded. "I did and I meant it. None of you are to try to be amateur providences and fix Jay's situation or anyone else's. This is about praying." *Though I'd like to wring Red Smucker's neck for him . . .*

Jay seemed to relax at Joseph's words and leaned back against the workbench.

And Joseph bowed his head and began to lead them all in prayer.

Priscilla plunged her hands into the sudsy water of the sink, then nearly jumped in surprise when Joseph knocked on the kitchen window directly in front of her.

"What?" she mouthed.

He motioned for her to come outside, and she

quickly dried her hands and slipped out the door while Abner and Hollie were deep in a game of checkers.

Joseph caught her close when she came out, so close that she shrieked, and he laughed softly, then let her go with a quick buss on her nose.

"How was your talk with Edward?" she asked low.

"Like a talk with Edward . . . frustrating. Hey, I'm afraid Daed will get riled if he sees me beat up, and I'd hate to lie to him. I thought I'd run up the mountain to Grossmudder May's and get some possible treatment for the bruises and swelling."

"You look like a pirate," she chided him gently. "But if you're going to go, will you take something to her from me? I promised Hollie we'd go over and see baby Rose today."

"Sure," he said, smiling.

Pricilla nodded and moved quietly back into the house, snatching up her sewing basket. But judging by the serious eyes of the two opponents at the checkerboard, she doubted she needed to worry about being noticed. She closed the door behind her, then withdrew the two hand towels from her basket.

Joseph bent to study her work. "Lilacs, hmm? Do you remember when . . . ?"

"Yes," she snapped, taking a flustered look about.

He laughed and kissed her again, lingering over the pulse point in her throat.

"Joseph," she hissed. "Anyone can see."

"And since when have you grown shy? Maybe we need a trip back to the secret pool, hmm?"

She had to smile and he took the lilac towels from her with an elegant bow and a rakish smile.

She put her hands on her hips and shook her head, unsure how he could be so battered and still look so good. She sighed aloud and watched him disappear into the treeline with longing in her heart.

Chapter Forty

Joseph knocked on the door of Grossmudder May's cabin, taking a deep breath of the delicious, herb-scented air. He was surprised when Sarah came to greet him; even after what she'd done for his *fater*, he still couldn't picture her in the *auld* healer's place. And he had no idea what to say to her on the subject of Edward.

"Joseph, Grossmudder's been expecting you. I'm sorry you're hurt. *Sei se gut*, *kumme* in."

Joseph had the strange, turned-upside-down feeling he normally had at the May cabin, but now it was Sarah Mast who was generating the odd energy that made his scalp tingle.

"Sarah," he began finally. "Look, Edward is—"

She waved him silent, then stirred a fragrant pot over the small fire. Then she straightened and rubbed her hands on her apron. "Joseph, your *bruder* must choose his own path, his own wife—there is nothing I can do. The demon that holds him now must be dealt with, but only he can do the dealing."

Joseph found himself agreeing. *Demon . . . It was a* gut *word for the drink, though he understood that drinking could be a disease; but maybe it was easier for Sarah to think of things in more straightforward terms . . .*

He blinked thoughtfully, then noticed Sarah was leaving. She looked at him once over her shoulder. "Grossmudder May is in bed. She'll tell you what to do. Have a *gut* day, Joseph."

He waved her off and turned in the sudden silence of the strange cabin, wondering what was next.

"Joseph King, would you have an *auld* woman ease your pain?"

He jumped in spite of himself, then went to the archway that separated the kitchen from the bedroom. He saw Grossmudder May without her *kapp*, her hair twined in a massive gray braid about her small head. She was tucked up comfortably in the feather bed, the quilts drawn up in cozy folds to her gnarled hands.

"Took a fair beating, hmm?"

He nodded, feeling uncomfortable standing in her bedroom.

"Well then, go on out to my cabinets and I'll

holler and tell you what you need to do to fix yourself up so Abner doesn't need healing again."

But Joseph hesitated. "Are you—unwell, Grossmudder?"

"Me? Naww . . . nothing wrong with me but dying, plain and simple."

Joseph stared at her. "What? What did you say?"

"You heard me fine, *buwe*," she sniffed. "Now go on to the herbs."

"I should get Bishop Umble and Sarah back here . . . Maybe she can—"

Grossmudder May held up a hand to silence him. "Joseph, Derr Herr has revealed to me that it is my time today. He said he'd send someone to be with me, and you're obviously the one. Now let's move along."

Joseph felt as if he'd entered some strange nightmare and blindly turned to the vast cupboard of jars and bottles and vials.

"Bilweed for the bruises and some arnica, mix them together."

Joseph braced his hands on the cupboard and shook his head in disbelief. He wanted Priscilla there with him . . .

"You're not moving, Joseph."

He looked up at the containers. "Where's the bilweed?"

"Under 'B,' *buwe* . . . What's wrong with you?"

He found the jar of the dried herb and opened it, promptly bringing on a sneeze.

"Bless you," she called.

He couldn't reply, but he was glad to have something to do with his hands. He dumped some of the bilweed into a stone mixing bowl and found the arnica cream. He mixed the two together with a small pestle. "Now what?" he asked, though his voice shook.

"Pour a little aloe in from the stone jug on the floor, then bring it all in here with a cloth."

He obeyed slowly, not wanting to go back into the bedroom. *But maybe she's simply* auld *and worried and is making up all this dying stuff in her head . . .*

"I can hear you thinkin' from here, young fella. *Kumme* in and let me help you."

He reentered the bedroom, carrying the bowl and a soft cloth.

"Sit down here in the chair beside me, *sei se gut*."

He sat and she took the items from his hands.

"Turn up the light a bit more, Joseph, and stop being afraid. I promise my eyeballs won't pop out nor anything too unusual."

"It's not that . . ."

"Lean over here," she commanded.

He leaned and she began to gently stroke his face with the cloth and the mixture.

He closed his eyes.

"Hurts, hmm?"

"*Nee* . . . but you . . . that hurts."

She dabbed at his mouth. "Well, that's right nice to hear, Joseph King. That I'll be missed when I'm gone from here . . . right nice indeed."

He didn't speak; he couldn't. His throat worked and he sat still, letting her heal his wounds.

"Her skin feels like petals, Mommy," Hollie marveled as Priscilla dried Rose with a soft towel.

"And you have a beautiful imagination, my sweet girl," Priscilla said, smiling down at her daughter.

Mary sat in a rocking chair nearby, her eyes full of admiration and wonder for her small baby.

"You're a good mother, Mary," Priscilla complimented her as she sat about dressing the doll-like, wriggling baby.

"Why do you say that? Sometimes I feel totally helpless and wonder how I will really help her grow."

"Well, for one thing, you let other people love and care for her. The more love she has, the better. I couldn't . . . well, never mind. But you'll see, God gives you wisdom with your children." She reached down to tug Hollie's braid. "Or else I'd never know what to do either."

Hollie giggled and stepped away to rub Bear, who sat like a giant, silent sentinel at the bath.

Rose cooed and Priscilla had to laugh. "She sounds like a dove."

"I know," Mary agreed. "She wakes Jude and

me each morning with her gentle sounds. It is truly a blessed way to begin the day."

Priscilla listened to the baby and wondered what it would be like to raise a child with someone by your side—like Jude was with Mary. She hugged Rose tight and mentally calculated days in her head for the tenth time that morning. *I'm late . . . Dear Lord, I'm late . . . but maybe it's nothing . . .* Yet when she considered Joseph's passionate, virile lovemaking, she had to smile to herself, like hugging a precious secret close, even though she felt herself flush at the idea of carrying his child.

"Are you hot in here, Priscilla?" Mary asked, rising to open a window. "Your face is a bit red."

Priscilla smiled brightly. "I'm fine. Truly fine."

Joseph took the bowl back when she'd finished.

"Now go on and get a *gut* chunk of ice from the box and wrap it in a linen towel. Top drawer on the right of the cupboard. And no considering some excuse to go for more ice and runnin' off down the mountain for help. I told ya, I'm fine . . . and you'll be fine too." Grossmudder May gave him a direct look from faded gray eyes and he got the wrapped ice as she'd told him and settled back in the chair beside her.

He struggled for something to say as he listened to her breathing, glad that it seemed soft and regular.

"Not yet, Joseph . . . let's talk. You tell me a secret and I'll tell you one."

He shifted the ice higher on his cheekbone. "I let Edward have at me."

"Ha! No secret there, nor that still of his. I've seen him pass by a-stumblin' on more than one evening."

"I destroyed the still."

"Well, he'll only build another, *buwe*. Do you really think you can save him?"

"I don't know. I can try." Joseph leaned his chin glumly in his hand, his elbow bent on the chair arm.

"Bah! Try to be Gott more likely . . ."

"All right. What's your secret? And it better not be some—"

"Your wife's pregnant."

Joseph nearly fell out of the chair. "What did you say? How do you know? Has she been to see you? Dear Gott, and I've been making lo—" He broke off, confused and excited.

Grossmudder May laughed. "What you know about women, Joseph, could fill a pea hull. You can make love as much as you want throughout the pregnancy, *buwe*, so long as there's no pain or bleeding."

"Right. Right . . . no pain or . . . right."

"And now you're a-longin' to go to her. Well, you ain't got but a few more minutes to wait. Tell me another secret."

Joseph noticed that she appeared restless and he quickly rose, then brought back the hand towels Priscilla had made. Grossmudder May fingered the embroidery with pleasure. "Lilacs . . . they say heaven smells of lilacs. Just like my grove every May . . ."

"I kissed Priscilla there," he whispered, telling the secret. "Showed her how I'd do it too, using a lilac blossom."

Grossmudder May laughed and Joseph noticed the strange beauty of sudden paleness that appeared to rest on her countenance. It was almost as though she grew younger and he could see the change before his very eyes.

"I can hear the angels, *buwe*, like roses and lightning all mixed together."

He reached out and held her hand, watching helplessly and with the grave knowledge that there was something truly greater than he in the cabin at the moment she passed on into the life to come.

He knew when it was over and sat, holding her hand, until it grew cold. Then he gently moved away, leaving the hand towels beside her on the bed and feeling as if he'd suddenly grown up a bit more in the wise woman's passing.

He banked the fire and closed the door behind him, then set off for the bishop's *haus*.

Joseph reached the stair steps of the bishop's home and was met with an unearthly wailing from inside; it took him a few moments to register that the bishop and his wife were in the middle of some kind of argument.

At any other time he might have felt amused by the reality that Bishop Umble did not always have all the answers—at least where Martha was concerned—but now Joseph decided he'd have to knock and interrupt.

He put his booted foot on the first step.

"Dear, this has nothing to do with me not loving you!" the *gut* bishop hollered, and Joseph winced.

Another step.

"I'm telling you, if my *mamm* was alive, I'd go back to her," Martha cried.

Joseph was within knocking distance of the porch door but held his hand when the bishop roared out his next words.

"Ya would not, Martha Umble! Your mother drove you crazy!"

Joseph shook his head and had just decided to knock when he saw Martha Umble *kumme* barreling toward the door like a freight train with no brake. He jumped off the steps in the nick of time and still almost caught the porch door in the face.

"Hello, Joseph," Martha murmured as sweetly as if they were in a church meeting.

"Hello . . . is . . . can I . . ." He watched her stalk off toward the barn, then peered cautiously back at the door.

Bishop Umble stood there, snapping his suspenders with a frown. "Suppose you heard all that, *buwe*. Well, she's got it in her head that we should go for a month, a month mind you, to visit Mary Malizza. A bishop's job is for life and she wants me to take off and go gallivanting like I'm some—"

Joseph nodded. "*Jah*, sir. But I must tell you—"

"*Ach*, women. They drive you mad, then make you think they're right. Well, I haven't had a vacation in some time and I—"

"Sir, Grossmudder May is dead."

"Hmm? What's that?"

Joseph shook his head, hating to be so blunt but seeing no other way around it. "I said that . . ."

The bishop came out and dropped down to sit on the top step, visibly stunned. "*Auld* May . . . who'd have thought. I just saw her last week for my knees and she fixed me up *gut* . . ." He cleared his throat, then took out his massive red hankie and blew his nose. "You were with her, *sohn*?"

"*Jah* . . . she spoke of hearing the angels singing. I didn't—she didn't want me to fetch you. I'm sorry."

"*Nee*, it should've been the way she wanted. Well, I'll notify the deacons. We'll have the funeral tomorrow, I expect."

"All right." Joseph struggled for something else to say, but the bishop seemed to want to be alone with his grief. "I'll go on home then."

"*Jah . . . danki . . .*"

Joseph walked away, feeling that he wanted nothing more than to be in Priscilla's comforting arms.

Chapter Forty-One

Priscilla bit her bottom lip and stared at the recipe she'd written down, not quite sure how to triple the brown sugar, which was simply to be measured "with a liberal hand."

"Priscilla, it's after midnight. Are you coming to bed?"

She glanced over her shoulder at Joseph as he stood, his black pants slung on over his bare, lean waist and his dark hair rumpled invitingly.

She sighed and shook her head. "I promised Frau Umble that I'd make apple dumplings for the funeral, and I'm going to do it. I wrote down what I can remember of my mother's recipe—I'm trying to figure out how to measure, that's all."

He came forward and slid his hands down her shoulders and pressed his mouth against her neck. She tried to swat him away with a floury hand but he only laughed.

"Come to bed, my sweet. I'll make it worth your while . . . Besides, there'll be plenty of food anyway."

"Joseph . . . I loved her."

"I know, but I don't want you to overwork yourself."

"I'm baking—it's not that difficult."

"*Jah*, but you're . . ."

"I'm what?" She looked up at him, putting a hand on her hip.

"Nothing . . ."

"What were you going to say?" She felt suspicious suddenly when he dropped his gaze. "Joseph?"

She watched him glance at his *daed*'s bedroom door; then he looked her in the eye. "All right," he whispered. "I wanted to wait—but you're, well, you're pregnant."

She blinked at him. He looked so handsome, his face filled with suppressed excitement, she didn't have the heart to disappoint him.

"What?" She dropped her spoon with a clatter and he caught her close against his chest.

"Grossmudder May told me before she passed. She said it was a secret, but you should know so you don't overdo."

He dropped to his knees suddenly and pressed his mouth against her belly. "*Ach*, Priscilla. I love you so much." She stared at his bent head and ran her hands through his hair.

"Well," she murmured, glancing at the mixing bowls and the sugar. "I suppose I could get up really early . . ."

He got to his feet and swept her up in his arms. "We'll both get up early—I'll help you."

"All right. Now what were you saying about making things worth my while?"

She loved how his eyes simmered with passion as he bent to kiss her, using his tongue to foray gently against her lips, then moaning deep in his throat when she allowed him access. He crossed to their bedroom door in long strides and was better than his word at making the night worth her while . . .

At five a.m., Joseph was up to his elbows in flour. He wasn't about to wake Priscilla and had decided that baking apple dumplings couldn't be all that difficult. He was frowning over the addition of vinegar to the milk on the recipe card when the front door eased open and Edward walked in.

Joseph eyed his *bruder*'s tousled appearance then looked back at Priscilla's handwriting. "Are you drunk?" he asked softly.

"*Nee.*" Edward shook his head. "I've been walking and thinking most of the night. Sarah won't have anything to do with me anymore, Joe."

Joseph stirred the milk and vinegar and remembered Sarah's words at the cabin. *A demon holds him* . . . "Well, maybe she doesn't feel there's been much to give her hope lately where you're concerned."

Edward hung his head. "I know that. I guess I expected her to wait and . . . well, wait."

"For what?"

"For me. I know it sounds arrogant, but I thought we had enough of an understanding . . . Well, never mind. It's probably for the best. What are you doing?"

"Making apple dumplings for the funeral. Priscilla's still asleep . . ." He drifted off, not wanting to explain why she was so tired.

"I'll help. I'm a *gut* hand at pastry."

Joseph raised a doubtful brow.

"Really, Joe. Grossdaddi taught me. Do you remember that I spent a lot of time with him when you and I were young?"

"I guess so," Joseph said, trying to remember. *I wish you'd spent a little less time with him if he's the one who also taught you to drink . . .* But Joseph didn't want to discourage his *bruder* so he concentrated on blending the flour and milk while Edward washed his hands.

Then they both took to peeling and paring the apples—sour crab apples that made the best dumplings with plenty of brown and white sugar added.

There was something soothing about the process, and Joseph rejoiced in this moment of accord with Edward.

"How's your face feel?" Edward asked after a few minutes.

"How's it look?" Joseph turned toward the lamp.

"Much better. I really am sorry, Joe."

"No worries. It gave me time to be with Grossmudder May when she passed."

"I heard at the store that you were with her. The only person I ever saw die was Grossdaddi—I ran and hid in a cave by the creek that day."

Joseph frowned at him. "You couldn't have been more than seven or eight. I didn't know you were with him alone."

Edward shrugged. "I never told anybody."

Pieces started to fall into place in Joseph's mind as he considered Edward's restless life and various troubles, and something niggled about their grandfather—something that seemed important for him to remember . . .

A quiet knock on the door interrupted his thoughts and he looked up in surprise. Edward went to open the door and Joseph was even more surprised to see Sarah standing in the early light of dawn.

"Sarah." Edward whispered her name.

Joseph sighed to himself. *I'll have to leave them alone, I suppose . . .*

"*Nee*, Joseph," Sarah said, reminding him eerily of Grossmudder May. "Please don't go. It's you I came hoping to see."

Edward swept his arm back with a flourish. "Then by all means, *kumme* in, Sarah Mast. I'll leave."

Joseph felt distinctly uncomfortable when Sarah didn't protest and Edward grabbed his hat and walked out.

Joseph cleared his throat. "What can I do for you, Sarah?"

"Do you know why I said I no longer wanted to see Edward?"

He shook his head. "I can guess, but *nee*, I don't know for sure."

"Well, it affects you and everyone on this mountain, all of us." Her big gray eyes welled with tears and Joseph shifted his weight uncomfortably.

"How so?"

She shook her head. "Edward apparently wrote to someone at the mining company where you worked. He actually went so far as to invite them to Ice Mountain to do geological testing."

"The gas rigs?" Joseph frowned. "I don't understand."

"I don't understand either. I only know that Edward has changed so much from the boy he used to be."

"I'll try and talk to Edward, Sarah. That's about the best I can do."

"*Danki*," she said and turned to go. "Oh, and Joseph, your first batch of apple dumplings are going to burn, so you'd better make extra dough."

He nodded and she left. *Great. Just great. I've got an errant* bruder, *and his girlfriend happens to use her powers for* gut *to tell me my dessert is going to burn.*

He turned as Priscilla wandered out into the kitchen.

"Joseph, do I smell smoke?"

Priscilla held Hollie's hand and glanced down at the neat white part in the little girl's hair. It was the *Amisch* way, Joseph had explained, not to shield children from death. And certainly Hollie had asked enough after Heath's death to understand some of the concept, not that Priscilla even felt she understood it fully herself. But even baby Rose was in attendance at the small graveyard near the foot of the pines for Grossmudder May's burial.

All of the community was dressed in their finest Sunday wear, and the bishop stood, holding his hat in his hands, once they'd all filed past the half-open coffin to say one last good-bye. Then the two lids of the coffin were closed and Bishop Umble began to speak.

"Part of living is dying . . . but for many of us, the idea of death has to be approached like very cold water. In other words, we put a toe into the thought of death, then pull back, feeling like we've got all the time in the world in which to adjust. Then we might get a whole foot in, stand ankle deep, and come to have some sense that who we are in this world will not last forever. But even then, we move away from the idea of death—it's not comfortable. Well, Grossmudder May knew when her time was coming—a gift from Derr Herr, she would call it. She knew and she faced it, faced it with the help of an *Amisch* man, Joseph King here. And we can only hope that we might face our own time with equal grace. Let us have a moment of silent prayer."

Priscilla closed her eyes and listened as a soft breeze stole gently through the pines. For some reason, she thought of her father's letter to her. She'd been trying to put it out of her mind for some time, but now, standing next to the open grave, she realized how short life truly is. *I want to forgive him. Help me, God. I want to forgive my father.*

She looked up, startled, when Joseph slid a comforting arm around her waist and began to lead her and Hollie away from the grave and back toward Grossmudder May's cabin, where the community would meet to remember their healer together.

Priscilla glanced back once and knew she had left her anger at her father far behind at the foot of the pines.

Chapter Forty-Two

A few days following the funeral, Joseph realized he'd still not been able to find time to talk with Edward alone about Sarah's concerns. First, he and Priscilla had gone down the mountain to get Mr. Ellis to drive them to see Dr. McCully, who'd happily confirmed the pregnancy. And now they were preparing for a picnic supper to let the family know about the new baby.

"Priscilla," Joseph said, watching her fry chicken with an easy hand, "I wonder if I shouldn't take Hollie out for a walk or something. I think I'd like to tell her our *gut* news alone, so she won't feel lost when we announce it this afternoon at the picnic."

"Oh, Joseph, I've been trying to think of a special way to tell her. Coming from you would be that something special, and I know it would be wonderful for you to tell her."

"Tell who what?" Abner asked, coming into the kitchen with an appreciative sniff.

"Never mind, Dat. You'll find out soon enough." Joseph laid a hand on his *fater*'s shoulder as the older man tried to pick some frying crumbles from the grease and Priscilla slapped his hand away.

Both men laughed, but Priscilla shook her

337

head at them. "Too many cooks in the kitchen . . ."

Abner sighed. "Well, I'm going fishing. Bound to starve if I don't, but I'll be back by two or thereabouts."

Joseph saw his *daed* out the door, then lifted his own straw hat from its hook. "I'll go find Hollie."

He found her in the hay mows, lying on her side, the faithful Bear beside her as they both watched a new mother barn cat wash her kittens.

"Oh, Daddy," she whispered in excitement. "Look!"

Joseph smiled. *Here's a Gott-given opportunity to explain things to her . . .*

"It's a fine sight, *kind*. Tell me, which one do you think she loves most?"

Hollie looked affronted, as he'd expected her to do. "Why, you don't know anything about being a mommy . . . She loves them all the same, of course."

"You're right, sweetling. You're so right. So it doesn't matter to her which one came first or second or third?"

"Nope."

"Well, if this mama barn cat can do such a *gut* job of loving more than one baby, how do you think your own *mamm* and *dat* would do?" He watched her small face as her quick brain processed, and loved looking at her.

"Wait a minute . . . Are you and Mommy going to have a baby?"

"Yep."

"Whoopee!" She threw her arms around his neck and squeezed tight, then pulled back to look him in the face. "Is it a boy or a girl?"

He laughed out loud. "I don't know, *kind.*"

"Well, when is she gonna have it?"

"We figure around next year in March." *Next year in the spring. Dear Gott, how my life will have changed from one year to the next . . .*

"Next yeeeaarrr!" Hollie moaned, looking crestfallen. "That's a long time away."

"*Ach*, but it takes that long for Gott to knit the baby together in your *mamm*'s belly."

"God knits?" Hollie wrinkled her nose in doubt.

"*Jah*, He does. It says so in the Bible and He knit you and me and your *mamm* together into a family when I never thought I'd have a family of my own."

Hollie leaned back against Bear. "Why did you think that, Daddy?"

Joseph smiled. "I don't know. I really don't know at all."

Mary Lyons sat nursing baby Rose in the kitchen while Priscilla made last-minute preparations. Jude prowled around, seeming unwilling, as always, to let his wife and new baby out of his sight.

"You know you are going to have to go back to teaching school in the fall," Priscilla teased him.

He adjusted his glasses with a smile. "I know that—I try to forget the subject though, as much as I can."

They all three laughed together; then Mary spoke up. "Jude, why don't you go look for Joseph and Hollie? I promise not to disappear from sight."

He bent and dropped a lingering kiss on Mary's mouth, and Priscilla smiled.

"All right, sweetheart. But I'll hold you to that promise."

He started to whistle, lifted his hat, and pressed Priscilla's shoulder before he left.

When he'd gone, Mary leaned forward in a conspiratorial whisper. "I think I can guess what your big announcement is for today, Priscilla."

Priscilla laughed gaily, then dropped to the table beside her sister-in-law. "All right. I promised Joseph I wouldn't tell until the picnic, but yes, I'm pregnant."

They caught each other's hands and smiled.

"That is so lovely, Priscilla. Praise Gott."

"Yes," Priscilla said. "And the funny part is, though don't ever tell Joseph, he was the one who told me I'm pregnant."

Mary looked surprised. "What? How did he know?" Her tone suggested that her brother was not the kind of man to be aware of such things, and Priscilla's smile deepened.

"I had my suspicions, but Grossmudder May told him before she passed."

"*Ach*," Mary said softly. "I will miss her so much."

"I know . . . a lifetime of wisdom and knowledge and so much compassion."

"But"—Mary brightened—"we have Sarah."

"Yes," Priscilla agreed quietly.

"What is it? You're thinking about Edward and her?"

"Yes." Priscilla bit her lip, not wanting to reveal what Joseph had told her about Sarah's early morning visit.

"I know things aren't right between them. But I've been praying for Edward."

Priscilla thought hard. "You know, Mary, I could get a lot better at praying for others. Mostly, I've been focusing on myself and Joseph and Hollie. And I—I've started praying for my father."

"Joseph told me about the letter he sent." Mary squeezed her hand sympathetically.

"Yes—I know I've forgiven him, but it's kind of scary to think where prayers will lead."

Mary nodded. "Scary but transforming and exciting."

Priscilla had to agree.

Joseph left Hollie and went to stand outside the enlarged woodshed. It was something to imagine a wood shop, a true furniture shop, and he'd been praying hard about it. It wasn't that he needed the money; he had plenty socked away from the rigs. But with a new baby coming, he wanted to have a steady income, though he knew that God would provide.

He turned to go, then heard a sound inside the shed and went to the door. He opened it and saw Jay Smucker kneeling on the floor in front of the hope chest. The *buwe* was polishing the box with enthusiasm, and the sunlight from the window made the highly lacquered box so beautiful that Joseph caught his breath.

"Jay, it's done. It's marvelous," Joseph praised.

Jay nodded, not lifting his head.

Joseph stepped closer and gave a low whistle of appreciation at the incredible workmanship the lads had done. "Hollie will love it."

"*Jah.*" Jay's voice was unusually soft.

"Is something wrong?" Joseph asked, touching the *buwe*'s shoulder.

Jay flinched and lifted his face into the sunlight.

Joseph caught his breath. The *buwe*'s right eye was swollen shut and he had a large bruise on his cheekbone.

"Jay . . ." Joseph choked. "Your *fater*?"

"I tried to stop him this time. I got between him and Mamm. I—I wasn't very effective."

"All right. *Kumme* with me." Joseph extended a hand to help him up.

"Everything stays within these walls, remember, Joseph?"

"*Jah*, but you need some treatment for your eye. We'll stay off the trail and go to Grossmudder—I mean, Sarah's cabin."

Jay nodded with visible reluctance, then took his hand.

Chapter Forty-Three

When Joseph and Jay got back to the woodshed, the *buwe* was looking much better and was able to hold his head up. Dan, John, and Ernest had shown up to look at the dried, lacquered chest and to see what Joseph had to say, but each took time to be awkwardly tender with Jay.

Then Joseph cleared his throat. "Before we give Hollie her gift, men, let's pray for Red Smucker."

John looked shocked and angry. "Pray? For him? Look what he did to Jay . . ."

"*Jah*," Joseph said slowly, his hand on Jay's shoulder. "He needs prayer. Prayer is transforming. We don't know what Derr Herr can and will do in Jay's *fater*'s life if we pray."

John nodded reluctantly but bowed his head in the ensuing silence.

Joseph listened to the quiet, sensing each *buwe* relax, feeling peace pervade the room. Then he lifted his head.

"All right. Let's take the chest in to Hollie and *danki*, *buwes*, for your amazing work."

Joseph watched with pleasure, his arm around Priscilla, as Hollie knelt on the floor in her bedroom, the large key in her hand. She fiddled with the lock, then lifted the beautifully painted lid.

"There's presents inside, Mommy! Besides the promise of the baby in your belly . . ."

"Really?" Priscilla strived to keep the laughter out of her voice as Joseph looked at the four *buwes* standing awkwardly in the background.

Dan smiled, breaking the awkward silence after Hollie's announcement. "Her first hopes. We couldn't give it empty."

Hollie lifted the first wrapped package. "From John." She read the card and opened the brown paper slowly and revealed a lace doily. "Oh, so pretty."

John shrugged. "It was the finest Ben Kauffman had—you can use it someday in your own *haus*."

Ernest's gift was a fine lantern, and Dan's a set of dish towels with tiny apples on them. "My *mamm* gave 'em to me to give to you."

"Oh, thank you! *Danki*!" Hollie cried then took the last package from the deep box. "From Jay."

Joseph watched Jay's face as his daughter opened the present. "Oh my!" Hollie exclaimed.

It was a beautifully carved boat with crafted paper sails.

"It's waterproof—I thought maybe we'd take it sailing sometime," Jay offered, his head down a bit.

Hollie scrambled to her feet and ran to fling her arms around Jay's legs. Joseph didn't miss the flush of pleasure on the *buwe*'s cheeks and it pleased him greatly. *And here I thought the kid was a pain in the neck when there's so much more to his story . . . Maybe there's so much more to everyone's story.*

Joseph nodded his thanks to his group once more, then turned back to the preparations for the picnic.

Priscilla felt a wave of nausea upon rising from the oven with a pan of shortcakes for the strawberries she'd picked that morning.

"What's wrong?" Joseph took the pan from her shaky hands and put an arm around her shoulders. "Are you sick? You're overdoing things. You know Dr. McCully said you could start feeling faint or sick anytime in the first three months." He was walking her away from the kitchen even as he spoke and led her to their bedroom. She was grateful for the light breeze coming in through the screened window.

"Lie down. I'll get a wet cloth for your forehead . . . Do you want some water?"

Priscilla had to smile at his attentions. "You know, Joseph King, I think you're going to spoil me silly."

"Yeah—like you don't deserve it," he muttered as he poured water onto a cloth from the pitcher on the dressing table. He came back to the bed and sat down on the edge, carefully positioning the damp cloth on her forehead.

"You know, you could help me forget this sickness for a while." She trailed her fingers up his arm.

He pulled back with a shocked look, and she burst out laughing. "What?"

"I know it's perfectly fine to make love during the pregnancy so long as there's no discomfort or bleeding," he said, almost as if repeating a lesson learned. "But you're sick."

"I think I'm better." She pulled his hand to her breast. "Feel my heart."

He shook her off and got up.

"Joseph!"

"I think you're not yourself. Now just rest until the picnic and maybe tonight we'll . . . never mind." He stalked out, closing the door behind him and she smiled and stretched languorously.

Joseph made the rounds of family and the few friends they'd invited, with Priscilla beside him.

"Where's Edward?" she asked as they sampled blueberry turnovers from Frau Umble, who was looking particularly at peace.

"I don't know," Joseph murmured low, then looked up as the bishop's wife touched his arm.

"He's going to do it, Joseph—take a month's vacation. He's going to announce it in church on Sunday."

"Great." Joseph smiled and bent to let Priscilla in on the secret.

Then he led her to the shade of a fine maple and looked out on the happy picnic quilts and was deeply thankful for those who had gathered.

"Priscilla and I have an announcement to make," he said, his voice carrying, and Hollie ran to their side. "I guess I should begin by saying I thought I'd never marry—but I was gladly wrong."

A few chuckles met his remark and he smiled. "And now, having been gifted with a wife and beautiful daughter, we have the pleasure of announcing that Priscilla's expecting . . . a baby . . . in about eight months . . ."

"Daddy!" Hollie cried as he stammered a bit. "Bear and me are gonna be a big brother and sister!"

Then everyone laughed and Joseph joined in, hugging Priscilla close, then gathering Hollie up into his arms. The people gathered buzzed with the *gut* news but then Joseph saw Edward, disheveled and unshaven, step from the woods, seemingly unmoved by the air of joy around him.

Joseph put Hollie down as his friends muttered, obviously noticing his *bruder*'s appearance.

Joseph watched Edward half saunter in their

direction and he instinctively knew his *bruder* had been drinking, but he also wondered what else he'd been up to, given the conversation with Sarah earlier that morning.

"What'd I miss?" Edward asked, slurring his words.

Joseph resisted the raw urge he felt to grab hold of him.

"Edward, why have you been drinking again?" he asked low.

"What d'ya mean, Joe?"

Joseph took a step closer to him and frowned at the odor of alcohol. "You know exactly what I mean."

Edward swallowed a hiccup. "So what if I do?" He spread his arms wide then slapped Joseph hard on the back. "You need to loosen up."

Joseph let out a low growl of contempt, then grabbed Priscilla and Hollie's hands and walked away from his *bruder.*

"Hey, Joe, where ya goin' in such a hurry? Joe!"

Joseph kept walking, stopping only here and there to thank people for coming as they quietly gathered their things to go, sensing something was not right.

When Joseph got to the door of the *haus*, he ushered Priscilla and Hollie and his *fater* inside.

"Dat, I'd like to talk to Edward alone."

His *fater* nodded without comment and took Hollie's hand. Joseph closed the door behind him and turned in time to see Edward come barging toward him.

Joseph put out a calm hand and stopped him still.

"*Kumme* on, Joe, don't make me beat you again."

"Edward, this can't go on. I've got an *auld fater*, a pregnant wife, and a child in this *haus*, and so help me, until you come clean about your drinking and sober up, you're no longer welcome here."

"You can't keep me from my home," Edward cried, giving an ineffectual swing.

Then emerald-green eyes met angry blue, and Joseph's gaze spoke the truth they both understood. *I can keep you from it and I will . . . with the last breath in my body.*

Edward let out an angry sob and pulled away, slinking off into the forest.

Joseph stood on the doorstep, unmoving but for the silent tears that crept down his face in the bright mountain sunshine, testament to a love that knew no boundaries and a hope that time would transform his *bruder*'s heart.

Epilogue

Later that night, Joseph breathed in the soft fragrance of Priscilla's hair as it fell across his chest. He could safely lose himself in her for a time and forget about the world outside. Whenever he loved her, he was caught up in the surreal feeling that he was floating, flying, only to be wonderfully tethered by the realness of her. He laid his hand across her belly, pressing lightly, in wonder of what she carried—part him; part her. And then her lips met his like the taste of mountain spring water, rushing fast and true through his veins . . .

"Edward will come around, Joseph," she whispered, and he knew he could hide nothing from her, least of all the worries that haunted him for his brother.

"Are you so sure, my love?" he asked as she leaned over him, half in shadow.

"Who was it that taught me about gifts in oilcloth?" She kissed him tenderly as he recalled his own words about faith with a rueful smile.

"Well, we unwrapped plenty of those," he admitted.

"And we can continue to unwrap and discover all that life brings us, Joseph, if we do it together."

He caught her close, then moved above her.

"*Jah*, you are right, sweet spitfire, and I will gladly take all from Gott's hand with your help and strength beside me." He kissed her with lingering heat until she arched against him.

"*Ach*, Joseph, as will I."

And then he forgot words as his body spoke of a passion that more than met the demands of her soul and heart.

Center Point Large Print
600 Brooks Road / PO Box 1
Thorndike, ME 04986-0001 USA

(207) 568-3717

US & Canada:
1 800 929-9108
www.centerpointlargeprint.com